Fallen Idyll

Les Dalgliesh

Copyright © 2013 Les Dalgliesh

All rights reserved.

ISBN: 978-1482625455
ISBN-13: 1482625458

DEDICATION

Thank you to Sarah, Adam, and Joe
without whom this story would still be rattling
around in my head.

CONTENTS

1	THE HOMECOMING	1
2	THE WILDERNESS	Pg 11
3	THE CAMP	Pg 17
4	THE VISITORS	Pg 24
5	THE PHILOSOPHER SPEAKS	Pg 30
6	THE PRISONER	Pg 40
7	THE VILLAGE	Pg 49
8	DEATH COMES CALLING	Pg 59
9	THE WAKE	Pg 66
10	FIGHT OR FLIGHT	Pg 74
11	THE CHOICE	Pg 84
12	THE LEAGUE OF JUSTICE	Pg 93
13	VENGEANCE	Pg 101
14	THE PATIENT	Pg 106
15	RECOVERY	Pg 118
16	THE RUNAWAY	Pg 124
17	DRAFT HORSES	Pg 131

18	PARTS UNKNOWN	Pg 139
19	PASSING THROUGH	Pg 150
20	REDWOODS	Pg 156
21	A HISTORY LESSON	Pg 167
22	A DEAD MAN	Pg 174
23	RESURRECTION	Pg 181
24	HOMELAND SECURITY	Pg 188
25	THE FOREST	Pg 198
26	THANKSGIVING	Pg 203
27	JORDAN SPEAKS	Pg 213
28	PORCUPINES	Pg 220
29	VALENTINE DAY	Pg 225
30	HEAVEN OR HELL	Pg 233
31	FIRE	Pg 239
32	THE PORCUPINE TURNS	Pg 246
33	PREPARATIONS	Pg 255
34	ARMAGEDDON	Pg 263
35	ESCAPE	Pg 275
36	SANTA CLAUS	Pg 282

Fallen Idyll

1 THE HOMECOMING

He reminded himself that the bicycle was a good idea. Okay, maybe it wasn't a great idea. After all, the road climbed through the forest for more than eight miles, twisting and turning up the mountain as if it couldn't decide which way to go. Heat waves danced like demons in the near distance. He was carrying way too much "stuff." And he was definitely feeling his age. But damn it, it was still a good idea.

How long had it been since he had ridden a bike up that horrible hill? He was surprised at all the changes, even though he knew he shouldn't be. The trees had grown. They were mostly second-growth redwoods and, in his memory, they were standing serenely around the charred stumps of their ancestors, whispering their family secrets in the soft, mountain breezes. But now they had grown into a great, dark forest that blocked out much of the July sun. For this at least, he was grateful.

Every foot of the shimmering blacktop road was familiar. Every switchback curve held a memory. Every postcard view of the jagged canyons called him back to earlier times. It was all the same, and yet somehow it had all changed... like the man. He was older, pushing fifty.

So much had happened in the intervening thirty years and yet now, in spite of all that, he was back in this place and in many ways, he was feeling as if he had never left it.

He had flown almost three thousand miles and ridden a bus for three hundred more because he wanted to find something he'd left here, all those years ago. It might have been freedom. It might have been simplicity or innocence or any number of things. Sometimes he even wondered if it was simply the pathetic longing of old age for lost youth. With his heart pounding and his lungs gasping for air, he was longing for lost youth, alright.

When he'd decided to make this insane ride up the mountain he had made an even more insane deal with himself that, no matter how tough it got, he would die before he would get off the bicycle and walk. It was the same insane deal he had always made with himself. See what you're made of. Push yourself to the limit and beyond. Damn the consequences.

He was hunched over the handlebars, staring down at his feet and willing them to make each revolution of the pedals, left... right... left... right... when he realized the insanity of it all and stopped. Change muscle groups. Die another day.

Why couldn't he just relax? After all, this was supposed to be a vacation. He was in one of the most beautiful, most peaceful places on the planet and yet inside, he was still in turmoil. For a long time now, his image of himself had been as a big soap bubble, all smooth and glassy and fragile on the surface, but inside, just below, was fire and screaming; clenched teeth and straining muscles.

Small birds flitted from branch to branch above him as he walked along beside the heavily laden bicycle. A blue jay sailed out on the hazy air of the canyon with its warning cry of, "Man! Man! Man!" The smell of the forest in the hot summer sun was intoxicating.

Suddenly he heard the sound of a car coming up the

hill behind him. He stopped, and knelt to examine his packs and panniers. The car whizzed by and, after it disappeared around a corner he stood, looked around, and walked on.

The justification had been automatic. He hadn't wanted anyone, not even the nameless driver of that car, to see his weakness; to see that he was too out of shape to ride that stupid bike up that stupid hill. He smiled as he walked. Some things hadn't changed all that much.

Kneeland isn't really a town. There is just an opening in the forest where a few houses huddle together on the side of a mountain. One of these houses serves as the post office. Four miles farther up the winding road, there is a pinkish, stuccoed, two-room elementary school. That's it. There are no stores, no restaurants, no beauty parlors, nothing.

As he neared the post office, the bold adventurer mounted up again and began to ride, partly because of ego and partly because the road began to level off a little. "Not just for show, but also for go," he thought. He hoped that there wouldn't be anybody outside to see him pass, and especially that he wouldn't be recognized by anyone who might remember him.

The post office and the smattering of buildings around it looked as tired as the man felt. He had remembered it as the "new" post office, but he realized with a shock that it was a forty-year-old building. Its mint-green paint was peeling and it could have used a new roof. At least they hadn't paved the gravel parking lot. An old, blue pick-up and a beige mini-van idled there, waiting for people who would return, carrying packages, envelopes, and a few juicy tidbits of local gossip. He rode past, unnoticed.

He suddenly realized that he missed the logging trucks. He missed the blat of their Jake-brakes and the smell of the fresh-cut fir and redwood logs that used to linger in the air as they roared down the mountain to the sawmills below. In the old days, they would have come pounding by every few minutes. So far, he hadn't even heard one.

Every revolution of the pedals brought a new memory. He could almost hear the laughter of the child he had been, running and climbing and exploring the brave new worlds of youth.

Here was the spot where he and his brother had found a full case of beer beside the road one hot summer day. They'd stashed it in the cool base of a burned-out redwood stump just down the hill. For weeks, every time they'd come hiking up the road from the post office, they'd stop and have a beer, posing with the cans and feeling all grown up.

There was the old power line road, steep and rugged. It had made a great sled run in the years when the snow was deep enough.

At the place where the Maple Creek road forked off to the left, he was truly home. He stopped to rest a moment and to have something to eat from his pack, but first there was something important to be done.

This was the spot where the county road crews had always stored great piles of gravel. They used it for filling pot-holes, and to bridge the gaps when these mountain roads took a notion to slide off into the canyons. But a few special stones waited patiently for a chance to fulfill a different destiny---a destiny of flight.

Thirty yards away was the stump. It was all that was left of a tremendous old redwood tree. Fifteen feet through and about twelve feet tall, it looked as if it had been through a war. The bark had fallen away on the near side and the bare, weathered wood underneath was covered with pockmarks. In the center of this bare spot, down low, there was what remained of a dinner-plate sized circle that looked as if it had been scratched into the wood with a pocketknife. Here the pockmarks were more concentrated, almost obliterating the circle.

He chose just the right stone. It was egg-shaped but flattened a little, and sized to fit comfortably within the natural curve of the forefinger.

Twenty yards... sixty feet. Begin with the stance. Check the runner at first. Wait for the signal from the plate. Wave it off. Fix the target in your mind. Follow the imagined arc of the stone to the stump as if it were a tracer bullet and fix that in your mind as well. Look away and continue to picture that perfect pitch.

Wind up and check the target again. Reach all the way back and throw from the ground up. Crack your body like a bullwhip to full extension, and bring your right leg around to follow through.

When the stone hit the center of his old target, it disappeared in a "poof" of redwood dust. The rotten wood splintered and collapsed inward with the force of the blow, leaving a gaping hole in the stump where the old mark had been.

It was as if the hours he'd spent chunking rocks at that stump all those years ago had been leading him to this one final, perfect pitch. The familiarity of the mental process and the motion of throwing had felt kind of spooky, as if he were in a dream instead of actually being here in this place. When he got back on the bicycle and rode past his parents' old driveway he felt far away, disconnected from the present, but totally connected to something else.

He thought about riding over the hill to the old house. But another family would be living there now, and he decided he didn't want to meet them and feel the need to explain himself. It was private property and he was no longer a part of it, not even today. He told himself that his old memories would be better off without being cluttered up with new ones. He wanted to be able to remember the home of his childhood without any overlays of what it might have become. So he was off to the Maple Creek Bridge.

He had been traveling east, following the ridge between Freshwater Creek canyon on the south and Mad River canyon on the north. The Maple Creek road led north, running down the east side of an intersecting ridge to the mighty Mad. It snaked down to the river, seven miles away, ranging around rugged side hills and through a thick forest of redwood and Douglas fir. On the right lay Black Creek canyon.

He stopped only once. There was an opening in the trees where he could look far down into the canyon and see a small, deserted cabin. It was just a one-room shack at the edge of a tiny meadow. He couldn't believe it was still there. These cabins could be found here and there throughout the region, left over from the great logging days of more than a century ago. He had even found a whole sawmill once, complete with iron tools and machinery. The shacks that had huddled around the mill building had still contained rude furniture and rusted woodstoves.

This particular cabin had always seemed to be the perfect place to live the simple life of a hermit. It was picturesque and romantic, and had always called to him.

He was reminded of Robert Frost's poem, "Stopping by Woods on a Snowy Evening." It ends with, "…but I have promises to keep, and miles to go before I sleep. And miles to go before I sleep." So down the mountain he rode, leaning and braking and feeling the hot breath of summer in his face. He was alive again. He belonged here.

The bridge is constructed of light-grey concrete. In the sunlight it looks almost white, its single arch standing out in stark contrast to the deep and varied greens of river and forest that surround it. The road angles down, makes a sharp left turn, crosses the bridge over the Mad River, then makes a sharp right turn, goes on for about fifty yards or so and crosses over Maple Creek.

Much smaller and older, the Maple Creek Bridge is

moss-covered and sleeps in the shade of a pair of ancient maple trees. Just beyond it, there is a gravel access road that cuts steeply down to the river.

For most of the year, the Mad River appears to be almost cheerful. The water riffles over gravel and sand, or pools and eddies around great boulders. But in winter, it takes on a different personality. It becomes a seething, hissing brown dragon, devouring small trees and thrashing its way madly toward the sea.

As he stood there on the bridge, gazing down at the peaceful river, the man remembered a spring day when he and a group of friends had tried to drive a Volkswagen up that creek. He couldn't remember why. Young men don't much concern themselves with the 'why' of things.

They hadn't realized how buoyant those little cars were. The creek was a bit too deep and the car tended to float. It was carried out into the river before taking on enough water to sink. They'd had to work all the rest of the day to get it out. He smiled as he recalled how relieved they all were when it miraculously started and they didn't have to walk home. Ah, youth.

About a half mile up the road was another trail down to the river. It was overgrown now, hidden in the underbrush. If he hadn't known it was there, he'd have missed it. He wheeled his over-laden bike down the tangled trail, around a small hill, and dragged it out of sight. When his belongings were well hidden, he continued on, carrying only a small pack, his sleeping bag, and a telescoping fishing rod.

He slept that night under the stars. After feasting on trout and huckleberries, even the excitement of being back in the forest couldn't keep him awake. He had no idea what time he had fallen asleep, as he had no idea what time he woke. Time was only important in that other world, the world of mortgages and taxes and buying and selling. He had left his watch in a locker at the bus terminal. Here it would always be now, daylight or darkness.

Well, it was daylight. He sat up, yawned and stretched. For the moment, the man was utterly content. It was as if he'd been misplaced, exiled for thirty years, and now he was home again. Just upstream from the sand bar on which he lay, a great, grey rock slumbered half in, half out of the water. It was as big as a house, or a brontosaurus. Fir Trees bristled the ridges that angled up from the river. The pale blue, morning sky arched over all, and mare's tail clouds hung motionless within it.

He didn't realize how sore he was until he tried to stand. His thighs and calves were the worst, but he was a little sore from the saddle, too. He walked around a bit, trying to stretch out his leg muscles and, leaving his clothes next to his sleeping bag on the sand, padded over to the rock. From a ledge near the water, he slowly lowered himself into the cool, swirling river. This was heaven. This was nirvana. This was home.

Upstream from his position, the river eddied into a deeper pool, where the boulder rose up from the water to a height of ten feet or more. Hand-over-hand, he worked his way around the rough stone surface until he no longer felt the tug of the current. Depressions in the stone provided hand and footholds. He remembered them well. Making use of these, he scrambled up the surface until he stood high above the water. This was not the time or place for a graceful swan dive. He jumped, tucked, and smacked the water in a not-so-classic cannonball.

Regretfully then, he allowed the current to carry him back to the ledge. Back on the sand, he dried off, dressed, and stowed his sleeping bag in its stuff sack. Then, using a branch as a broom, he erased every trace of his having been there from the soft sand that had been his bed. A couple of granola bars would do for breakfast.

When everything had been repacked carefully onto the bicycle, he set about extricating it from its hiding place in the bushes. That done, he started up the road, walking

Fallen Idyll

at first, and then riding more as his stiffness began to ease.

The impulse to hurry was strong, but for the next three weeks, maybe for the rest of his life, he would try not to give in to it. Now was the time, and that was enough.

After a few miles, the pavement ended. Riding was more difficult on the dusty gravel, so he alternated riding and walking more frequently.

He could feel it beginning. There is a mental or spiritual phenomenon that occurs in the wilderness. Vision seems to get clearer. Awareness is heightened, and the mind shakes off the chains of linear thought. Thoughts seem to take wing, flying free of motive and intent. In some ways he was there in the present moment more fully than ever, and yet, on another level, his mind felt free of its connection to that moment, free to ramble and create. He was free of himself! That was it. And in being free of himself, he was freed from the constraints of expectation. Each perception was sufficient within itself. Even if the present moment were disconnected from all other moments, it would be complete. The eternal now; maybe this is what he had come three thousand miles to find.

For thirty years he had been settling for a life in which he had substituted accomplishment and the fleeting, fragile elation that comes from the acquisition of possessions, for this intangible but satisfying sense of actually being alive. He sighed and pushed on. The frantic activity under the surface of the soap bubble was beginning to ease.

All day he traveled that lonely gravel road. With each mailbox he passed, with every driveway that forked off to the right or to the left, the road became narrower.

Finally it was just one lane, two wheel ruts through the woods and fields. It continued on this way for miles.

The road ended at a ravine. It had washed out once, years before, and there had been no reason to repair it, no reason to go beyond that point. It was the boundary line of the civilized world.

2 THE WILDERNESS

First, he unpacked, carrying everything across the gully, one bag at a time. He had purchased a folding, three-wheeled baby stroller, the kind used by joggers. He removed it from its place on the bicycle, set it up on the far side of the gully and loaded it with his things. Then he walked the empty bike through the tangled brush, and up the hill. When it was well hidden, he covered it with a camouflaged plastic tarp and set off, pushing the stroller.

He kept to the hills, far above and out of sight of the river. Another, larger ravine had to be crossed, this one containing a swiftly flowing stream. This meant another portage, unpacking and then repacking the stroller.

As he entered a big meadow, he surprised and was surprised by a small herd of black tail deer. He stood for a moment, watching. He counted seven before they disappeared over the hills. Soon he was back in the forest again. It was slow going. Here there was no trail. He had taken "the road less traveled by," left it behind, and struck out on his own. There was that poet again.

He was on the edge of a deep, rugged canyon. Over countless centuries of erosion, the river had carved a winding path, shifting its bed of fine sand one grain at a time. At a certain spot though, it cuts between tall cliffs. The sheer rock faces rise directly out of the water, continuing for almost a mile before gradually diminishing in height, giving way to gravel and sand bars once again.

The traveler had never ventured beyond these cliffs. Following the river upstream, the water is too deep and swift to swim and the rock faces are too sheer and tall to be easily climbed. He had always thought that, if he could just get beyond that point, he would make for the river and find a place that was completely isolated from the civilized world. And whether he spent a few moments there or a lifetime, he would know true freedom.

Darkness was coming on. In the shadow of the mountains, dusk seems to start in the middle of the afternoon, so nightfall can happen suddenly. Once again, he didn't bother to set up his tent. He simply rolled his sleeping bag out upon a fairly level, grassy spot for a dry camp under the stars. He awoke early, or so it seemed, breakfasted on some crackers and resumed his journey, turning south, toward the river.

Dragging the stroller full of supplies and equipment through the thick underbrush began to wear through his cheerfulness. He figured that he must be beyond the cliffs, and he wanted to get down to the river and set up a base camp. He had been struggling for most of the morning and neither he nor the stroller looked new anymore. They were both scratched and dirty and maybe leaning a little to one side. Finally, about mid-day, after struggling and working his way toward the river, he burst out of a particularly tangled mass of vines and shrubs at the top of the cliff.

There was the river far below, sliding silently between the rock faces, mocking him with its serenity. He knew that his anger and frustration were due to his inability to abandon linear thinking. He had set an arbitrary goal and allowed his progress toward that goal to act as the barometer by which he measured his happiness and sense of well-being.

The goal was still there, but now it seemed even farther away. This meant that he would have to backtrack through the woods for a while before heading east again. It was almost unthinkable. A whole morning wasted. Or was it?

It was while he was kicking himself for wasting the morning, that he realized just how spoiled he had become. Does anything worthwhile come without a price? Is life simply a series of snapshots, a disconnected chain if high and low points? Somehow, he had forgotten that the process of working toward a goal is the foundation, the substance of the experience.

There was as much value to be found in his struggle through the woods as there was in the possibility of setting up a base camp. There was no intrinsic, qualitative difference between the two. There was only his spoiled-child desire to have what he wanted, when he wanted it.

It suddenly came to him that he was possibly the only human who had ever been dumb enough to push his way to the top of that cliff. The view alone was almost worth the trip. Massive grey stone cliffs held back dark green, forested hills. Beyond the hills, slate blue mountains stood high against the deep, azure sky of summer. And far beneath it all, the river flowed, giving rhythm to the scene. It filled his senses.

The serenity that had mocked his frustration gradually began to soothe, even to inspire him. He went to his packs and searched until he found a notebook and pencil. This was to have been his journal, a record of his time here, but so far this would be his first entry. It was a poem:

> I was born here in these mountains
> Like the dust between my toes
> I've got holes in all my pockets

> I've got patches on my clothes
> And I've never owned a dollar
> And I've never worked for pay
> And sometimes you'll find me sleeping
> In the middle of the day
> And sometimes you'll find me waking
> When the moon is on the rise
> At the magic hour of midnight
> With the starlight in my eyes
> And sometimes you'll find me laughing
> Like the ripples on a stream
> And sometimes you'll find me weeping
> At the memory of a dream
> And some people think it's sinful
> Living careless and so free
> But deep inside I think that they're
> Just wishing they were me

Smiling to himself, he packed the journal away and started back, away from the cliff. Instead of retracing his steps to the north, he followed a more easterly line, intending to describe a wide circle that would bring him to the river at a point farther upstream. He chose his trail carefully, but again, progress was slow.

He found that, as long as he concentrated on the task at hand, he was okay. As long as he could keep from thinking about his difficulties in terms of his goal, he could remain relatively content. He wasn't always content,

There was one especially steep slope where the stroller got caught in the branches of a Tan Oak bush. He pulled lightly, trying to free it. Becoming frustrated, he pulled harder and harder until it suddenly broke loose.

He heard the branch snap and suddenly eighty pounds of stroller, packs and provisions were airborne. As it sailed over his head, something hit him hard in the nose, causing him to lose his precarious footing on the grass-covered hillside.

The stroller bounced a couple of times, rolling end-over-end to the bottom of the hill.

The man was spinning side-over-side, but since his angle of trajectory was lower than that of his belongings, his progress was halted abruptly by the presence of another bush. He would think of it later as a kind of slow-motion tragic-comical ballet: packs and bags pirouetting down the slope in time, the stroller breaking free of its burdens like a terrestrial comet, leaving a tail of grass and dirt, as the man whirled down the hill with arms and legs flailing the air.

A colorful and creative string of cusswords echoed around the canyons and up and down the river, ending with, "damn, damn, damn, damn, damn!"

Looking around, he saw that it could have been worse. The packs had held together. He sat for a few minutes with his head tilted back until the nosebleed stopped. There was blood on his face and shirt, spattered from the rolling. The bad news was that the stroller handle and the front wheel were bent and that he had seriously damaged two innocent bushes.

He would have to be more careful. What if he had been badly injured, maybe even broken a leg? It was critical that he stop planning and thinking ahead to the exclusion of the present. Once again, he had been impatient to find a spot to set up base camp.

Why? Because he was tired and bored with dragging that damned stroller all over the country. So what? How is a moment in the imaginary future more important or worthy of attention than the moment of now?

So the first words he had spoken in three days, perhaps the first words ever spoken in this area of the canyon were yelled in anger and frustration. He wished he could take them back.

The wheel looked like the brim of a cowboy hat. He was able to straighten the handle, but from now on he would have to apply downward pressure, keeping that front wheel off the ground. This would make his progress that much more difficult. "Progress to where?" he thought.

All he needed was a level place to roll out his sleeping bag. That and a tall tree for "bear bagging." Black bears in the wild aren't particularly dangerous, being shy and avoiding humans when they can, so he hadn't bothered so far, but if he were going to spend more than one night in a camp he would suspend his food in a big sack, out of their reach.

In fact, he was tired of dry camps and snack food. He wanted to cook a meal.

He secured his duffel bags, his packs, and the panniers from his bicycle and started dragging the stroller down the mountain once again. A few hours later he reached the floor of the canyon. He was tempted to set up camp right there.

Following the river upstream though, he found the perfect spot. It was a wide bench, on the outside of a long curve of the river. Here it was level and open under a high canopy of alder trees. The sandy ground was carpeted with dry leaves.

3 THE CAMP

The trees were tall and straight. Mossy columns supported a crown of branches and leaves high above the forest floor. The river had flowed here at one time, but now it had cut a deeper channel, flowing past about ten feet below the level of the bench.

At the eastern end of this bench, over against the foot of the hill, stood a huge moss-covered rock. It was, appropriately, the size of a large camp trailer. At one end, a tree had grown up through it, fracturing the stone. Between the two pieces there was a sand floored "room" about six feet wide, the perfect place for a shelter.

The man unpacked the now-hated stroller, folded it up and stashed it out of sight under a log. He stretched a camouflaged tarp over the space between the rocks and tied it down, covering it with moss and leaves. Inside, he placed all of his belongings, leaving enough room to roll out his ground sheet and sleeping bag. He found a short piece of tree limb, tied it to one end of a nylon line and threw it over a high branch. He then removed the limb from the line, tying it instead to his duffel bag full of food. This he suspended about ten or twelve feet above the ground, tying the other end of the line to the trunk of a tree within his reach. This was his "bear bag."

The next few days were spent fishing and exploring the area near the camp. He gathered up dead twigs and branches until he had a big pile of firewood. He was king of the world, master of all he surveyed.

The man figured that it was probably seven or eight miles back to the place where the road had ended. That would be due west. By the end of the week he had ranged a mile or two up the river to the east and maybe a mile north and south. He found a long-abandoned cabin to the north. It sat at the top of a sloping meadow, and against a grove of ragged white oaks. Skirting the field, he crept up until he saw that there was no glass in the windows. He walked cautiously over and peeked inside. A rusty old cookstove stood against the far wall and a bed of sorts had been built into a corner. The bed was a pallet of rough lumber, supported by legs made of peeled logs. There was also a small table and one broken chair. Leaves had blown in, gathering around and under the bed.

He went around to the small, covered porch and tried the door. It creaked open, scraping the floor as it went. There was something tacked to the wall near the window. In the darkness of the cabin he couldn't make out what it was until he walked over to look more closely. When the light from the window reflected off his shirt, he saw that it was a calendar, with a picture of a woman sitting on a rock and a hound at her feet. There was a village in the distance and a biplane flying overhead. The year was nineteen twenty-six.

There was no evidence that anyone had been there since. There were no candy wrappers, no cigarette packs, and best of all, no graffiti on the walls. He went outside and looked for footprints, finding none but his own. These, he wiped away before he left.

Just how big was this kingdom of his, this uninhabited valley? He resolved to find out. The next morning he put his collapsible fishing rod, some food and his sleeping bag in the daypack. He straightened up his campsite with the idea of making it invisible and, satisfied that it could be passed by unnoticed, he set off to the north, away from the river.

As he climbed and hiked, he was struck with the realization that he had been right about this place. He was truly free. He thought about the world at large, and it made even less sense than it had before. This world, this existence made sense.

Early in the afternoon he reached the top of the first ridge. It was thickly forested with Douglas fir trees, so he took off his pack and climbed one. He chose a big, gnarled one, with limbs that grew almost to the ground and were about the thickness of a man's leg. As he climbed, the branches and the massive trunk diminished in size until, at the very top, he could feel the great tree sway with the breeze, and some of the small, brittle branches broke off under his weight.

From here he could look out over both sides of the mountain. Unbroken forest stretched away to the horizon in every direction. Far to the north, on the side away from the river, he could see a house or a barn. It was just a speck in the distance, really, too far away to make out. It may have been another of those abandoned cabins. He looked for the one he had discovered the day before, but it was hidden by the slope of the hill.

His hands were all sticky with pitch, and during the climb down, they became even worse. He tried to clean them using all of the water he had left in his plastic bottle, but without much success. They weren't so sticky anymore, but the sap had turned from a honey color to black. "Black as pitch," he said to himself.

He needed more water. In this country, if you want water, all you have to do is go downhill. Sooner or later you will find a stream. Sure enough, after walking south for a few minutes, the man could hear the music of water dripping. He followed to the source of the sound and discovered a tiny spring. After digging a hole under the drip and waiting for the water to clear again, he filled his bottle.

There is no more satisfying drink than the cold, clear water of a mountain spring. The solid rock of the mountain imparts to it a sweetness, a flavour that can be found nowhere else. Distilled water may be more pure, technically, but it lacks something. It's like the difference between instant oatmeal and the kind your mom used to make. He decided that the difference was love. Chuckling to himself, he also decided that he was getting a little loopy.

It made sense that so many primitive cultures worship the earth as mother and the sun as father. The sun engenders life in the earth and the earth gives birth to life, teaching and nourishing it. Yes, he was getting loopy all right.

As he followed this little brook from its source it grew and grew. It was joined by tributaries from innumerable ravines, becoming a small stream as it babbled merrily on its way.

Night was coming on. Still the creek was too small to contain fish, but he found a salmonberry patch. Salmonberries look somewhat like large blackberries, only they have a golden color and grow on sparse vines. They can be found only on the banks of shady streams, with their large, pale green leaves hanging over the water.

Since his belly was full and the evening was warm, he didn't bother to build a fire. As he had in the past, he simply found a fairly level spot and slept. In the morning he resumed his journey down the creek and, before midday, began to see fish in some of the pools.

These pools were still too small for any of his fishing lures, so he climbed a side hill in order to search for bait. There was a field some way up the slope where he hoped to find grasshoppers. They would do nicely.

A log slanted up the hill between the man and the

meadow. He could have walked around it, but he was feeling particularly adventurous and decided to climb over. Better yet, he would balance upon it, walking this fat "tightrope" up the hill. About halfway up, at a spot where the log crossed a small gully, he slipped. Actually, it was the bark that slipped. No matter.

He fell off the log. It really was easy.

For one split second he thought he would be okay. He landed on his feet, but the bank was too steep and he couldn't quite get balanced. He pitched out into the air, coming to rest with a splash in the creek. His natural reaction was to jump immediately out of the water, whereupon he slipped and sprawled face down on the bank.

At this point, he realized that sudden movements were not helping, so he lay where he was, collecting his scattered thoughts.

Somebody giggled.

The man jumped up, listening.

"Hello?" he said, "Is someone there?"

There was a rustling in the dense brush to his left, followed by the sound of something scurrying away through the forest. He followed for a while, but finding no tracks or trail, he gave up and branched off toward the field.

All of his senses were sharpened and alert. He was sure that the sound had been a giggle. Or was it? Could it have been some kind of bird? Maybe he had been up here alone too long and his imagination was running away with him.

Until now he had been utterly at ease, sheltered in the invisible arms of a loving Earth. Suddenly he was alone. Whatever that sound had been, it had shattered his contentment. It disturbed him to realize how fragile it had been. He forced his thinking back to the task at hand.

Catching grasshoppers can be a challenge. One method is to take off your shirt and scan the grassy ground until you spot one, spread the shirt like a parachute in front of you and dive to the ground, catching the grasshopper underneath. Then you feel around the spot where you think he was until you find him wriggling under the shirt. Pinch him gingerly in a fold of fabric, turn the shirt over and there he is. The problem with this method is "bug juice." Frightened grasshoppers secrete a liquid that has the color and consistency of soy sauce and, after you've caught a dozen or so, your shirt will have little brown spots all over it. Besides, if your shirt happens to be soaking wet from falling into a stream, all the grass, leaves and dirt will stick to it, making it really uncomfortable later on.

The man's preferred method was cleaner, but less efficient. He simply spotted one of the little varmints and dove to the ground, trapping the little guy under his cupped hands. He missed a lot. In about half an hour he caught seven. It was fun.

Back at the stream, he caught three nice trout, cleaned them and built a small fire. He cut green willow sticks, stuck the fish on the sticks and stuck the sticks in the ground, leaving them suspended over the fire.

He was sitting on the bank, eating his fish and watching the sunlight flash and sparkle on the flowing water of the creek. Just upstream he could hear a little waterfall, and downstream there was another, larger one. The sounds they made, added to the other sounds of the surrounding forest; here a buzzing cicada, there a flock of small birds twittering, became a symphony. His contentment had returned.

Somebody said hello.

The man jumped up, heart pounding, and said something like, "whaah?"

There was a man standing on the bank above him, silhouetted against the sun. He was a little less than medium height, lean, and dressed in overalls.

"Sorry if I startled you, 'mind if I come down and

talk?"

"Of course," said the man, "I just thought I was alone out here."

The stranger jumped easily down from the log he had been standing on and walked over. "I'm Henry." He appeared to be in his late thirties, with sandy hair and a friendly smile. There was a look of merriment in his eyes, as if he knew a really funny secret. "We don't see many strangers around here, and the ones we do see are usually lost," he said. "Are you lost?"

"Nope," said the man, "Just fishing."

Henry seemed to like that answer. "Fair enough," he said, "Got a name?"

"Of course I do," said the man, "I'm Thomas."

Both men stepped forward to shake hands. Each was impressed with the firm grip and clear, searching gaze of the other.

"Glad to know you, Thomas. So, are you heading to, or running from?"

"Both, I guess, or maybe neither. I'm on vacation. Am I trespassing?"

"A good question," Henry said, "Right now I'd say no. You're welcome to stay here as long as you like, just try not to burn the woods down. I notice you're packed kind of light so you must have a camp somewhere. Who knows, maybe I'll stop by and we can talk some more."

Henry turned to go. "Oh, by the way, if you keep playing in the water you'll probably scare all the fish away. But I guess you already knew that." Again there was that knowing twinkle in the eyes.

"Yeah thanks," said Thomas. He watched as Henry strode away, disappearing among the trees. It was a disappointment, finding another human in his world. He had been feeling like a pioneer or a mountain man exploring virgin territory. The creek led him down to the river and he followed the river back to his camp.

4 THE VISITORS

For the next two days Thomas stayed close to his shelter. Somehow he had lost his taste for exploration. After all, what might he find next? There was probably a resort, or maybe even a whole town out here.

He only ventured far enough to check on the trap he had made. It was a "dead fall," whereby a log is supported by three notched sticks, which are arranged to form the shape of the number four. When the horizontal member is disturbed, the device collapses and the log falls on whatever was unwary enough to disturb it. In this case it was a rabbit.

After stretching the hide to dry in the sun, he set about cooking up a meal. He was elated. It wasn't a fish.

His elation was tempered by feelings of sadness, humility and gratitude. The rabbit, recently alive and scampering freely through the forest had been sacrificed, only to be burned upon the altar of Thomas' appetite. He began to see the fish he had been living on in the same light. Each plant or animal here was dependent upon all of the others. Even the elements were part of the whole, adding the uncertainty of weather and climate to the mix. It was, in fact, like a great, swirling dance, spinning with the seasons; animal and plant populations growing, shrinking, appearing or disappearing in a great ballet of life.

Somebody said, "Smells good!"

It was Henry. He was standing about fifty feet away, and another man was with him. The other man was about Thomas' age, dark hair graying, thinning on top. There was something familiar about him.

"Thomas, meet Martin. Martin, this is the man I was telling you about."

Martin's face lit up into a big grin. "Well if it isn't Tommy Graham," he said, "I should have known."

Thomas jumped up and held out his hand. "My god, Marty, is that you? Look what happened. You're an old man!"

"I don't know what happened to you, but I'm still just a pup," Martin laughed, "and I can still kick your butt."

"Yeah, like you ever could. Remember the time…"

The men had brought corn bread, butter, and a pot of cold beans to add to the meal.

They sat around the campfire and talked into the night. Tommy and Marty appeared on the faces of Thomas Graham and Martin Tyler as they recounted adventures from their early days, beginning in elementary school and ending when Thomas moved back East.

"I always wondered what happened to you," Martin said, "You moved out to… where was it, Ohio? And we never heard from you again."

"It was Michigan. And at the time I thought I either had to get out of here or die. I was drinking too much, along with other things, and I kept trying to change, but I always seemed to wind up with a hangover. I had to break the pattern. I needed a new environment, a new job, and even new friends."

"Yeah, that's what I always figured," Martin nodded, "One of the things you had to get away from was me. It kind of ticked me off for fifteen years or so, but then I realized that I needed to make the same kinds of changes and that's how I ended up here."

"You live up here?"

Martin glanced over at Henry before answering. "I guess you could say that. But let's talk about you. What have you been up to all these years? Didn't you miss this place? You never even came back for a visit."

"Well, I'm here now, aren't I? I must have thought about calling or writing a thousand times. I don't think a day went by that I didn't dream about this part of the world and my life here. But with the business and all, I just never seemed to be able to find the time. I've spent the last thirty years doing what was necessary and not much else. Hell Marty, this is only the second vacation I've ever had."

"The cost of comfort," Martin said. "Since the beginning of time, man has sought to insulate himself from the realities of life. He gathers things around himself in order to make his life predictable and safe, but in the end he finds that it's only boring and repetitive. The price we pay for comfort is our freedom."

"Whoa, big fellah!" Thomas laughed. "You're preaching to the choir here."

"Sorry Tommy, I get kind of carried away sometimes. We were talking about you."

Thomas pulled his wallet from his back pocket. He drew out a faded photograph and handed it to Martin. "This was my family," he said. "Helen and I were married for eighteen years. A couple of years ago, we lost a long, difficult fight with cancer.

"I'm sorry man," Martin said. "Is that your son?"

"Yeah, That's Tyler. He's grown and married, and living in New Jersey. I don't hear from him much. What with his mom's illness and me running the business, I wasn't able to spend a lot of quality time with him and I guess he kind of resents it. I've made a few mistakes in my life. Maybe that's why I'm here."

"Well, what do you know... You named your kid Tyler?" A mischievous look stole into Martin's brown eyes. "I named a dog Tommy once, but he ran away. Kind of an interesting coincidence, I thought."

As the night wore on, the conversation flowed as easily and smoothly as the river close at hand. The two old friends talked and laughed and remembered.

The sun was rising somewhere. The eastern sky had that weird combination of blue and green and yellow and pink that only the early morning sky can have. Direct sunlight was still a long way from the bottom of the canyon. Henry was sound asleep, rolled up in a blanket by the dying fire.

"I have a proposition for you, Tommy. We have what you could call an experiment going on here." Martin was poking the remnants of the fire with a stick, sending sparks up into the morning air. "I guess, in a way, you've always been a part of it, because it's based on ideas that I got from you. Remember our conversations about the four basic needs? We need water, food, shelter and companionship. All of our institutions, governments, corporations, everything that touches our lives, is centered around the satisfaction of those four necessities."

"Yeah, I remember," said Tommy. "I even wrote it all up once. The theory was that, knowing this, you could cut through all the crap, concentrate on satisfying those four needs in the simplest possible terms and have a richer, fuller life."

"Good. You were right."

"Sure I was, in a way. But in this electronic, digital society it's not very realistic to think you can live that way. Freedom is only possible for the extreme top and bottom ends of the human food chain. Homeless people are free, but they pay the price of being nomadic. It becomes very difficult for them to have permanent relationships or any kind of continuity in their lives. At the other end, the wealthy have the opportunity to be free, but they usually become chained to their excesses and the emotional rush that comes from acquisition and power. The people in the middle are the drones, the workers upon which the whole mess of society rests. If they were truly free, it would all collapse. They really have no options."

Martin continued to poke the fire. "That would be the rule," he said. "But every rule has exceptions." He paused for a moment, collecting his thoughts. "Haven't you been wondering what Henry and I are doing up here, wearing homemade clothes and eating cornbread and beans?"

"I just figured you'd get around to telling me sooner or later," Thomas said. "You looked as if you'd bust if you didn't."

"This is serious." Martin tossed the stick onto the coals and turned toward Thomas, looking very serious indeed. "This is the most serious thing I've ever done," he said. "Henry and I and some others are involved in something really important.

A few years ago, I met a man out here in the woods. I was doing just what you're doing now, taking a vacation and trying to make some sense of my life. This guy had just bought the whole valley. I guess he had a lot of history here, family roots or something. Anyway, he bought the place, several thousand acres.

He told me that he'd made all of his money by exploiting the weaknesses of others and that he wanted to make up for it somehow. We hiked and camped together for several days, talked a lot of philosophy and ate a lot of fish. One night we were sitting by the campfire and he came up with this idea. He'd let people homestead his land."

Henry rolled over and sat up, sleepily rubbing his eyes. "Have you guys been talking all night?" he asked. "I'm hungry."

"Well good afternoon," Martin said. "I thought you

were going to sleep the day away. It was your snoring, kept us awake. I was afraid you were going to bring the mountain down on us. How about you rustle us up some breakfast while Tommy and I go down to the river and talk some more?"

"Good idea." Henry got up and began rummaging through the small packs that he and Martin had brought.

5 THE PHILOSOPHER SPEAKS

The two older men stood, stretched and started walking slowly toward the river. "Now, where was I? Oh yeah, the Homestead Act. So this guy got all this money by exploiting the weaknesses of others, whatever that means. I figured it had something to do with drugs. He said that the problem with profiting from peoples' weaknesses is that you soon discover that you have weaknesses of your own. He felt like he was headed for a big fall if he didn't make some big changes, so he bought more land south of here for himself and opened this place up for people like me."

They came to the riverbank and sat down on the grass, feet dangling over the water. "He had decided that all of his negative actions had created a domino effect of negative energy that aught to be stopped. Since he had no way of stopping most of it, his alternative was to start some positive domino effects that he hoped would make up for the things he had done before. I know it sounds all weird and metaphysical, but, the way he put it, it's more natural than supernatural. More inevitable, like gravity."

"Anyway, he set up some sort of annuity to pay for taxes and such, so the whole thing kind of runs itself.

Would you look at that."

A Great Blue Heron came sailing low over the river, his long neck looped into a "U." "They always remind me of pterodactyls," said Thomas. "I could watch him all day. You were saying?"

"Okay, here's the deal. This property started out as a cattle ranch, or rather several cattle ranches. Around the turn of the century, they were all bought up by a lumber company. I'm not sure, but I think it's something over six thousand acres. Anyway, it's all split up into quarter sections and if someone is interested, say someone like you, all he has to do is pick out a spot. Then he's given a conditional deed to that spot and the hundred and sixty acres surrounding it. He has five years to prove up on it, at which time it becomes his property, free and clear."

"You're kidding, of course." Thomas flipped a small stone into the water. The splash it made was carried away by the swiftly flowing river. "In my experience, there are two kinds of dreams, the kind that are supposed to come true and the kind that are supposed to remain dreams. Reality can never compete with fantasy, and if you want something too much, the getting of it will always be a disappointment."

"Wait a minute, Tom. Didn't you say that you've been dreaming about coming back here ever since you left?"

"Yeah, so what?"

"Well, are you disappointed?"

"Of course not. This trip has been everything I had hoped it would be. But taking a vacation, and living out a fantasy for the rest of your life are two very different things. Then there's my life in Michigan to think about. What about the business I've been working on for all these years?"

"Oh, I see. You're just scared. That was always your problem. You always think too much. By the time you've made your mind up about something, it's too late and the opportunity slips though your fingers."

"Yeah, well at least I'm not like you. With you it was always 'Jump right in and to hell with the consequences."

"Oh yeah?... Oh yeah?" Martin stood up as if he wanted to fight it out. Then with a grin he said, "My way is more fun," and dove into the river.

Thomas muttered, "Oh hell," took off his shirt and shoes, emptied the pockets of his shorts and dove in too.

The water was surprisingly cold. Not so surprising was the quickness with which both men climbed back onto the bank.

"Do you see a couple of lumps up by my shoulders?" Thomas asked.

"No, why?"

"Because I think my nuts are up there somewhere. Wow! That water is cold!"

"Refreshing, ain't it?"

"Hey! Are you guys ready for some breakfast?" It was Henry from the camp, banging on a frying pan. Thomas and Martin smiled and walked back toward the fire.

"It looks like you two fell in the river," Henry said. "That seems to happen to you a lot, Tom."

With a look of surprise and obvious pleasure, Thomas accepted a steaming tin plate of ham and eggs. "This time I was pushed in," He said. And with a glance at Martin, he added, "Peer pressure."

The next few minutes were spent enjoying Henry's considerable skill with a frying pan. When the last bit of yolk had been sopped up, Thomas laid his plate aside. Sighing contentedly, he said, "I don't know what you did or how you did it, but that was bar-none the finest breakfast I ever ate."

"He does it every time," Martin added. "Maybe if you decided to stay up here, you could eat like this again."

"Marty, if it was just me, you couldn't pry me out

of this place with a crowbar. But I have responsibilities. I have to do what's right for my business and the people who depend on me. We're not little kids anymore. There's a real world out there and I have to deal with it."

"Okay, Tommy, let's look at your 'real world.' Whatever this country started out to be, it has become a nightmare land of greed and deception. Government and big business, through P. R. Firms, manipulate public opinion by putting a spin on the truth. By the way, that's impossible. If you spin the truth, it's not true anymore. Anyway, people are so used to being lied to, that the line between fact and fiction gets all blurry and truth becomes an idea instead of being a simple fact. People believe whatever version of truth fits their particular agenda.

Governments lie in order to further their interests, whatever that means. Liberals and conservatives feel justified in lying to themselves and to each other because they're so right and everyone else is so wrong. Let's face it, liberals are socialists and conservatives are profiteers. One group sides with big government while the other sides with big business. We call America the land of the free, but try not paying into social security and see what happens. Try not paying your property tax, sales tax, fuel tax, income tax, road tax, bed tax and on and on and on.

If you want to build a house, you have to get permits for every aspect of the project. This helps pay the salaries of the inspectors, commissioners, and official pains in the butt who make sure you build it their way.

Someone tells you when and where to smoke, drink, eat, sleep, spit, walk, or go to the bathroom. People have been convinced that they are incapable of making the simple decisions of life, or even of solving their own problems. How can anyone, by any stretch of imagination, call this a free society? I'll tell you how. You just have to choose to ignore the truth and believe the lies."

"So your solution is what, to run away?"

"You bet it is. I'll run, I'll hide, I'll fall through any

crack in the system that's big enough. I don't want to start some kind of a movement, I just want to be left alone.

I built my house way out in the woods where nobody will notice it. If I have to pay for a license to drive a car, then I just won't drive one. I don't pay income tax or social security because I have no income. Out here we grow our own food, make our own clothes, fight our own fights and live our own lives with no apologies to anyone."

"Yeah, but at what cost?"

"All we've given up is technology. We don't have electricity, so we can't watch TV, talk on the phone, eat processed food, use a microwave... By the way, what does a microwave oven do for you? It gives you the ability to do in twenty seconds what used to take twenty minutes. And what do you do with the eighteen minutes you've saved? I'll tell you what you do. You work, so you can make more money, so you can buy more crap like microwave ovens.

In the meantime, what does that eighteen minutes cost you? It robs you of the experience and possible pleasure of everything connected with cooking a meal; the aromas, the tactile sensations, the satisfaction of doing something well, and the possibility of sharing that experience with somebody.

Everything that you possess, possesses you. If you own a car, you have to keep it filled with gas. You have to change the oil. You have to replace tires, brakes, everything that wears out. You become its servant. To one degree or another, the same is true of everything you own."

"Preach it, brother Martin!" Henry said, laughing. "Hallelujah!"

"I'm sorry, but it just makes me mad," said Martin. "Technology has taken all of the life out of life."

Thomas was intrigued. "No, go on," he said. "This stuff is great."

"Okay, but remember, you asked for it. "Let's take

TV. Television trivializes important things and elevates trivia to a position of seeming importance. A commercial showing you which deodorant is most effective is presented with the same intensity, and seems to have just as much value, as news coverage of an earthquake that destroys a city where millions of people are killed. Using the wrong laundry detergent seems just as catastrophic as a stock market crash. How can a person or a society keep their priorities straight when they are constantly bombarded with this monotone of drivel? Obviously, they can't.

As human beings, we have very small circles of influence. We work with our hands, our hearts and our minds, doing what we can to make our lives, and the lives of those around us a little better. Mass electronic communication brings us too much information. The fact is that we don't need a particular deodorant and we don't need to know about an earthquake unless it affects us directly. Sure, we could send aid to the earthquake victims, but how many of us do? How many of us would even give aid to a neighbor down the street? The way I look at it, if I'm doing what I can about the things within my circle of influence, then that's enough. If we would all do that, the world would be a lot better off."

"Maybe so, but in reality, we all don't do that." Thomas was thinking that he could see a flaw in Martin's theories. "There's no way to make sure that the people outside of our immediate area are getting the help they need if we aren't aware of their situation."

"That may be true enough. But maybe their situation isn't any of our business. We're always trying to second-guess and circumvent the laws of nature. The world exists most efficiently when it is in balance. Each species of animal, and even the plants, live in a finely tuned balance between the availability of food and water, and the presence of predatory enemies.

Let's say there's a great year for acorns. Maybe a

mild winter and optimum conditions cause the oak trees to produce an unusual abundance. The squirrels in that part of the forest are healthier than they've ever been. Since there's so much to eat, an unusual number of squirrels survive to reproduce. The following spring, the country is overrun by millions of baby squirrels.

Squirrels are the staple food for coyotes. That year, the local coyotes have an over abundance of food, so more coyotes survive to reproduce. The following spring, the country is overrun by millions of baby coyotes.

The baby coyotes grow up, and along the way, they eat millions of squirrels, decimating the local squirrel population. Now we have too many coyotes, and not enough tasty little squirrels to feed them. Hunger and disease come along, decimating the coyote population. With fewer coyotes around, the squirrel population increases again, and on, and on, and on.

Animal populations wax and wane continually. Barring great catastrophe, the numbers only vary by a small percentage. But, through scientific and medical advances, people have been able to short-circuit the system. Without the natural checks and balances of predators and disease, the human population continues to grow, unchecked."

"So, what's your point?"

"My point is that the world is overpopulated, and it's going to get worse. When too many people live too close together, they act irrationally. In a small group, people can see the advantages of acting for the good of the group. But in a larger group, people tend to do only the things that make them feel good. They tend to abuse whatever freedom they have through self-interested, and even self-destructive behavior. The group becomes too unwieldy, and the dynamics of the group become too complex. People can't see the responsibilities they have toward their actual circles of influence, and they become confused. They try to spread their influence so thin, that it disappears."

"Okay," said Thomas. "Suppose you're right. Suppose there is an earthquake and people die. Suppose this creates a typhoid epidemic. As the epidemic spreads, each person deals only with his immediate circle. What's to stop the disease from wiping out everyone on the planet?"

"There you go. You've been conditioned to think in terms of corporate responsibility and corporate response. If each individual acted responsibly there would be no epidemic. It is just that attitude of letting some overarching authority deal with individual problems like disease and crime and racism, sexism, stupidity, greed, sloth, gluttony, acne, whatever, that allows these problems to continue.

Freedom in this country was never meant to be anarchy. Without individual responsibility for the greater good, there can be no individual freedom. America was founded on the idea that each person has an innate knowledge of right and wrong, and that each of us, given the freedom to act according to the dictates of conscience, has the capacity and the ability to rise above self-interest and act for the greater good of the group. When people depend on government to solve all of their problems, they become wards of the state, children who give up the right to make their own decisions."

"Yeah, I know," said Thomas. "Then the idea that people are too stupid to make their own decisions becomes a self-fulfilling prophecy. If you first take away their power to decide, it won't be long before they lose the ability to decide."

"Exactly."

"So here we are, three guys sitting on a log in the middle of nowhere, discussing things that the whole world ought to hear. How can we get this message out? How can we show the people of this country that they've been sold a bill of goods, that they've traded away their freedom for comfort?"

Martin sadly shook his head. "We can't," He said. "People don't want to hear this stuff. Freedom involves risk. If you make your own decisions, you have nobody to blame if it all goes wrong. All we can do is decide what's important in our own lives and set examples in our own limited circles of influence. By coming up here to the mountains again, you've entered my circle and brought me into yours. When you make the decision to live up here, the circle will be complete."

Thomas let his friend's gentle coercion slide. "So you're advocating revolution?"

"No. A revolution wouldn't solve anything. No matter how it starts out, a revolution can only trade one kind of oppression for another."

The three men sat in silence, allowing the subtle noises of forest and river to carry their thoughts along. A soft breeze played among the tops of the alders, the river babbled secret things and the next few minutes passed slowly by.

Thomas sighed and spoke. "I'm leaving tomorrow."

"Oh come on!" said Martin. "I had so much to show you."

"I'm sorry old pal, but there are people in Michigan who are counting on me. I have promises to keep."

"And miles to go before you sleep. I know, but why not just hang out for a few more days? You could see what we've done up here, meet my family and the others. Hey Henry, we could put together a barn dance, do it up right."

Henry looked hopefully at Thomas. "It wouldn't be that much trouble. We're always looking for an excuse to have some fun."

"I really am sorry guys, but we'll have to save it for next time. I'll try to get back up here next year, maybe have a little more time. Who knows? Maybe I'll even take you up on your offer and join your little band of merry men. But tomorrow I've got to hit the trail for home."

6 THE PRISONER

Martin stood up, smiling. "Well, I guess if you have to, you have to. The truth is, we should be heading back, too." He picked up the frying pan and handed it to Henry. "Why don't you take this down to the river and rinse it out. I'll gather up the rest of this stuff and we can get going." He turned toward Thomas.

"Tommy, it sure has been good seeing you again." He held out his hand.

As they shook hands, Thomas thought that Martin's grip was a lot stronger than before. He caught a flicker of movement out of the corner of his eye, but it was too late. The frying pan. He had just enough time to feel his knees buckle before the lights went out.

When he came to, the lights stayed out. His hands were tied and he was wearing a ski mask. Some kind of opaque material had been sown over the eyeholes. A spot on the back of his head was throbbing and his ears were still ringing. Quasimodo came to mind. The frying pan had sounded just like a church bell, and it still seemed to be echoing in his head. Gradually, other sounds began to make their way through the ringing.

Henry said, "I think he's waking up." Then

Martin said, "Good."

The sound of footsteps came toward the spot where he lay. "I'm really sorry about all this old buddy, but there's a lot more going on up here than I let on." Martin grabbed Thomas' bound hands and pulled him to his feet. Thomas was a bit dizzy and needed help standing.

"This isn't funny," Thomas managed to say. "What the hell are you doing, Marty?"

"We can talk about it later. For now, we're walking."

The rope that tied Thomas' wrists had been made into a kind of leash. He was dragged forward and the three began hiking through the woods at a pretty fast pace. Every so often, Martin would yell, "Limb!" And it wasn't long before Thomas learned that this was the signal for him to duck. He could taste blood where the first of these logs or branches had split his lip. They walked for hours and, after numerous attempts by Thomas to find out what the hell was going on, they moved along in silence except for the occasional, "Limb!"

Everything had changed. When he wasn't ducking or stepping over obstacles, Thomas was racking his throbbing brain, trying to piece together the things that Martin had said. What red flags had he missed, what clues had he ignored that might have prepared him for this bizarre possibility? He tried again. "Marty, this is ridiculous, why don't you stop all this dramatic crap and turn me loose?" No answer.

They walked on all day, or so Thomas thought. They crossed seven streams. Or did they cross one stream seven times? Or three streams twice and one stream once? Or were a couple of those streams actually the river? Thomas was hopelessly lost.

After hours of walking, the two men had a brief, whispered conversation. Thomas couldn't make out what was said, but he had the feeling that one of them went off somewhere and he was left alone with the other. "Marty?"

No answer. "Henry?" No answer, just the continued pressure on the rope that kept him moving forward.

He thought they must have found some sort of trail. There were fewer obstacles and he hadn't heard, "Limb!" for quite awhile. Then, suddenly they were inside.

Thomas could feel a plank floor and there was a musty smell of old pine timber. Besides, the sound of their movements had a slight echo. Someone loosened the knots on his hands, but before he could remove the ski mask and turn around, he heard a door close and he was alone in the dark.

The room was large, and made of squared pine logs. Moonlight came in through small openings, which were cut into the timbers at regular intervals about eight feet off the floor. In the corner farthest from the heavy door, he could make out a bed and night table, an enameled pitcher of water and a tin cup. There was nothing to do but sleep. He drifted off, into an unsettled slumber, filled with strange dreams.

He was awakened by a knock at the door. It was Martin. "Hey Tom! Are you okay in there?"

"What do you think, you dumb sonofabitch? Of course I'm not okay! I've been knocked on the head with a frying pan, blindfolded, dragged through the woods and locked up! I'm the Count of Monte-freakin' Cristo!"

"Yeah, I figured you might be pretty upset."

"Upset? Why no, Marty. I'm enjoying your fine hospitality. Come on inside so I can thank you properly for all you've done to me."

"That's why I'm talking through the door, old friend. We need to reach a point of understanding. There are a few things you're going to have to learn to accept, and the sooner you can do that, the easier it will be for all of us. I brought you some breakfast."

A small door opened near the floor and a plate of ham and eggs appeared. Thomas realized that the openings in the upper part of the walls had corresponding holes near the floor. They were covered by little trap doors, hinged at the top. Where had he seen this sort of design before? Oh yes, in Virginia. Tobacco barns have ventilation holes like these to permit air circulation for drying the leaves.

"Why don't you eat something," Martin said. "Maybe you'll feel better."

"I'd feel better if I had your neck between my hands." Thomas listened as Martin began walking away. "Hey Marty!" He said. "What about a bathroom?"

"There's a chamber pot under the night stand. Just put the lid on it and slide it out when you're done." Martin was gone.

Through the walls, Thomas could hear the sounds of activity. Hammers beat out a semi-regular rhythm. Voices laughed and chattered. He removed the pitcher of water and the chamber pot from the night table and slid it over beneath one of the openings in the wall. By standing on the table and crouching a little, he had a pretty good view of what was going on outside.

His timber prison was perched on the top of a grassy mound of earth. From it, the ground sloped gradually away and into a dense forest of what appeared to be old growth Douglas fir. Among the giant trees were scattered several small cabins, one of which was still under construction. Three men were nailing shingles on the near side of the roof. On the ground, another man was splitting more shingles from a large block of wood with a knife-like tool and a wooden mallet. These cabins were similar in appearance to the one Thomas occupied. Each was roughly the size of a two-car garage, with a second floor under a steeply pitched roof. They all had covered porches, some attached to the gable ends, and some on the eave sides. A few had windowed dormers.

Saddle horses were tied to hitching rails in front of several cabins. It was as if he had gone through some kind of time warp, ending up in the old west.

Looking up, Thomas was surprised to see a half-dozen tree houses of various sizes, some with multiple levels and fantastic shapes, conforming to the irregularities of the trees. Stairways snaked and spiraled up to these at weird angles, giving the entire scene an other-world quality. In spite of himself and his situation, Thomas was impressed.

In and around these odd structures, people moved. Several children laughed and played. Three women chatted near what appeared to be a well house. A group of men worked on some kind of wooden machine. Well, two men worked on it. The others seemed to be heckling and offering advice. Thomas watched for a while, trying to make some sense of what he was seeing, in light of the fact that he was a prisoner here.

Everyone seemed to be completely at ease. He sensed a familial bond. There was merriment in this place. It was almost as if these people were on vacation. They all seemed to be having fun.

Thomas however, was certainly not having fun. Actually, he felt rather numb. His predicament was so bizarre, so far outside the limits of normality, that he had no real way to process it. Besides, for the moment his fate and future events were completely beyond his control. Whatever the future held could mean a return to normal, logical life, or a quantum leap into something even more bizarre than this. He realized that he was lost in every imaginable way---physically, emotionally, spiritually, even intellectually. He had no idea where he was. He jumped down from the night table and sat on the floor with his back against the wall. How symbolic was that?

Wait a minute. His secretary expected to hear from him today or tomorrow. She might wait a few days, but then she would report his absence to the authorities! But he hadn't told her exactly where he was going. They could trace him through airline and bus tickets to Eureka, but there was no way they would be able to know where he had gone from there. What a mess.

Martin knocked at the door again, but this time it swung open and he stepped inside. He was carrying a plate of food. Someone behind him closed the door and Thomas could hear a bar being dropped into place on the other side.

"Give me a chance to put down your lunch, and then you can go ahead and hit me," Martin said. "I know you want to and it'll probably make both if us feel better."

"I don't want you to feel better. I want you to drop dead." Thomas remained on the floor, staring across the room at nothing. He had never been so angry.

Martin sat down beside him, placing the plate on the floor. I can't tell you how sorry I am about all this," he said. "But I didn't know what else to do. I knew you were dead set on going home, and I didn't know how else to stop you."

"Stop me? Why would you have to stop me? If it was a question of my keeping a secret, all you had to do was ask. You know me well enough to know that."

"I used to know you. I couldn't take the chance."

"So what do we do now? Are you going to keep me here, locked up forever? You still don't know what to do with me, do you?"

"Oh, I have some ideas, but you're right. By doing this to you, I've destroyed any loyalty you may have ever felt toward me, haven't I?" The two men sat for a moment, one trying to figure a way to manipulate the situation, one just mad as hell.

Thomas blinked and turned toward Martin. "How can you sit there and talk to me about loyalty, you pompous bastard? You wonder if you can trust me? I wouldn't trust you now if my life depended on it, and I have this terrifying feeling that it does! If you won't trust me enough to let me go, then you have to either keep me or kill me. And you're sitting there talking about loyalty while you try to decide which one serves your purposes best! What a hypocrite!"

"Hey, look at this from my side for a minute. When you saw Henry's kids up by the creek, he couldn't just let you go back thinking they were runaways or something, maybe report them to the cops. So he had to find out who you were and what you were doing up here. When he did, he came and got me, and I was curious too. We watched you for a while and, when I recognized you, I had to say hello. I wasn't thinking. After that, things just got carried away somehow and here we are. Now we have to come up with a plan that works for both of us, and doesn't do any harm to all the people who live up here and depend on me."

"How's this for a plan? Let me go."

"I can't. You're mad and I don't know what you'll do. Give me a few days to work this out. In the meantime the door is open, at least during the day. Obviously, I'll have to have someone watching you, but you'll be free to wander around and enjoy what we've done here. How's that?"

"Screw you."

"Yeah, screw me." Martin grunted and stood up. "If I can't figure a way out of this, I'm afraid we're both screwed." He crossed to the door. "Hey V. D! You want to let me out?"

Thomas heard the bar being lifted and the door swung open. He continued staring at the wall until Martin said, "Tommy, meet V. D." Filling the doorway was a very large man.

At a little over six feet, it wasn't his height that was so impressive, it was the bulk of the man. If the Incredible Hulk was in his fifties and not green, if his arms were covered with tattoos, and if he sported a grey ponytail, he would look a lot like this man. He crossed the room and stuck out a great paw of a hand. "Pleased to meetcha," he growled.

Thomas stood and shook the offered hand, or

rather he was shaken by it. When he looked into the eyes of this great pro-wrestler-looking, lantern-jawed, hand-smashing freak with the scary name, he was surprised to see kindness. The hulk was smiling.

Martin was smiling, too, probably at the look on Thomas' face. "V. D. will act as your guide and companion for a while."

The monster spoke again. "Most people just call me V." he said. "Martin seems to get a big kick out of calling me V. D. It's a name I picked up in another life." After a long silence, during which Martin just stood there, grinning, V. added, "You're a quiet one, ain'tcha? Well that's okay, people get used to me, after awhile. I'll be outside if you need anything."

The big man walked out, momentarily filling the doorway again. Thomas looked at Martin, who was still grinning like an idiot, rolled his eyes and sat down on the bed.

Martin turned toward the door. "Why don't you have some lunch, Tom. Then go do whatever you want. If you have any questions, I'm sure V. D. will be happy to answer them. 'See you later." And he was gone.

Thomas stood up and waited a few minutes in stunned silence. Then he sat down on the bed and began to eat. He also began to realize that his situation here was not unlike some of the lessons he had learned on the trail.

If he could get past the "what-ifs" and see this turn of events as a complete experience, rather than as an obstacle in the way of his path toward the goal of getting home, he might be able to think his way out of it. He reminded himself that frustration and emotional turmoil are counterproductive, and that they have the power to make a bad situation even worse. He knew that he had to let go of his anger and try to see the present more clearly. Anger unchecked turns into bitterness, bitterness turns to hatred, and hatred turns inward, coagulating into despair. Somehow, he had to stop feeling sorry for himself, stop asking, "Why me? Why this? Why now?" and most pathetic of all, "How can they do this to me?" and try to be bigger than even this gigantic mess.

7 THE VILLAGE

"Hey, V! You still out there?"

"Yeah boss, whatcha need?"

Thomas heard the front legs of a chair coming down, heavy, on the porch floor. The big man appeared again, looking even bigger than before. As frightening as he was, Thomas had a good feeling about him.

"Am I really allowed to go outside, or will I be 'shot trying to escape' if I do?"

"Ain't nobody here gonna shootcha, Boss."

Thomas stood and walked to the doorway. V. D. stepped back and let him pass through. He was looking amused, but wary. Thomas could sense a benign power, like a he-bear, playing with a cub.

There were two wooden chairs on the porch. Thomas sat in one, and V. D. took the other. As he surveyed the scene before him, Thomas was again impressed. "Wow!" he said. "This is quite a place."

"You got that right," said V. "I don't think Heaven could hold a candle to it."

The view was pretty much as it had been from the hole in the wall. People continued to move and talk, the picturesque cabins and those fantastic tree houses dominated, everything softened by the deep green shadows of the forest.

"Would you mind answering a question or two?"

With a long, contented sigh, V. tipped his chair back against the rough timbered wall. "Not a'tall," he said.

"Okay, first of all, where'd you get a name like V. D.?"

"Everybody wants to know about the name. I kinda wish Martin would stop callin' me that. Like I said, it's left over from another life. My real name is Valentine Day. They tell me I was found on a doorstep in L. A. on February fourteenth. Some smart-ass in the court system or social services must have given me the name as a joke. Anyhow, it ain't easy growin' up in foster homes with a handle like Valentine, so I tended to get into fights with the other kids. When I got a little older, it seemed kinda natural for me to make my livin' kickin' ass, so I worked as a bouncer in some pretty rowdy south-side bars. Well, one night some bikers came into a place where I was workin' and started makin' a fuss, so I had to toss 'em out. The next night, the parkin' lot was wall-to-wall hogs. The next thing I know, the joint is full of bad-ass mother… 'scuse me, bikers lookin' for a fight. I started workin' my way through 'em from one end, but there was just too many and I got tore up pretty bad. A bunch of 'em came up to see me in the hospital, said they was sorry and asked me to join up with 'em so I did. They were the ones that give me the name."

It was as if V. had told the story so many times that he was reciting a memorized speech. Thomas, by way of response, said, "Remind me never to piss you off."

V. sighed again and stretched his tremendous arms up toward the ceiling. "Oh," he said, "Them days are long gone. Your grandma could prob'ly take me now. I wouldn't have the heart for it anymore. 'Nothin' to prove."

"Okay," said Thomas, "I'll take your word for that. Now for the serious question, what the hell is going on around here?"

"You're lookin' at it." The big man made a sweeping gesture toward the cabins. "I think we better let Martin explain it to you when the time comes for that. You bein' here has got him all worked up. I don't think he's figured out quite what to do about it yet, but he will. And when he does, it'll be the right thing."

"I wish I shared your confidence. The last time he decided to do something about me I got knocked on the head and locked up in here."

"Ah, you're all right. He was just buyin' time, is all. What's a little lump on the head between friends?"

Thomas frowned and rubbed the back of his head. It was still tender.

"That's the spirit," said V. "Maybe you'll be able to pay him back some day."

"What makes you think I want to pay him back for anything?" Thomas asked.

"Bouncer's intuition. When you make your livin' by keepin' the peace in hell, you learn how to read minds. You have to be able to guess where the trouble is gonna start."

"Trouble? The last thing I want is trouble."

"Yeah, I'm not too worried about you. You're one of the good guys. But it all depends on how mad you get. In a bar crowd, there's usually at least one loud mouthed troublemaker. They're easy. The fight doesn't run too deep in 'em 'cuz it's just showin' off. But you take a nice fellah, such as yourself, and you push hard enough to make him fightin' mad, why he'll take it all the way. His fight goes clear to the bone. If you take a guy like that head-on, somebody's gonna get hurt. The best thing to do is to reason with 'em. Try to talk 'em down. Cut the fuse off before the blast."

"Is that what you're trying to do now?"

"Oh, hell no. I'm just passin' the time of day, is all. What do you say we go for a walk? You could prob'ly use some air."

"Why not?" said Thomas. "Air is good."

The two men stood and made their way down the path that led to the village. It was a narrow, well-worn trail, bordered by various kinds of shrubs and ferns. A footbridge, built of rough beams like the cabin, crossed a small brook, at which point the path began to rise toward the buildings. It curved around great tree trunks and followed the contours of the ground. "Pretty, ain't it?" It was more of a statement than a question, and needed no response.

Thomas was struck by the paradox formed by the rough, graveled voice and the gentle, innocent question. It reminded him of something, but he couldn't quite put his finger on what it was. It was more of a feeling than a memory, more intuition than thought. Whatever it was, it would have to wait. They were approaching the first cabin.

They walked onto the low porch and went inside. The door handle was more ornate than the one on the Jail, but made the same way. It was an old-fashioned grab-handle with a thumb latch that passed through a hole. This raised a steel rod on the inside of the door, which fitted into a corresponding slot attached to the jamb. Thomas noticed that there was no provision for locking it.

"This here's my shop." V. stood smiling while Thomas scanned the large room. In the middle of the far wall there was a stone hearth. Nearby stood an old iron mechanism with a hand-crank that must have been a bellows. Among the rafters lay various kinds of steel rods and bars. There was a great, heavy anvil in the center of the room, and an assortment of hammers, pincers and pliers hung on a wall behind a thick, plank workbench.

"All you need is a spreading chestnut tree."

"Well," said V. "In my other life I did a little

welding, and when I came up here, I found out I had kind of a knack for smithing."

"So, you made the latches and hinges I've seen?" Thomas asked.

"Yeah, and tools, hardware, everything we have that's metal, these old hands made it."

There was a childlike pride in the big man's voice and demeanor as he spoke, an innocence that Thomas found intriguing; a paradox. "You do nice work."

"Thanks, man."

From the blacksmith's shop, the two men proceeded up the trail to the next cabin and the next, until they had covered the whole village. Thomas met Sarah, Millie and Jean who were spinners, dyers and weavers of wool. Arnie and his son, Jim were heavyset, redheaded, frecklefaced tanners of hides and makers of shoes and other leather goods. Adam, Daniel and Jason McGrath were the three carpenters who were shingling the roof of the new cabin, while their brother James was splitting the shingles, actually called shakes, with a froe. They lived on a farm nearby. They were tall, capable and full of life, laughing and joking as they worked.

Joe and Steve were working on the machine that Thomas had seen through the window. It looked like a big wooden box with helicopter blades attached to the top. V. explained that it was for grinding grains and just about anything else. He had made the grinding mechanisms, which were tapered cylinders, geared together to operate on the same principle as a pencil sharpener. What looked like helicopter blades were actually long poles that could be pushed in a wide circle by man or horse, to power the thing. It was mounted on a horse-drawn wagon and could be transported from farm to farm. According to V. even though it didn't have the capacity of a water-powered mill, its portability would suit it for a variety of small jobs. If it worked, that is.

Thomas was curious about the tree houses. With

their steeply pitched roofs and their arched windows and doorways, they looked as if they came from a fairy tale.

Some had ornately carved balconies and bay windows that added to their charm. They were perched in the giant trees at various heights, stairways spiraling up from the ground. Their wood siding, shingles and trim were greyed with age, in contrast to the newer wood of the cabins on the ground. The only cabin that appeared to be of their same vintage was Thomas' jail. He was looking up, admiring a particularly ornate tree house when the fight started.

One of the men who were watching the progress on the grain mill must have gone too far. Whatever he said seemed to have offended young Steve, who reacted rather suddenly. Like a cat, Steve dove off the top of the machine and punched the offender in the nose, which began to bleed profusely. The other man reacted in kind, and the two punched and kicked and wrestled around the yard until they wore each other out.

In the end, dazed and bloody, through swollen lips, the older man said, "Is that all you got? You ain't so tough."

Steve was in about the same condition as his adversary, and as much the worse for wear. "You look sorta tired, old man. Maybe you aught to rest a minute."

"Done?" the man asked.

"Done," Steve replied.

The bystanders crowded around them then, slapping them on the back and recounting the highlights of the exchange. V. turned to Thomas. "That young hothead gets into more scraps... At least this time he held his own."

Lions came to mind. The fight between the two men reminded Thomas of documentary footage of young male lions testing the strength and authority of their elders. It had the same animal fury, the same honesty and respect. Each man had fought with passion and resolve, but the damage they inflicted had been limited to cuts and bruises. It had obviously not been a fight to the death, only a kind of physical negotiation. Once a mutual understanding had been reached, the battle was ended and the two had retired from the field, limping and throbbing and satisfied.

"Well," V. said, "I'd better get you back to the barn. It's gettin' late and I have things to do."

Just inside the door of the barn/prison, Thomas found his packs of clothing and food neatly arranged. His propane stove and lantern were there too. His knife and axe were not.

V. said goodnight and closed the door. Thomas listened as the big man lowered the heavy bar into place, and suddenly he was alone. The noise of activity outside had ended and the silence was oppressive. He fished his journal and pencil out from one of the packs, sat on the bed and wrote a note to his secretary. He didn't write about his captivity or this weird place with its even weirder people, only that he had been delayed and that he was okay. She must be worried by now.

Martin arrived with breakfast in the morning. "Well," he said, "What do you think of our little Garden of Eden?"

"Do you think they had fistfights in Eden?"

"Oh, that. Well, you see, around here, people are free to solve their own problems. We hold a court of mediation to help settle really serious disagreements, but for the most part, it's up to each of us to be responsible for his own affairs."

"So the strongest always wins, eh?" Thomas was remembering the "pecking order" of his elementary school playground.

"You'd be surprised how well the system works. We have a closed society here. Each of us realizes that the survival of the group takes precedence over his or her immediate wishes and desires. I hear that yesterday, Al lost control of his mouth and pushed Steve too far. Steve got mad and felt the need to defend himself. It was all perfectly natural and correct. Nobody got hurt, and an understanding has been reached. There's been tension between those two for quite some time and now the air has been cleared."

"What do you mean, nobody got hurt? I'll bet those guys are both all bruised up and sore as hell today."

Martin chuckled, "Yeah, I'll bet they are. In fact, with them walking around all black-eyed and swollen up, things will probably be real peaceful around here for a while. But they're not really hurt. They'll both be fine in a few days.

Tom, I think it's time I laid all my cards on the table. You've been real decent about all this. V. D. likes you and says you can be trusted, and if he trusts somebody I know they're okay. Back in the day, he could go into a bar and tell you what everybody in the place was thinking, who was going to make trouble, who was going home with whom, even what kind of drink each new customer would order. And he'd be right."

"Yeah, bouncer's intuition. He told me."

"Well, just like most everyone else up here, he's got secrets."

"What's that supposed to mean?"

"He grew up the hard way, being shuffled through foster homes and juvenile facilities, and somehow never got a formal education. I think he set himself up against anything they wanted him to do, so he never learned to read. I've tried to teach him, but he claims he can't get it, that his brain doesn't work that way. He has this gift for reading people, but he can't read books. And up here, that's just fine, but out in the world, not being able to read is quite a handicap. He was at the mercy of a system over which he had no control and which he couldn't understand. Needless to say, living that way, he was filled with rage against that system and the people who could control him through it. His rap sheet is about a mile long and includes about every crime you can think of, including murder."

"So that's why you couldn't let me go?"

"Just about everyone here has a secret or two."

Thomas walked over to the door. "What about you, old buddy?"

"Yeah, me too," Martin said. "You might as well know. There is no mysterious benefactor who makes this all possible. This place belongs to me. I started out up here growing the best pot on the planet. Most of these people were part of the operation. This building was the barn where we hung the plants to dry. We made obscene amounts of money. This was a pretty wild place in those days." Martin was speaking quickly, as if a dam had burst and his words were spilling over.

"Then a funny thing happened. The more we became separated from the world, the more we were able to let go of the world's excesses. We slowly began living a simpler, saner life together. I had started a whole slew of dummy corporations to run all that money through, and over a period of a couple of years I sifted through them, legitimizing a few and getting rid of the rest. We stopped growing dope. We began to grow food instead. We set up this little village, and the people who had marketable skills other than farming started bartering their trades. Maybe for the fist time, our lives started to make sense. Isn't it strange that our checkered past has become the glue that holds us together?"

"That's all well and good, but knocking people on the head and kidnapping them still seems like a strange way to recruit new members."

"Geez! You're just like a hound dog, aren't you? I told you about all that. I panicked! Look, even though we've built this Paradise up here, we still break the law every day. We didn't get permits to put up any of these buildings. Nothing is built to follow current codes or specifications. We hunt deer and catch fish when we're hungry. We educate our own children and we don't use a state-approved curriculum. We don't even license our pets! The law may be actively trying to find any of us, and if they are, they could force you to reveal our location. For myself, I could have just let you go, but the lives and freedom of all these people depend on absolute secrecy."

"Look Marty, I probably shouldn't tell you this, but the fact is, nobody knows where I am. I just said that I'd be gone for a couple of weeks. Your secret is safe with me."

"Thanks, man. Does this mean you forgive me?"

"I'll let you know."

8 DEATH COMES CALLING

The two men were standing just outside the door, watching the morning activities of the villagers. The four brothers were finishing up their roofing job, Joe and Steve had taken their grinding machine off somewhere to test it, doors were open and people were moving about, everyone seeming to be busy and content. V. appeared on the path beyond the houses, walking fast. His head was down and his massive shoulders seemed to be bent under a great, invisible load. Something was obviously very wrong.

He strode up to the cabin. Looking to Martin, he said, "You better come. They found Carl."

"Is he alive?"

"He was when I left, but I don't think he's gonna make it. He's all busted up.

By this time, all three men were on their way back up the trail. "What the hell happened?" Martin wanted to know.

"You know that big bluff up on Baker Creek?"

"Yeah, the one that goes right down into the water?"

"Well, I guess he was on his way back up to the house, and he decided to go up and over, instead of wadin' through the water. It was gittin' dark, and he stepped in a hole or somethin' and fell off the cliff. After bouncin' off the rocks a few times, he got hung up in a bush and laid there for two days 'til Henry found him. We set his legs, but his ribs are stove in pretty bad and he's lost a lot of blood. I'll be surprised if he's still kickin' when we get up there."

"Damn!"

They made good time, but it was still almost two hours later when they arrived at the cabin. It was built much like the others, only taller. It had a full second storey with two windows on each side, directly above the ones on the main floor. It was built on a small, timbered hill, overlooking a vegetable garden and an orchard of moss covered old apple trees. Back in the forest behind the house stood a barn and a corral. Two brown and white Guernsey milk cows were there, with a pair of young calves.

Two women, one in overalls and one in an old fashioned yellow dress, talked with a man on the covered porch. The man was Henry. 'Mornin' Tom," he said, almost, but not quite smiling. In answer to an enquiring look from Martin, he simply shook his head, just a little.

The woman in overalls wrapped her arms around V. as far as she could, and the other woman ran to Martin. Haltingly she said, "He's almost gone."

Martin strode across the porch and knocked at the open door. "Ginny? Can I come in?"

"Is that you, Martin?" came the tired voice from inside. "He wants to talk to you. Come on in."

Thomas followed the others into the house. The front room served as a kitchen, living and dining area, and the other was a bedroom. A narrow stairway ran up one wall to what Thomas assumed were two more rooms upstairs.

The man on the bed was nearly the same color as the sheet. His upper lip was swollen to twice its normal size, one eye was blackened and swollen shut, and dried blood was matted in his graying beard. "Marty," he rasped, "I'm glad you're here. Ginny, put on some coffee."

"I don't want any coffee," Martin said. "I just stopped in to say hello."

"Goodbye, you mean. Marty, I screwed up." He paused to gather strength and a tear squeezed out when he momentarily closed his eyes. "We had a good life here. Because of you and Ginny I was finally doing things right and now I've blown it all. Maybe everyone was right about me."

"Yeah, maybe Ginny and I were right about you. You're a good man who just needed someone to believe in you. Look what you've accomplished here. You've raised two fine sons and built this place up with just your two hands and the power of your will."

"I'm scared, Marty. I'm prob'ly goin' straight to hell."

Ginny had been kneeling by the bed. With a sharp intake of breath, she stood and turned to the woman in the yellow dress, who held her while she quietly cried. "My god!" thought Thomas. "It's Virginia."

"Carl, if I know anything about anything, you won't be going to hell." Martin laid a hand on Carl's arm. "Like I said, you're a good man. Whatever happened in the past is over and done. You've more than made up for it. You can rest easy."

"Yeah, rest. That's what I need. I'll just take a little nap. Then we can talk." The last few words seemed to take a lot of effort. A moment passed and he was gone. Thomas was surprised at the difference. There he was, Carl Wilson, sleeping on the bed, and suddenly, Carl disappeared and in his place there was just an empty grey husk. Somehow, it reminded Thomas of a schoolyard, when recess is over and the swings and the slides, recently teeming with laughing children, stand vacant and silent.

Two younger men were sitting on wooden chairs in the corner. Thomas took them to be Carl's sons. One of them continued sitting, jaw clamped tight, eyes staring into space. The other jumped up and stalked outside. Thomas followed him out.

He had felt like an intruder. The grief these people shared was deep and personal, the result of years of association. Thomas, not having shared in the joys and sorrows of their lives, would not impose upon this, their most intimate and personal moment of all.

He sat down on the porch and watched the young man walk quickly down the path and then break off into the woods. These were tough times.

Thomas was alone on the porch. Everyone was inside, and this would be the perfect opportunity to escape! He had no idea where he was, but all he had to do was hike downhill until he came to the river and follow it out to civilization. With enough of a head start, he could even stop by the jail and pick up his things.

"One day back to your camp, and two more days from there to the coast. That about right?"

"You're doing that bouncer's intuition thing again, aren't you V.?"

"A blind man could read your face right now, my friend. And I guess if you want to go, you can go. You made a promise to Martin that you wouldn't give us away, and from what I've seen that's good enough."

"For a big man, you can be pretty sneaky," Thomas said. "I didn't hear you come up."

"Old habit. I must've forgot I don't have to watch you any more."

"So I'm free to go?"

"Free to go, or free to stay, it's up to you." The big man walked over and sat down on the step beside Thomas. "Ya see that hill over there?"

Thomas looked and, framed by the trunks of the fir trees nearby, he saw a grassy knoll. Some kind of yellow flowers, probably just dandelions, were scattered about, but the color appeared brighter when seen from the shadows. It glowed and sparkled in the sunshine.

"That's where Carl wanted to be planted. What say you and me go up there and dig a hole? You can always leave tomorrow."

It was early afternoon, a poor time to begin a long journey. Besides, here was this gentle giant, asking for help. Besides which, the activity of digging the hole would be just the thing to clear the dark cloud of loss that seemed to hang over the cabin. Thomas stood up. "Why not?"

V. stood up too, smiling. "That's the spirit! Let's head up to the barn and see if we can scare up a couple of shovels!"

When they reached the top of the hill, V. paced off a rectangle three paces long, by two paces wide. They marked it out with the shovels and began to dig. This didn't just look like the warmest place around, it really was. Soon, both men had removed their shirts and were working with a will. Thomas matched the big man spadefull for spadefull, but he noticed that he was breathing harder. As the hole got deeper, the piles of dirt and small stones around it rose in proportion. He stopped several times to wipe the sweat from his eyes. "How deep do you want to go?" he asked. They had already dug down about four feet.

"Oh, prob'ly just another foot or two. I figured to make it a little oversize in case she decides to cave in. This prob'ly could've waited 'til later, but I needed to do somethin'. Hey, you dig pretty good, for a city fella."

"My god, you must have had some kind of life," Thomas observed. V's huge upper body was roadmapped with scars. Most of them looked like centipedes, showing the marks of the stitches that had held them together.

V. grinned and shrugged, "I guess I used to be kind of accident prone, always bumpin' into things."

"I'm glad you never bumped into me."

They dug down another two feet and squared up the hole. Thomas suddenly realized that there was no way to get out of it. "Maybe we can dig footholds into the wall," he said.

V. seemed to have it all worked out. "Why don't you just go over to that end and get on one knee. Lean the outside of your other knee against the wall, and I'll use that as a stepladder."

Thomas did as he was asked, and V. took two quick steps and a jump, pushing off from Thomas' knee on the way up. With his hands planted on the grassy lip, he muscled his way out of the hole. Then he reached back down with one hand and pulled Thomas out. The sun had set and a cool breeze was blowing. They took the shovels to the barn and went back to the house. Martin was on the porch.

"Did you boys have a good time up there?"

Thomas eased down onto the porch step. "I think I've pulled every muscle in my body! My legs hurt. My arms hurt. My back, stomach, chest, hands... even my eyeballs hurt!"

Martin laughed. "I watched you, trying to keep up with this animal. You were doing pretty well, too. But you'll probably be sore as hell for a couple of days. I know I would be."

"He dug a real nice hole, didn't he? I mostly just stood up there and watched him work." If V. was sore, it didn't show.

"I sent Carl's boys out to gather everybody in. We'll have a wake tomorrow, 'give their dad a real send-off. The McGrath boys'll make the casket, and there'll be lots of food. Speaking of which, aren't you fellas getting kind of hungry? I think there's something left over from dinner." Martin stood and entered the house, motioning for Thomas and V. to follow.

There was nobody inside. In the warming shelf of the woodstove they found bread, gravy, and some kind of meat that Thomas hoped was rabbit. The bedroom door was closed.

"I'm sure you boys can sack out upstairs if you like. I had Maggie take Ginny home to our house, and I don't think Carl will mind."

"Thanks, Marty," said Thomas, "but I think I'll just make myself a sandwich and head down the hill. The walk might loosen up my legs a little."

V. agreed. "I'll go with you. Carol Ann'll be expecting me home tonight and, after the day she's had, she won't want to be left alone."

Martin looked only a little disappointed. "You're gonna make me stand watch here all by myself, aren't you?"

A sly look passed between Thomas and V. "Yep, but like you said, you won't bother Carl much. Besides," Thomas added, "I don't think I've ever needed a bath more than I do right now. I think I'll take a dip in the creek before I turn in."

9 THE WAKE

Even with the cool comfort of a three-quarter moon, following the trail took a lot of concentration. The open places weren't so bad, but in the places where it meandered through thick woods, the two men had to rely on instinct and the feel of the ground in order to keep to the path. After half an hour or so, V. took the side trail toward his house and Thomas was left to find his way alone.

God, he was tired. Every step was a painful effort. As he limped down the trail, his mind tended to wander aimlessly on its own. It seemed to stumble around through an intellectual thunderstorm. Flashes of memory and insight danced and flickered through his mind.

He was mildly surprised to find that he wasn't impressed. It was as if his memories belonged to somebody else, someone he didn't even care about. During his wife's long illness, his life had revolved around her comfort and the challenges of balancing that and his business. He realized now that, since her passing, he had been drifting steadily downhill. He had lost interest in everything; in his business, in any kind of social life, even in his son.

Rather than being the freakish nightmare that he had initially thought it to be, the past few days had actually been a welcome change. Somehow, over the years, he had lost his passion for life. Was it fear? After his great loss, was he afraid to invest himself and his weary old heart in anything or anyone? "My god," he thought. "That's what I came out here to find! Freedom isn't the only thing I was looking for. My life had no passion. I needed to care about something."

He walked through the sleeping town, across the bridge and into his ex-prison. Rummaging through his packs, he found a bottle of biodegradable camp soap and limped back outside. He went downstream to where a bend in the creek had created a deepish pool, stripped off his grimy clothes and waded in.

The creek wasn't large, but this pool was deep enough to lie down in. He rested his head against a smooth, driftwood log and let the cool water soothe his aching muscles. Moonlight danced and sparkled on the surface of the stream. Stars too, peeked down among the branches of the ancient firs to add their sparks of light. The water chuckled and babbled over sticks and stones. Thomas soaked it all in. His thoughts drifted with the current to things past; to youthful dreams and choices made; to Virginia.

Had any of the townsfolk been awake about an hour later, they might have seen a naked figure, carrying his clothes and limping up the sandy creek bed. When he reached the bridge, he climbed out and up the path to the old barn. Once inside, he dried off and slept, weary and contented, until the morning noises of the village gradually drew him from his dreams.

The first big challenge of the day was what should have been the simple act of getting out of bed. Bending enough to get dressed was the second. Thomas stretched out as many of his knotted muscles as he could, but there were a bunch of them in his upper back that were just too balled up to release. Someone had left a covered plate of food near the door, some kind of sweetbread baked with apples, and a cup of coffee. The coffee was cold. He didn't mind.

Thinking that a walk might help his condition, Thomas headed out the door and up toward the village. A few fleecy clouds dotted the sky above the forest.

The horse-drawn wagon that Thomas had seen before was pulled up in front of the blacksmith's shop. This time, instead of the grinding machine, it held a rectangular pine box. V. was installing the fifth of six wrought iron handles, three on each side of the box. "Well, look who's still kickin'," he said. "I figured you'd either died or gone home."

"I'm just hanging on by a thread," Thomas admitted. "And I probably won't be healed up enough to leave for a few days now."

"Well, that's just fine with me. If you want to wait just a minute, I'll get this last handle on and we can go for a ride."

Thomas was fascinated by the wagon. He had noticed before that it was unusual, but the fight had taken his attention at the time, and he hadn't really looked it over. It was built on shortened car axles, and had radial tires. It was only about four feet wide and built low, with a flat wooden bed that came out over the wheels. It had one green bucket seat, mounted on the front of the bed, and the back of the seat rested on a wooden box with a hinged lid.

The horse was built low to the ground, too. Stocky and brown, a little sway-backed, placid and mature. She seemed to like having her ears scratched.

"That about does it," V. exclaimed when the last handle was nailed firmly in place. "Hop on."

The wagon's old bucket seat looked racy, like it had come from a sports car. Thomas thought it looked as if V. should be going through the gears instead of handling the reins. "Let's go, Daisy," said the big man.

The old horse came to life. Her slow gait was rhythmic and easy. Even seated on the wooden box, Thomas was impressed with the relatively smooth ride of the wagon. It was a good design, retaining the original springs and shock absorbers. "Nice wagon," he said, "yours?"

"Yep, I've made six of 'em. They're narrow enough so we don't have to brush out the trails much, like big roller skates. The only problem is they tip over easy. They're no damn good on a side-hill. There's a couple of places up ahead where we'll have to get off and walk."

There were actually a lot more than a couple of places. Thomas would lead Daisy up the trail, such as it was, while V. walked along on the downhill side of the wagon. Three times, the big man had to lift it so that two wheels dangled in the air until they reached more level ground.

At last, they reached the Wilson place. People were already arriving. There were two more of V's giant roller skates in the yard, and long tables had been set up near the porch. The white tablecloths looked cool in the dappled shadows under the trees.

Thomas eased himself down from the wagon box. The two Wilson boys stepped off the porch and, after the customary greetings and handshaking, carried the casket into the house. Several of the other men, including V. followed them in, emerging a few minutes later with the obviously heavier casket. They brought it outside and rested it on one of the long tables. The wooden lid was then removed, and there was Carl, all spiffed up. He was wearing a Hawaiian shirt and, had it not been for the ashen pallor of his skin, and the cuts and bruises on his face, looked as if he was all set to go on holiday. As it was, what with the garish colors in the shirt and the almost total absence of color in Carl, it was a pretty grisly sight.

More people had arrived and were arriving. Another table had been set up and, what had begun as quiet and subdued conversation had increased to a steady hum of voices with even a few guffaws of unrestrained laughter here and there. Thomas guessed that there were upwards of thirty people, milling about the house and grounds or seated around the porch. Children raced and climbed in happy chaos, seemingly unimpeded by directives from their parents to "settle down."

Martin and Carl's wife, Ginny came out of the house and stood on the top step of the porch. "Folks!" he said loudly. "Can I have your attention for a minute?" The conversation trickled off. "You all know why we're here. We have to say goodbye to our friend, Carl. Does everyone have a drink?"

There were a few murmurs as several people, including Thomas, headed over to one of the wagons to get what turned out to be a bottle of homemade rootbeer. When they were all attentive again, Martin continued. "The way this works is, I'll start it off, then anybody who wants to say something, come on up here and say it. Okay?" Another murmur passed through the crowd.

"Carl, old buddy, it's been one hell of a ride. Just like everyone here, you may have had kind of a rocky start, but with guts, determination and character, you turned it all around. You will be missed by every one of us. Good journey, old friend!"

Ginny had been standing beside Martin as he gave his toast. She looked small and frail, her black dress making her appear even more so. Martin turned and gave her a hug, then stepped off the porch. V's wife, Carol Ann, brought a wooden chair from inside and motioned for Ginny to sit. Then she began. "Carl was a good man," she said to the crowd. "And a good friend. And, like Martin just said, you're all going to miss him. But every time you think about Carl, I want you to remember that, now that he's gone, Ginny and the boys will have to pick up the slack and work that much harder. The boys have their own lives to live. It won't hurt any of you to stop by once in a while and help out." She raised her bottle, "We love ya, Carl!"

Fallen Idyll

Thomas was in the background, leaning on the wagon. He watched as each person made his way up to the porch and said his piece, ending it with a toast. There were humorous stories, tales of adventure, character sketches, and simple salutes. In the end, Ginny stood and thanked them all. Martin, V. and four others placed the lid on the casket and carried it up to the meadow, followed by the rest of the company.

They lowered it into the ground, Martin said some words about Carl going home to a better place, and Carl's sons stayed to fill in the hole while the others strayed back toward the house.

Platters of food were brought out from the kitchen, and the long tables were filled with meats, vegetables, fruits and breads. The hum of conversation returned, punctuated by the clink of forks and knives on china and tin. Thomas felt as though he were looking through a lens into the past. In this place there was no fear. They had accepted the death of their friend as a continuation of his life, as they accepted the death of a deer or some other wild thing.

They seemed to have no reserve. Men were conversing, one with his hand on the shoulder of the other. Women walked arm-in-arm. People were laughing or crying, sharing and communicating on a deeper level. There was nothing sexual about this; it was simple familiarity. There was common concern. There was that familial bond that Thomas had seen through the hole in the wall of the barn when he first arrived.

Two guitars appeared, along with a fiddle, a banjo, and a hand drum. The players sat or stood on the porch, and soon the air was filled with the sound of their playing. They played traditional songs, homemade songs, songs about life and love and freedom. The food was cleared away and people began to dance.

They danced with abandon. It seemed, to Thomas, that the intensity of their playing and dancing was out of respect. They had just seen how quickly the flame of life can be snuffed out, and they felt a responsibility to fan the fire, to make it burn as brightly as possible. Several times, hands appeared to pull him into the whirling crowd. He tried to dance with abandon.

The band took a break about mid-evening. Thomas took the opportunity to pay his respects to the widow. "Hello Virginia."

There she was, as beautiful as ever. The fine lines that had appeared around her pale blue eyes seemed to add wisdom and character to the face he remembered. She had put up her long brown hair in the way she had always worn it. He recalled how, with one slight movement, she could release it, sending it cascading onto her shoulders. Looking at her somehow made his life of the past thirty years as if it were a dream, and he had just woken up.

Several chairs had been set up at the edge of the yard, and she was seated in one of these. She stood and hugged him. He hugged back.

"Tom," she said. "I can't believe you're here."

"I'm having a little trouble believing it, myself," he said. "This is all very strange."

They sat down in adjoining chairs. "I'm so sorry about your husband. I wish I'd had the chance to know him."

"Me too. I think you two would've been friends. He was a good man, a good husband, and a good father to the boys."

The music started again and he thought about asking her to dance, but he knew it would be inappropriate. Instead, he asked, "Can I get you anything?"

"No thanks." She smoothed a fold on the knee of her long black dress. "But why don't you stop by in a few days? I'll fix you some dinner and we can have a chance to really talk. You've been gone a long time."

Thomas was a bit overwhelmed and didn't notice Martin coming up behind them. Suddenly, he was there, and with his hands on their shoulders, he said, "Hey there!

I was hoping you two would have a chance to get together." And to Ginny, "I was afraid Tommy was going to leave us again without saying goodbye."

"I'm still all crippled up from my little workout with V," Thomas said. "I won't be able to go very far for at least a couple of days."

"Well that's just fine." Martin turned to Ginny. "Do you mind if I steal him for a minute? We have a few things to talk about."

"No, you boys go ahead," she said. "I have some things to take care of in the house."

10 FIGHT OR FLIGHT

Martin and Thomas started walking toward the meadow and the newly covered grave. "So, old buddy," Martin began. "Are you starting to realize that you belong here?"

"Well, given the manner in which I arrived, I'm a little surprised at how comfortable I've become, but I don't know if I belong here."

"It's all about the size of the puddle," Martin continued. "The world is such a big puddle that a little duck can't make much of a splash in it. But up here we have a little tiny puddle. Just about anything you do makes a difference. One life more or less in the world has a very small impact, but here, Carl's death is going to affect the whole community."

"Okay Marty, Even after thirty years, I can tell when you want something. Just spit it out."

"It's about Ginny. It's going to be almost impossible for her to handle this place by herself. Her boys'll be here as much as they can, but they have their own lives to run. Especially right at first, she's going to need a lot of help. I was wondering if you'd mind looking in on her once in awhile, at least for the next few days until you leave us."

"You really are a sneaky bastard, aren't you?" Thomas stopped on the trail. "You are faced with a possible problem, and in your twisted little mind, I become the perfect solution. It doesn't matter what Virginia wants. It doesn't matter what I want. It doesn't matter that I have responsibilities and commitments back home, you just want your problem to disappear."

Martin let out a quick, exasperated sigh. "You don't have any idea what you want! Ginny probably does. Women are a lot more practical than we are. But just take a look at your situation here.

You were knocked on the head and kidnapped! You were held prisoner, locked up in a barn for two days. For most people, that would have made them mad enough to fight, but not you. You started to enjoy it. You came out here looking for adventure and a change of pace, and that's what you got.

If you really wanted to go back to Michigan, you would've taken off the other day when you were left alone on the porch. But no, you hung around to help V. D. dig a hole, and you've been making excuses for not leaving ever since. You can accuse me of manipulating you and your circumstances if you like, but the fact is, I've just been giving you what you wanted the whole time."

"How the hell do you do that?" Thomas was incredulous. "How can you twist everything around until, in your warped little mind, being whacked on the head with a frying pan and locked up in a barn was something I wanted?"

"Like I said before, you don't know what you want, or won't admit it. Are you going to tell me you don't want Ginny?"

"Are you kidding? She just watched her husband die! How can you even think like this? People aren't gamepieces that you can just move around on a board. She needs time to grieve. Then, if she wants to get involved with somebody, it's up to her to choose who and when."

"You were always such a blockhead. She made her choice already. Thirty years ago, she chose you. Then you pulled your disappearing act. Nobody knew where you went or why. There were rumors: that you'd gotten busted and were going to narc us all out, that you'd joined the army, lots of stuff. I figured they'd find your body in a ditch somewhere, or floating in the river. It wasn't until years later that we found out you'd gone back east."

"I was such a mess. I had no future, no direction, she deserved better."

"Aha! You sneaky bastard! You're such a hypocrite! Without regard for anyone else, or what anyone wanted, you made a decision that affected all our lives and just took off. You manipulated the situation to suit yourself, and justified it by thinking it was the best thing for her."

"Whenever I discuss anything with you I feel like I'm in a war." Thomas started walking again.

"That's because I don't let you get away with all your bullshit. You have all these layers of protection and misdirection. If people were panes of glass, some would be clear and some would be clouded. You, my friend, would be a prism. Nothing is where it appears to be. Your words aren't reflections of your thoughts, they're refractions. You never approach anything head-on. Most people get sucked into your games, I don't."

"Oh shut up. If I'm a prism, you're just a pane. You're babbling, and I have questions for you."

"Alright, if you're out of your comfort zone, we can change the subject. Shoot." Martin had an infuriating smirk on his face.

"Whatever… First of all; root beer?"

"It's kind of a long story, but the short version is that we decided that drugs and alcohol were just ways that we'd found to distort reality. Out here, our existence depends upon our ability to cope with things as they are. There are certain things we've had to give up for the good of the group."

"Okay, now for the important one. Why didn't somebody take Carl into town for medical attention?"

"We knew there was no hope for him. There wouldn't have been enough time to make the trip."

"How did you know that? How could you know what his injuries were, or what to do about them?"

"I trust Henry's judgment. In his other life, he was a doctor. I guess toward the end of his residency, something went wrong and he lost a patient. There were allegations of misconduct, allegations of drug use, and he lost everything. Nothing was ever proven, but it was enough to get him fired. After that, he just gave up. He drifted up here and we took care of him for a while. I got in touch with his wife, and she brought the kids up. They've been here ever since."

The two men had walked and talked their way to the gravesite. The freshly turned earth smelled musty and alive. The dandelions flashed yellow in the sunlight. The fir trees near at hand soughed in the light breeze. "I don't know how to get you to understand," Martin paused and searched his mind for words. "Everything here is connected. We raise crops and animals for food. The cows, pigs, chickens, and what have you, need food too, so we have to raise that. The animals contribute milk, eggs and meat, but they also contribute fertilizer to help grow the crops. You see the circle?"

Thomas nodded.

"Everything and everyone here that takes something, gives something back. It's the way of the universe, the way of the natural world. In this community we try, as seamlessly as possible, to fit into that world.

Now, we're going along, the world is turning, the seasons pass, and here comes Tommy Graham, with this confused, 'how did I get here' look on his face. Three days later, Carl falls off a cliff and dies, leaving a vacancy. As it happens, the best person in the world to fill that vacancy is

Tommy Graham! The way I look at it, thirty years ago, you made a mistake. You took yourself out of the circle. Now you've been given a chance to make up for it. For once in your life, Tom, take a chance."

"Things always look so simple to you. Everything falls into a straight line that leads to whatever you want. How can I put this so it will penetrate that thick skull of yours? I have a life. I have a business. I have responsibilities. Right now, there are people in Michigan wondering why I haven't returned. If they haven't done it already, soon they'll report that I'm missing. People will come looking for me."

Martin was unmoved. "What I'm trying to tell you is that you don't need any of that anymore. You don't need the headaches or the responsibilities or even the money. Everything you need is right here. And by the way, nobody's looking for you. The night I brought you here, I went through your stuff and found your address book. I sent someone out with a telegram that said you were having a really good time, and that you would be staying on for a while."

"Here we go again. What made you think you had the right to do that? Who put you in control of my life?"

"Well, at that point I did have control of your life. We had just kidnapped you and I wasn't sure what to do with you."

"Oh, so now you've figured it all out, is that it?"

"This is getting us nowhere. I brought you up here to tell you something, and your paranoia has gotten us off track."

"It's only paranoia when you think someone is out to get you and it's not true."

Martin walked a few paces toward the house and sat down on the grassy hillside. "Here's the deal. A couple of miles from here, there's a big, flat, open field. Back in the day, an airplane used to land there in the middle of the night to pick up our produce. While the Feds were patrolling the skies for planes that were bringing drugs into the area, we were flying them out."

Thomas sat down and Martin continued. "What I wanted to tell you is that, on the fifteenth of every month, all summer long, that plane still comes. Only now, instead of taking stuff out, it brings stuff in. We make up a list. If V. D. is going to need some iron for a particular project, or the McGrath boys need nails, or we're low on flour, or cloth, or whatever, it all goes on the list. When the plane comes, we pick up our previous order and drop off the list for next time. He can also take things out for us, like correspondence, or even a passenger."

"You are, without a doubt, the most infuriating sonofabitch I ever met!" Thomas shook his head in disbelief. "Just when I think that maybe you've figured out a way to force me to stay here, you offer me a chance to leave."

"Well, like you said, it's your life."

"That's right, dammit, it is! How long do I have?"

Martin looked at his wrist, where a watch would have been. "I'd say you have about four or five hours. If you want to get your stuff, you'd better get moving."

"The fifteenth is today? You waited to tell me about this until now?" Thomas was infuriated all over again. "Okay, that's it!" he said. "I'm outta here!" He sprang to his feet. "I'll meet you back here, and then you can take me to the field."

Martin just sat and watched as Thomas walked quickly down the slope and back to the house. The crowd was breaking up and people were saying their goodbyes. Thomas didn't even pause, but stalked on past, taking the trail back toward the village.

Anger carried him. The path followed the brook that flowed from the spring that provided water for the house. In places where intersecting ridges caused the stream to make wide turns, the trail would cut across, going up and over them. The canopy of trees shed a soft green light on everything around him, but he didn't see it. The stream talked and chattered along the path, but he didn't hear it. He was busy remembering slights and atrocities. He kept going over the long list of wrongs and indignities he had suffered at the hands of his friend. He replayed these in great detail, projecting them upon the screen of his pure, white innocence. Rather than the melodious songs of birds in the trees above him, he heard only the Hisses and Boos of his wounded pride.

After several long and dramatic encores, the tragedy ended. His active mind shifted into rehearsing future conversations with the villain. He pictured Marty being shamed into repentance as the result of a few well-chosen words. His arguments were rapiers, cutting and slicing until Martin, dazed and bleeding, begged for mercy. But gradually, the world around him began to eat away at the world within.

That outcropping of rock signaled the trail that branched off toward V's house. This great, dead snag held a red-tailed hawk's nest high above the surrounding forest. Even now, the hawks were circling overhead as they always did, making sure their children were safe from whoever was walking past. Up ahead, the trail wound through a thick patch of salal and huckleberry brush.

A flash of movement caught his eye. The path made a long, U-shaped curve, and at first, it was just a flicker of color through the bushes that drew his attention. Then it came into full view. A bobcat was padding towards him on the trail. It was huge. It walked with the stately grace and unconcern of royalty. He could see the muscles rippling its mottled coat as it came, apparently lost in thought. Perhaps it was busy recounting the slights and atrocities of another bobcat. Whatever the reason, Thomas couldn't believe that it hadn't spotted or scented him yet. He continued, quietly walking forward, wondering what would happen next.

He lost sight of it, momentarily as it approached the

point in the curve where they would meet. Suddenly it reappeared in the trail ahead. Still it came on. Thomas was beginning to get a little bit worried. This great, powerful cat wasn't afraid of him, didn't even notice him at all.

They were about fifteen feet apart when the bobcat looked up. Its yellow eyes widened in a look of shock and disbelief. This lasted for about half a heartbeat. It sprang into the air, spinning as it rose to a height of about six feet so that, when it hit the ground, it was facing back the way it had come. Thomas caught a glimpse of its bobbed tail and it was gone. There was an instant of decision, fight or flight. Thomas was amused and quite relieved that the cat had chosen flight.

He was reminded of a night, years before, when he had been walking home in just such a state of mind. There was just the sliver of a moon, and he was lost in thought. Suddenly there was a violent commotion right in his face. He had jumped up, just as the bobcat had done. When his senses cleared, he realized that a he had startled a vulture in the process of enjoying a midnight snack. He had been surprised to find that he, unlike this bobcat, had jumped forward and, when reason returned, found himself standing with fists clenched in an aggressive attitude. He had chosen fight. Luckily, the vulture too had chosen flight.

That night, he had learned that the line between heroism and cowardice is so fine as to be almost imperceptible. There are times when fight or flight is not a decision, but an impulse; an involuntary reaction. The hero is lauded as someone possessing great character and bravery, and the coward is sneered at as one possessing neither, when in fact, they each simply responded differently to the same impulse, a response over which neither of them had any control.

He was approaching the deserted village. The houses were scattered among the trunks of the fir trees, looking like a lumber camp from the old days, except for the tree houses. From the beginning, Thomas had been intrigued by the tree houses. One in particular had piqued his curiosity. It was larger and more ornate than the others, having balconies with carved balusters, and a third level observation room. Nobody was around. He was the first to return from the wake. It would just take a minute to check it out.

The first level was a good twenty feet off the ground. Thomas climbed the spiral staircase that twisted like a corkscrew around the trunk of the tree. At the top of the stairs, a trap door had been cut into the tree house floor. He was surprised that it opened at a light touch. It looked a lot heavier than it was. When he entered the room, he saw the reason. The door was counterbalanced, like an old-fashioned window sash. A section of heavy iron bar was suspended by a rope and pulley against the tree, which made up part of the interior wall. The door could be either raised or lowered with the pressure of one finger.

The room was slightly pie-shaped, about eight feet wide at the tree, and ten feet wide at the far end, about twelve feet away. Another stairway spiraled up over the one that led to the ground, and Thomas followed it to the next level. The trap door was rigged up the same as the one below. The room was a little smaller though. It had the same basic shape, and the same pine paneling. It was offset, following the contour of the tree and the rise of the stairs. The third level was smaller yet, tapering from about five feet at the tree, to the wider end at about seven feet. It contained a desk and chair, dusty and apparently unused for some time. As a matter of fact, everything about the place looked and smelled as if nobody had been up there for a long time.

Each room had a large, dusty window and a balcony. The middle floor had a big built-in bed, and the lower one contained a table, a couple of chairs, and an old tin stove. Spider webs were everywhere. Thomas guessed that the spiders came and went along the exposed bark of the tree.

He was a little disappointed. This great, fantastic looking, mysterious structure that had called to him from his first sight of it, had turned out to be, not exactly ordinary, but not all that exciting, either. He took the stairway back to the ground and went to get his belongings.

11 THE CHOICE

He figured to take only what he would need for the trip back, and leave the rest. His small daypack would do. When he had filled it with a change of clothes, a few toilet articles and his neglected journal, he started up the trail once more.

People were arriving. Everyone he met had a smile and a word of greeting for him. He trudged on, leaving them all behind.

As he walked along, feeling the slight weight of his pack, and enjoying the solitude of the trail, he began to wonder about certain things. It crept into his mind that, maybe he was making a mistake, here. He tried to sort out his feelings and his options into some kind of order. What was it that he really wanted? This kind of life had always been his fondest dream. When the pressures of his business or the fears that accompanied his wife's illness had gotten to be too intense, he had always taken a mental journey to this place. Peace was here. Simplicity was here. But that sonofabitch Martin was here, too.

Then there was Virginia. When he had left for Michigan, actually for parts unknown at the time, she had consumed him. She had been in his every thought. His feelings for her had been so intense that he'd had to get away from her and from them in order to function. He'd known, at the time, that he wasn't ready for any kind of commitment, that he had nothing to offer her. That knowledge had been the force that had propelled him away from there.

He thought about his life in Michigan and the pressures and accomplishments of his business. For the past few years he had been downsizing. He had laid-off his crews and had been using subcontractors for all the hands-on construction. His only employee now was his secretary, who wanted him to call her his administrative assistant. She was a survivor. Finding a new job would be no problem for her.

He'd have to sell his house. That wouldn't be a problem. The market was still pretty solid and he wouldn't need to get top dollar.

There was his son, Tyler to consider. They didn't communicate much as it was, but he wanted to be there if Tyler ever needed him for anything. Would the monthly airplane be enough? Sadly, he thought that it probably would.

He suddenly realized that he had already made his decision. As he had been considering his options, he had been thinking, not about whether he wanted to go or stay, but about how he could justify staying. This was what he wanted, this flowing water, these growing trees, this open sky. This made sense. Everything else was just detail.

Finally, he allowed himself to consider living out the rest of his life here. It was as if the bottom of his pack had just ripped out. Suddenly the weight he had been carrying was gone.

He could see now, that the incident involving the vulture was the only time in his entire life that he had chosen fight over flight. And of all the times he'd had to choose, that was probably the one that mattered least.

All this time he had been running away. He had run

from his feelings for Virginia. He'd gone halfway across the country, gotten married and settled down. When his wife had gotten sick, he had run away by filling his life with his work, and lost his son in the process. When his work no longer seemed to hold any satisfaction, he had run back here to the woods. It was definitely time to stop running and face whatever it was that he had been running from.

Martin was on the porch, waiting for him. Virginia was there, too. Everyone else had gone home.

"Okay Marty," Thomas began. "Let's talk. Exactly what is it that you have to offer me?"

"Everything I have, Buddy." Martin was beaming. He jumped up from the porch steps and reached out to shake hands. "What made you change your mind?"

"I don't know, maybe I'm just tired of splashing around in the big puddle. Hello Virginia, are you okay?"

"I will be," she said. "Maggie and Carol Ann are going to take turns staying with me for a few days. Then I'll just take it one day at a time. I thought about leaving, but I love it out here. I don't think I could move back to the world now. I'm too set in my ways."

"Well, if there's anything I can do, I'll be glad to pitch in. I'll be around for at least a month. Right now though, I think Marty and I have a plane to catch."

"Yeah, we'd better get moving," Marty said. "He should be landing within the hour." He turned toward the open door of the house. "Hey Maggie! We're taking off now! You want to come along?"

"No thanks," Maggie appeared in the doorway, wiping her hands on a towel. "Ginny," she said. "You can go, but I think I'll just stay here and finish cleaning up."

"I think I'll stay too. It's been a long day. You boys go ahead."

The women went inside. Thomas and Martin went up to the barn, where a horse and wagon waited. Martin settled into the bucket seat, and Thomas climbed up onto the box. They clip-clopped down the path, past the house and on toward the main trail.

It was twilight when they arrived at the big plateau. The trail brought them to a kind of fire pit, next to a stack of cordwood. They stopped here and built a roaring fire. They built a similar fire at the other end of the field and waited.

Stars had begun to show when they heard the plane. It circled once, and then landed on a direct line between the two fires. Thomas commented that he was surprised at how quickly the plane slowed down, requiring very little runway. "Randy is an old Navy pilot," said Martin. He can land that thing on a dime."

When the engines had been shut down, Martin and Thomas walked over to the plane. The door opened and Ichabod Crane jumped out onto the wing. He was tall and skinny, with a prominent Adams Apple and a long, pointed nose. "Howdy, men," he said. "How they hangin?"

He was all business. Introductions were made, a half-dozen large cardboard boxes were transferred from the airplane onto the wagon, and he was off again, bouncing down the makeshift runway and climbing steeply into the night sky.

Martin removed a shovel from the wagon box and proceeded to cover the fire with earth. They did the same with the other fire.

The moon was rising red in the East, but the darkness on the ground was nearly complete. "Too bad these things don't come with headlights," Thomas ventured as they started off.

"Maisy knows her way." Martin was lying back in the seat with his hands clasped behind his head. "Who needs headlights when you have autopilot?"

Back in the forest, there were places where Thomas couldn't see his hand in front of his face. He tried a couple of times. But the horse continued on with the same, steady pace, and brought them directly back to the Wilson house.

The two men put the boxes on the porch, unhitched the wagon, and walked Maisy up to the barn for a trough of grain. "Unpacking those boxes can wait 'til morning," Martin said. "It's getting kind of late and I'm just about wore out."

Back at the house, they found Maggie and Virginia seated at the kitchen table. Maggie looked up as they entered. "I'll bet you boys are starving," she said. "And I think I know just what you need."

From behind the stove, she produced a miracle. "Here you go." It was a huckleberry pie. "V. dropped this off just after you left. He said he wanted to talk to you about something, said he'd be back in the morning."

They sat down at the table then, and began to dig into that wonderful pie. Virginia looked across the table at Thomas. "Well hello there, Galahad."

She remembered. He always used to greet her with, "Good morrow, Your Highness." And she would answer with, "Well hello there, Galahad, slain any dragons lately?" To which he would reply, "Silly girl, it ain't dragon season."

He just smiled, said, "Silly girl," and ate his pie.

When the pie was all gone, the dishes had been done, and the lamps had been turned down, Maggie said, "Tom, it's all set. There are two extra rooms upstairs. Marty and I will take one, and you can have the other. Right, Ginny?"

"That'll be just fine. There's no sense going out again, late as it is."

As Thomas lay in the single bed, drifting off to sleep, he had the feeling that all was right with the world. At the same time, however, he felt as if he were in a Dali painting. He dozed off to the echoed tick-tock of a melting clock.

He awoke to the sound of voices downstairs, voices

and breakfast cooking. The aromas of bacon, eggs and coffee made their way up the stairs. Breakfast was just what he needed: breakfast, a toothbrush, a bath and a change of clothes. Breakfast would have to do.

V. had just arrived and was pouring himself a cup of coffee. Maggie was frying eggs, and Virginia was placing a platter of crisp bacon on the table. Martin opened a tall cupboard door and offered Thomas an ironstone cup. "Oh, I see how it is," he said. "You're the kind of a guy who sleeps 'til all the work's all done."

"That's right, I may not be real clever, but I've always had great timing. Hello V. Good morning Virginia, Maggie, this food smells wonderful. I thought maybe I'd woken up in heaven."

"You may be right," Martin said. "Have a seat."

The eggs were ready and everyone sat down to breakfast. Between mouthfuls, Thomas said. "Yeah, this is heaven, all right." This was followed by the clink of silverware on plates and the hum of genial conversation. Thomas felt as if he could just sit there and soak it all up. With a piece of toast, he wiped up the last bit of yolk from his plate. He glanced over at Virginia, who was, for the moment, staring into space. Staring through a window into the past, he thought. Her still-beautiful face wore an expression of sad resignation. But Thomas also thought he detected a sense of peace and even of contentment. When she caught him staring, the sadness disappeared from her eyes and her slight smile widened into a grin.

"Had enough?" she asked.

"Oh, I'm okay for now. This will definitely get me through the morning. What a feast!"

Everyone agreed, thinking he was talking about the meal.

Thomas stood, and began clearing away the plates. Maggie protested. "Why don't you just sit back down and relax? I'll take care of this mess."

"No, you and Virginia cooked all this. The least I

can do is help clean it up."

V. slid back his chair, stood up and began to help. "Good idea, Tom. I'll fetch the water." He picked up a pair of large buckets from under the kitchen counter. A third one, already full, had been heating on the stove.

"Oh hell," said Martin. "I guess I'll dry."

When V. returned with more water, he emptied the heated bucket into a washtub on the counter. Then he added cold water to this until he achieved the proper temperature, took a big bar of soap and a washrag from the windowsill, and began washing the dishes. He handed the clean dishes to Thomas, who rinsed them by pouring a little water over them from the remaining bucket over the empty one. Thomas then handed them to Martin, who dried them with a towel and put them away in the cupboard. They laughed and joked while they worked, and in no time at all, the dishes were done.

"You know," said Thomas when they were finished, "A microwave oven and a dishwasher would have saved us from having to do all this work."

Martin began to speak, but V. quickly interrupted. "Don't get him started! If you get Martin talkin' about that stuff, we'll be here all day!" He turned toward the table, where the women were still seated, enjoying the last of their coffee. "Ginny, thanks for the breakfast," he said. "Carol Ann'l be here later on. She had a few things to take care of up at the house, but she figgered to be done by about mid-day."

"I'll be here for a while longer," said Maggie. Maybe the three of us can take a walk or something this afternoon. I know! We'll pack up some food and have a picnic up at the falls."

"Good idea!" Martin said. "Pack enough for all of us. I was just going to take Tommy around and show him the lay of the land. Maybe we can meet you up there this afternoon"

They said their goodbyes then, and the three men

walked out onto the porch. From smiling and jovial, V. suddenly turned serious. "Martin," he said. "There's something I wanted to talk to you about." He looked significantly toward Thomas.

"Don't worry about him," Martin told him. "He's one of us now."

The big man grinned. "Good," he said. "Welcome to the family, Tom." He stuck out his great paw of a hand.

Thomas felt as if he'd stuck his hand in a trash compactor. And as if that wasn't enough, he suddenly found himself locked in a bear hug that squeezed the breath out of him. As soon as he could speak, he said, "Thanks V. Don't ever do that again."

Chuckling, Martin asked, "What was it you had to say?"

"Oh yeah. Well, I've been thinkin' about Carl. There's some things that don't quite add up. He said he fell down that cliff, but to me, it looked more like somebody beat the hell out of him and threw him over. He said he'd been fishin' but I looked around a little, and I couldn't find his fishin' pole, nor any fish. I figgered maybe somebody aught to poke around up there and see if they can come up with some answers."

"Yeah, I know. It felt kind of funny to me, too," said Martin. "But if you say somebody beat him up, that settles it. Let's go up there and take a look around. What worries me is, if Carl was protecting someone, it could have been one of us."

Baker Creek lay two ridges to the east. The three men had to cut across country, and steep, rugged country it was. There wasn't much open ground. Thick forest covered all but the most vertical and rocky surfaces until they crested the last hill. They were hiking along, getting ready to make the descent into Baker canyon, when V, who was in the lead, found something. "Well, I'll be damned!" he said. "Would you look at that."

Tire tracks showed where someone had driven a jeep down the ridge, running parallel with the canyon. Martin sighed. "How is it you and Henry didn't find these before?"

"We came up the creek from the south," said the big man. "Maybe we should head back to the house and pick up some artillery."

"No, there's two sets of tracks here. Whoever it was drove in and back out."

They followed the tracks to a place where the field ended in a tangle of brush. Here the vehicle had turned around. About fifty yards away was the cliff. There in the field, the grass was matted down and the ground torn up as if there had been recent activity. Sure enough, there was a place where the men found streaks of blood in the grass.

"Outsiders," said Martin. He sounded relieved.

"This is a cold trail," V. observed. "Maybe we should go pack up some grub and some gear and check it out. These tracks could go on for miles."

"Yeah, maybe we can catch the girls before they leave for the falls. It looks like there'll be no picnic today."

12 THE LEAGUE OF JUSTICE

Carol Ann was there when they reached the Wilson house. "Hey!" she said, "I thought you boys were planning to meet us up at the falls! You just couldn't stand being away from us, could you?"

The three women were making up a lunch basket and getting ready to start their hike. V. picked up a sandwich and looked inside. "Whatcha makin?"

Carol Ann grabbed it away from him. "Put that down, you big gorilla. That's our lunch! Here I thought you missed me, and all you're interested in is the food!"

"You know better'n that, Darlin." He grabbed her up in one of his bearhugs.

Thomas thought she must be made of iron. Those hugs hurt.

Martin turned to Virginia. "Can we talk for a minute?"

"Sure we can," she said. "What's up?"

"Well," he said, quietly. "I hate to ask this, but had you noticed anything unusual about Carl lately? Had he been spending a lot of time away from the house?"

"Come to think of it, yes he had." They walked out onto the porch. "For the past six months or so, he'd go out overnight every couple of weeks. When I asked him about it he'd tell me he just lost track of time, or something lame like that. He kept saying he was going to take me away from here and buy me nice things, and I never thought much about it until… Come on up to the barn. I have something to show you."

The barn contained two large stalls and a tack room, with grain bins and shelves for various things. The loft above provided storage space for hay. There was also a lean-to shed on the back of the building with more shelves and cupboards. The lean-to looked newer than the rest of the building, and had a wood floor that proved to be a false bottom. Virginia removed this and pulled out a large, nylon gym bag. Inside was money, lots of money.

"I don't know what made me look in here," Virginia said. "It's just that Carl had been acting so weird and secretive, I thought he was up to something. We talked less and less, and whatever he was doing seemed to take over. Toward the end, he seemed like a stranger."

"Damn!" Martin said. "I'm really sorry. I had no idea. How much is here?"

Virginia stood, staring at the bag. "I don't know. What difference does it make? It's not mine, and besides, I have no use for money. I thought that's one of the things we stayed up here to get away from."

Martin placed the bag back in the hole under the lean-to floor. "I think maybe we all had different reasons for staying up here," he said. "For some of us, it was the dream of a simpler, fuller life. For others, it may have been something else, I don't know what. I just hope we can get through this, and that it doesn't wreck everything we've done here. Don't tell anyone else about it."

"What are you going to do?"

"I don't think we have much choice. We have to go back up there and check it out some more. We still don't know what Carl was into or what kind of people he was dealing with, so you should probably stay with Carol Ann 'til we get back."

"I'm so sorry. I kept thinking that he would come around, and that whatever he was doing would just blow over and things would go back to the way they were. Maybe if I'd told you about this in the beginning, he'd still be here." Virginia was trying not to cry.

Martin placed his hands on her shoulders and looked into her eyes. "Don't even go there," he said. "You were his wife. You wanted to believe in him. Carl made a bad choice, or a series of bad choices. Most of us are up here because we couldn't stand up to the temptations of the world. We thought that, with fewer opportunities to make bad choices, we could learn to make good ones. It just looks like, for Carl, the pull was too strong. One more question, was anyone else involved in this?"

"I don't think so," she said. "You should probably talk to the boys. I know they were as worried about him as I was. Maybe they found out something."

"For now, I think Tom, V. D. and I are just going to follow up on some things we found at the cliff." Martin started walking back toward the house. "Why don't you pack some clothes and move in with Carol Ann. Hopefully, we'll be back in a day or so with some answers."

V. was waiting on the porch with Thomas. "We're all set here," he said. "Let's get moving."

"Just a minute." Martin walked past them and inside. He went to the bedroom. From under the bed, he produced a deer rifle, a shotgun and a twenty-two. "Who knows what we'll run into up there. These might come in handy."

Thomas suddenly felt like John Wayne. Here he was, holding a rifle in the kitchen of a rustic farmhouse, preparing to embark on a foray into outlaw territory. Virginia pressed a box of shells into his hand and said something about being careful. Part of him wanted to put the gun down and walk away. This wasn't some old western movie. This was real. He could feel the smooth, polished wood of the gunstock and feel the weight of it in his hands. Even after what he'd been through for the past few days, this was surreal. In his best John Wayne impression, which wasn't very good, he drawled, "Rest easy, Ma'am, me and the boys is gonna ketch up with them varmints and bring 'em in."

Martin's Impression of The Duke was much better. "Wal fellas, we'd best quit jawin' and be headin' out. We're burnin' daylight, an' them critters has got a three day head start."

The feigned joviality lasted for about five minutes on the trail. It ended in a grim silence that continued until they reached the field where Carl had been beaten.

From the footprints, it looked as if there had been three of them. Apparently two had held him while the third man did the work. They couldn't tell if Carl had met them there or if they had all arrived together in the vehicle. They talked about the idea that this could have simply been a random act of violence, but Carl's recent actions made it look more like some kind of deal gone wrong. Martin didn't mention the money.

Martin set a pretty fast pace on the trail. Thomas figured that they made about three or four miles before it started getting too dark to see the tracks. They camped without a fire and were hiking again before the sun appeared.

It was beautiful country, steep and rugged. They crossed open fields and threaded their way through forests of White Oaks where mistletoe grew like green crowns among the upper branches. Sometimes the tracks would lead them into deep green glades of Jack Pine or Douglas fir, or among great rocks where narrow waterfalls poured into emerald pools. By the sun, it was about mid afternoon when they saw the cabin.

The faint tracks they had been following had turned

onto an old logging road. It really wasn't much of a road, just two dusty wheel ruts with grass and weeds growing up between them, but it had been well traveled recently, and was easy enough to make out.

They had crested a ridge, and the road angled down into a small, bowl shaped valley that formed the headwaters of a creek. Tucked into the edge of the bowl, and surrounded on three sides by tan oaks, the cabin had two tall windows facing the valley, and between them stood an old, glass paneled door. The door was open.

A beat-up Jeep station wagon was parked outside. It was camouflaged in green and brown patterns, and the passenger side door, facing the house, was open, too. Thomas could hear voices coming from inside the cabin, but he couldn't make out what was being said.

They left the road, ducked down, and began working their way toward the house, using stumps and bushes for cover. Thomas was finding it hard to breathe. His arms and his legs felt weak. It was as if all the blood in his body had gone racing back to his heart and stayed there, building up pressure like a steam boiler. His fingers began to hurt, and he realized he was gripping the twenty-two rifle with all his might. They were close enough now to make out what the voices inside were saying.

"How the hell should I know? It could be anywhere. We don't even know if it's out here in the woods or back in town," said one.

"I think it's out here," said another. "That tough old bastard was living out here somewhere, and that's where we'll find it."

"Bullshit! We've been looking for three days and haven't found squat!" said a third. "The old coot probably buried it somewhere. I think we aught to just cut our losses and get the hell out of here."

"Yeah, maybe you're right. It ain't going anywhere. We can pick up some supplies and come back later."

Three men emerged from the cabin. They were

mid-to-late twenties, ragged and unshaven. One was tall, over six feet, and skinny. His brown hair was tied back in a ponytail. The other two were about five feet seven or eight. One was bow-legged and slim, and the other was well over two hundred pounds, his belly hanging over his belt.

"Don't move!" yelled Martin.

They moved. Their reaction was instantaneous. All three men dove for the house. Martin fired a warning shot as they disappeared inside, too late to have any effect. The loud crack of the deer rifle echoed around the canyon.

"You missed, asshole!" came a voice from inside. "What's going on here? What the hell do you want?"

"Justice!" yelled Martin.

That caused a lot of whispering and grumbling from inside. It sounded, to Thomas, like the men were arguing about whose fault it was and saying "I told you so." After a few minutes of this, the man shouted again to Martin. "What's this all about? We haven't done anything!"

"That man you beat up is a friend of ours," said Martin. "And it's time to pay the piper!"

A nasally voice from inside said, "Oh shit, Tony. It's not the cops!"

"Shut up!" said the first man, obviously the leader. To Martin he yelled, "Walk away, man! If we come out, we come out shootin!"

"Give it up!" Martin yelled back. "You're surrounded!"

Thomas was getting that feeling again. He looked over at Martin, who was crouched behind a stump with his gun at the ready. He looked over at V. who was standing behind a tree, and if that wasn't a shotgun in his hand, you would think that the big man hadn't a care in the world. He looked down at the rifle in his own hands and was somehow jolted back to reality.

It reminded him of when they were kids. Tommy and Marty playing cops and robbers in the woods behind the schoolhouse. "Bang bang, you're dead!" But this was no game. These were real guns with real bullets, and if things were allowed to continue as they were going, there was a good chance that someone was about to get killed.

He ducked down and scrambled over to where Martin waited behind the stump. "Marty," he said. "What do we do now?"

"How the hell should I know? This really sucks! All this time, I've just been thinking that we had to catch these guys, and that they shouldn't get away with what they did to Carl. But I never thought about what to do after we caught 'em." He motioned to V. who walked over to join them. "What do you think, big guy?"

"Well, I'd say we're in a kind of a spot here. We have to figger out whether to bring 'em down, or let 'em go. The way I look at it, we're damned if we do, and damned if we don't."

"Yep, that's what I was thinking. There's no way out of this, is there?"

"I sure as hell can't see one. If we let 'em go, they'll come back. It looks like Carl had something they want. If we capture 'em, well then we have to live with that. Oh, we're in a pickle, alright."

"I wonder what they're after. Thomas said. "Maybe we could find it and give it to them."

"Who knows?" Said Martin. "Whatever it was, they killed him trying to get it. We can't just let them get away with that!"

"So, we're back where we started."

Thomas had an idea. "Hey! Why don't we take them back and lock them up? I know the perfect place, and it's not like you fellas haven't done it before."

"Wait a minute, that's not so bad, considering our other choices. At least it would buy us some time, while we figure out what to do with them." Martin looked relieved.

"Good, it's settled then." Thomas stood up. They had

a plan. That's when the cabin door flew open.

13 VENGEANCE

The three men burst out of the cabin, heading in a mad dash for the jeep. The one in front, the one with the ponytail, had an automatic rifle and began firing, as fast as he could pull the trigger, at the group behind the stump. The first bullet caught Thomas in the left hip.

As Thomas went down, he reacted by bringing the twenty-two around and squeezing the trigger. Martin and V. reacted as well, and the valley echoed like thunder. The shotgun boomed. The rifles cracked. The noise was deafening. It only lasted for a moment.

The heavyset man made it to the jeep. He was lying half in, half out of the open door. He was still moving. The other two lay where they fell. The bowlegged one had a big patch of blood on his chest that was quickly spreading. Ponytail had one eye open. The other one was gone.

The man at the jeep was crying.

Thomas was lying on the ground with his shirt pulled up, staring at the blood that was seeping out of the hole in his hip. He pressed down on it with his left hand, trying to stop the bleeding. He didn't realize that more was coming out of the larger exit wound behind him.

Martin came running over. "My god Tommy, you're Hit!"

"I'll take care of him," said V. "Why don't you go check on the other one?"

V. tore off Thomas' shirt and folded it into a makeshift pad. Then he took off his own shirt and used it to hold the pad in place, covering both the entrance and exit wounds. When it was wrapped around Thomas' middle, he asked if it was too tight. Through clenched teeth, Thomas said that it was okay, thanks. Then he simply said, "Ouch."

Martin walked over to the heavyset man, who was still crying. Between sobs, the man said, "I can't move!" His head was on the floor of the jeep and his right arm was extended at an odd angle behind his head and under the passenger seat. His left arm hung over the running board and his legs were splayed out on the ground. He looked up at Martin, and like a child he said, "Could you please help me? I'm stuck." There was quite a bit of blood on his shirt, a big spot at his chest and another one lower down.

After making Thomas as comfortable as possible, V. came over to help Martin. They dragged the wounded man out of the jeep and laid him on the ground. "Who're you guys?" he asked.

In his gravelly voice V. answered, "Just a couple of pilgrims, is all."

"I'm dyin' ain't I?" he asked.

"I'm afraid so," said the big man. For once, Martin was silent.

"I got to tell you something." There was still that childlike urgency in his voice that V. recognized as a symptom of shock.

"Me and Tony and Mike did something bad. Tony said that since we did all the work, we should get all the money. But Carl said he already paid us and that was enough. I didn't want to hurt him, but Tony went kind of crazy. He hit him and hit him and other stuff, but Carl wouldn't tell him where it was." He was crying again. "I didn't want to hurt him. He was my friend! I wanted to stop but we didn't. We threw him off the cliff. Tony said he was dead, but maybe he was wrong. You've got to go find him! Maybe he's just hurt. Maybe he's all alone out there by the cliff. Go find him, please? His name is Carl, and I need to tell him I'm sorry."

"Don't worry, I'm sure he's fine," said V. "We'll find him and tell him you're sorry he got hurt. Everything'll be okay. We'll fix it for you."

"Thank you," said the man. "I didn't mean to hurt him. He was my friend."

A pool of blood was growing around the man as he lay on the hard ground in front of the cabin. His skin had blanched to the color of ivory and his voice had become no more than a hoarse whisper. "You'll tell him," he said. "Tell him I'm sorry."

A few minutes later, the man was dead.

Martin finally got his voice back. "My god, what a mess!" he said.

"I'll check on Tom," said V.

Thomas had rolled over onto his side, and was trying to get up. The pad that V. had made for him was bright red in the back. He was grunting with the strain and the pain of trying to rise, but not having any real success.

"Whoa now, Hoss." V. laid a giant hand on his shoulder. "You just rest easy 'til we get organized. We'll figger a way to get you outta here. Martin, why don't you check around in the cabin, and see if there's anything we can use for a stretcher. Tom, if you'll just keep still for a minute, I have a few things I need to do. We'll be outta here before you know it."

He gently helped Thomas to lie back down, and set to work. He piled the three bodies in the back of the jeep. Martin came out of the cabin with a canvas and aluminum cot, and they raised Thomas onto it, complete with a pillow and a blanket. V. climbed into the jeep and drove away.

"I'm sorry I got careless," said Thomas. "I can't believe I went and got myself shot."

"What do you have to be sorry about?" asked Martin. "This was all my doing. I had to be the hero and go after these guys. Now look what's happened. You're shot and three more men are dead. Carl made some mistakes and put our whole community in danger. I tried to fix everything, but I've just made it worse. I'm the one who should be sorry!"

"What, exactly, did Carl do, anyway?" Thomas wanted to know.

"Carl always thought he was really good at only one thing." Martin sat on the ground, next to the cot. "He was a great farmer. He could grow better pot than anyone, anywhere. He was probably just doing what he did best. It looks like he brought these guys in and paid them to run his operation. I still don't know who he sold the grass to, or how he made the exchange, but I have a suspicion or two."

Thomas sighed and lay quiet, then. He knew that he was weakening. He felt helpless in the face of whatever might happen, as he had been unable to control the situation when the guns went off. Panic and regret took turns beating him up, while his imagination buffeted him with images of what had occurred and what was to come.

V. returned in the jeep, and he and Martin loaded Thomas in the back, stretcher and all. They drove back over the trail they had followed coming in. V. was still driving, slowly and with great care, trying not to jostle the cot in the back any more than was necessary.

They rode in silence, each man lost in his own thoughts. Finally, Martin said, "I'm glad you're here, man. I don't know what I would've done."

"Oh, I'm just like a big old Canada goose," said the big man. "I'm not too bright, but I've got good instincts. Hey Tom! Are you okay back there?"

There was no answer but, judging by his heavy, regular breathing, Thomas appeared to be asleep. It had been a long day.

By the time they arrived at the field, the sun had set behind the mountains. The sky was the color of burnished brass, and the field was in shadow. They got out of the jeep and V. yawned and tried to stretch some of the tension out of his back. Feeling the cool breeze, he said, "Fall's comin'"

"Yeah," said Martin. "It won't be long now. And then comes the winter. Are you ready?"

They opened up the back of the jeep and unloaded the cot, and the still sleeping Thomas. "Pretty close," the big man said. "I still need a little more firewood, but I finished the root cellar, and I already have quite a bit of stuff stored away. Me and Carol Ann canned up most of the vegetables from the garden, and I have a bunch of jerky smoked up. How about you?"

"Oh, we're alright."

Thomas groaned when they laid the cot on the ground, but didn't seem to wake up. Martin felt for his pulse, and it seemed strong enough. "As soon as we get back to the house, one of us should go get Henry,"

"Yeah, that's a pretty nasty hole," said V. "I think he'll come out of it all right, but he won't be runnin' any foot races for awhile." He climbed into the jeep and backed it into the shelter of a stand of young fir trees. Then they picked up the cot and started off.

They stopped once, just before they crossed a small stream, and Thomas opened his eyes. "I'm thirsty," he said.

"We'll get you a drink as soon as we get to the house," Martin said. "It won't be long now." But he was sleeping again.

14 THE PATIENT

Even though it was dark and deserted, the cabin was a welcome sight. Martin lit the big oil lamp on the kitchen table, and V. lit a fire in the stove. There was a linen closet at the top of the stairs where they found a couple of old sheets and tore them into pieces suitable for making proper bandages.

"Damn!" said V. Blood had soaked through the material of the cot and was dripping slowly onto the wood floor. Thomas was looking tired and pale, and when they tried to wake him up, he only groaned and continued sleeping. V. looked worried. "Martin," he said. "Go to my place and saddle a couple of horses. Tell the girls we're here and then go get Henry. He'll know what to bring. I'll stay here and clean out the wound as best I can. And hurry. He doesn't look so good."

As tired as he was, Martin ran for a good portion of the way to V's cabin. V. was right. Thomas had looked awful.

V. was sitting at the table, drinking a cup of coffee when Virginia and Carol Ann arrived. Virginia said, "Oh my god!" when she saw Thomas, and Carol Ann said, "Valentine, what the hell have you boys done now?"

Trying his best to look hopeful, V. said, "Aw, he'll be okay. He lost a little blood is all."

"Well, you both look like hell, if you ask me. Ginny and I'll take over. Why don't you go upstairs and get some sleep?"

"Henry should be here soon, and he might need some help," said the big man. "There'll be plenty of time for sleepin' later on."

"Oh, stop trying to be such a tough guy!" she said. "And just go on up and take a nap. We'll call you if anything happens."

With an expression that left no doubt as to the seriousness of his resolve, he looked deep into her eyes and softly said, "No."

She paled at that. "Ginny," she said. "Is there anything here for these boys to eat? I'll bet they're starved."

"I think we can come up with something. Let's go out to the cellar and see what we can find." She removed a lantern from its hook on the wall near the door, lit it, took Carol Ann by the arm and led her outside and around to the back of the house. The cellar was just a hole dug into the hill with a door framed over it. Inside were shelves filled with canned goods. Jars of fish, meats, vegetables, jellies and jams lined the walls. Each jar was labeled with contents, month and year. They chose a quart of stew and a pint of dill pickles. As she reached up to get the stew, Virginia said, "I don't think men ever outgrow their need for a mommy."

"Yeah," said Carol Ann. "And the hell of it is, I don't think we ever outgrow our need for a daddy. But maybe it's not so bad, this needing each other."

A sad, wistful look stole across Virginia's face.

"Oh, I'm sorry honey." Carol Ann laid an arm across her shoulder. "Sometimes I don't seem to have a brain in my old head. Let's go see what those damn fools have gotten themselves into."

Back in the cabin, Martin and Henry had arrived, and with V's help, had turned Thomas onto his stomach. Henry had cut away the bandage and had begun his examination of the wound. "Well?" Martin asked.

"I guess it could've been worse. The bullet didn't hit anything important, but it'll take some cleaning up. The problem is, it took so much meat with it when it passed on through. This hole is too wide to stitch together. Since it would be out of the question to try a skin graft out here, we'll just have to keep it clean and irrigated, and let it heal from the inside out. That's going to take some time. How 'ya doin' Tom? Have those pain pills kicked in yet?"

Thomas' voice was muffled by the pillow. "I'm not sure. It still hurts like hell, but it might be a little better."

"Let's give it a few more minutes. I'm hoping they'll at least take the edge off the pain. 'Sorry that's all I have. This won't be much fun."

He was right. Thomas tried to think of pleasant things. In his mind, he recounted the happiest times of his life. Mostly he thought about Virginia, and the time before he went away. Whatever pain killer Henry had given him seemed to intensify the power of his imagination, but the pain wasn't killed. Hell, it was barely wounded. His eyes and his jaw were clamped shut and he fortified the bulwarks of his will to endure.

There were times when he would think, "Hey, it's only pain. I can get used to this." And then Henry would hit a nerve and skyrockets would explode behind his eyeballs once again. Several times, he heard himself groaning.

Virginia was holding his hand. He wasn't sure if she was really there, or if he was imagining her being there, and he was afraid to open his eyes and maybe find out she wasn't. Real or imagined, that hand became his lifeline, a beautiful, compassionate presence that kept him from descending into a well of pain. He wanted to cry.

The skyrockets exploded again as he felt himself being rolled onto his side. Cleaning up the entry wound only took a few moments, and soon he was bandaged and wrapped up again. Henry was speaking to Virginia. "These will have to be changed everyday, and the wound will need to be irrigated. I was able to stitch up some of the interior muscle tissue, but I'll have to leave the rest to heal on its own. The important thing was removing all that dead tissue and those bits of fabric and lead.

Make sure he takes one of these every day as long as he's here. I'd move him to my place, but I don't think he's up to it." He began to wipe off his instruments. "I'll come over and check on him and, as soon as he can handle it, we can set up another place for him to stay until he's better."

Thomas felt the hand withdraw from his, as Virginia stood up. "Oh, he's fine right here. I can use some company right now. As a matter of fact, I was thinking he might be better off if we moved him into the bedroom. He'd have more privacy, and we could get rid of that nasty old cot. I can sleep upstairs until he's better." The hand had been real.

It seemed like an appropriate time to protest. "Wait a minute," said the patient. "Don't I get any say in this?"

"You just try not to move around too much," said Henry. "Especially for the next few days."

"Boy! You doctors are a bossy bunch."

"That's right, and if you do as I say, you might just get well. For now, I'm going to give you something that'll help you get some sleep."

When Thomas woke up, he was alone. The bedroom door was open a little, and he could hear Virginia, doing something in the kitchen. He was lying on his stomach, so he couldn't see much of the room. He noticed that the pillow smelled fresh and clean, and that his hip was on fire.

It was as if someone was pouring molten lava into

the hole. He made a half-hearted attempt at rolling over, but using the muscles in his back just made things worse.

He needed to get his mind off the pain. He thought about the lady and the tiger. That story was a metaphor for all the choices we make, but it was incomplete. Most of our choices don't bring immediate consequences. It's like sledding.

When he was ten years old, he had a sledding accident. He crashed his sled into a tree and broke his arm. He didn't choose to hit the tree, he simply chose to ride the sled down that particular hill. Up until the moment when the tree appeared in front of him, he was having the ride of his young life. The choice had seemed to be a good one. By the time he hit the tree, he was moving too fast to have any choice. So the trick, in life as in sledding, is to plan for eventualities. Look before you leap. "But then again," he thought. "That was one hell of a ride. And if we spent all of our time looking, there wouldn't be much leaping in the world."

"Hello, Galahad." Virginia had entered the room so quietly that he hadn't heard her open the door. "Slain any dragons lately?"

"Good morrow, Your Highness," he said. "I'm afraid the dragons are winning."

"Well, sometimes that's just the way it is with dragons," she said. "Nobody ever said being a white knight was easy."

"I'm just sorry that I'm putting you to all this trouble."

"Ah, gallant to the end, I see." She knelt down so she could look into his face. "Believe me, Sir Knight, this is no trouble. I learned a long time ago that the best way to get through a hard time is to get your mind off yourself and help someone else. This gives me the opportunity to do that." She placed a hand on his shoulder.

His focus moved instantly from the fire in his hip to the warmth of her hand.

"Besides," she said. "I have a feeling that you were wounded in the service of the crown. Martin told me what happened."

"Oh, really? What did he say?"

"He said that he was ready to shoot it out with those guys, but that you stopped him, and made him see that justice was more important than revenge for what they did to Carl. You tried to talk to them and that's when they shot you."

"And what happened then?"

"Oh, that's right, you were shot, so you probably missed it all. Martin and V. started shooting, and made them surrender. Then they gave those guys a good thrashing and told them if they ever come back, they'll get more of the same. He said they probably won't stop 'til they get to Mexico."

Thomas wondered if she really believed Martin's version of the story, or if she had just willed herself to accept it. She had withdrawn her hand while she was speaking, leaving a cold spot on his bare shoulder. His mental focus returned to the pain in his hip. "So where's Marty now?"

"He and V. went back up there. They're going to dig up the road so nobody else can use it."

"Good idea," said Thomas.

"Do you need another of those pain pills?" she asked. "You don't look so good."

"I'll take all I can get. I probably look better than I feel right now."

She brought the pill and a cup of water. In the cup she had placed a piece of glass tubing, to be used as a straw. She held it up so he could drink.

"Very ingenious," he said when he was finished. Where did that come from?"

"In the old days, Carl and I used to make water pipes. We kept a box of tubing in the cellar. Out here we never throw away anything that might be useful."

"Well, thank you. I'm glad you saved them."

"I need to go up to the barn and take care of a few things. Do you need anything else, before I go?"

"No thanks." Thomas still felt a little overwhelmed by the nearness of her. She had knelt down again and was looking into his eyes. God, she was beautiful. He couldn't look away. Her long dark hair and dark lashes intensified the awesome power of those pale blue eyes. She leaned in and kissed him on the cheek.

"I won't be long," she said as she disappeared through the door.

Inside, he was screaming. He wanted to jump up and run after her, to take her in his arms and tell her… tell her… what? Something incredibly romantic that would weld her soul to his. He felt like a teenager with his first crush. He closed his eyes and could still feel her breath, her moist lips on his face. "What a sap I am!" he thought. "She makes an innocent, friendly gesture and, in my mind, I turn it into this big fairy tale romance."

He tried to force her out of his mind. There were other things that needed thinking about, things like murder, and sledding, and unexpected consequences. What had they done? Three people were dead. Someone would miss them. Somebody, somewhere, cared about them. Sooner or later, there was a good chance that someone would come looking for them. If justice demanded their deaths in return for Carl's death, what would justice demand in return for theirs?

On the other hand, these were people who had allowed greed to induce them to take a life. Maybe they would have done it again. Maybe they would have come back up there and killed until they found what they wanted. Was the act of murder less significant than the motivation behind it? Could homicide ever be justifiable? His head was beginning to hurt. Lying there, unable to move, he had a powerful urge to jump up and run, and run, and keep running, and never stop running. He had come there in search of a simpler, clearer reality. Well, this was just too damn real.

Henry dropped by a little later to check on him. He showed Virginia how to irrigate the wound, which was a painful ordeal, and bind it up again. "Tom, the next few days are critical," he said. "But so far, it looks pretty good. Don't try sitting up until I say it's okay. The pain will give you more instruction than I can, though. If it hurts to do something, stop."

"Did they teach you that in medical school?" Thomas asked. "Or did you come up with that all by yourself?"

Henry smiled. "Medical school," he said. "Don't I wish… As far as I can tell, medicine is about sixty percent science, and about seventy-five percent common sense."

"Maybe you should've taken more math classes."

"Believe it or not," Henry said. "I think there are times when science and common sense overlap, just a little."

"Well, that's a comfort, anyway."

"I can't make it back here for a couple of days. I've got hay to cut, and it can't wait. Ginny, you know what to do, and what to look for. I stopped by on the way out and asked Carol Ann to be in charge of making sure someone's here in case you need to send for me, but everything looks even better than I'd hoped, so you shouldn't need to. Where the hell are your boys? I thought sure they'd be here helping out."

"Oh, Joshua came by while I was up at the barn, and I sent him away. They were going to take turns looking after me, but I told him that I'm a grown woman and I don't need a babysitter." She struck a defiant pose, hands on hips, feet apart.

"Well, it's not a question of what you need or don't need," he said. "It's just a simple problem of physics. You can only occupy one space at a time, and if anything goes wrong, it's not possible for you to go get help and be here too. It's more about what Tom might need."

"Oh," said Thomas. "You mean Tom the lump, Tom the slab of meat."

"No, I mean Tom the helpless smart-ass. Up until today, I thought you were the serious, scholarly type. Under the surface, you're just full of sarcasm."

"Or something," said Virginia.

"Well, my surface has a pretty big hole in it right now, so stand back. Who knows what might come boiling out of there."

"I can't stand any more of this," Henry said. "It's getting late, and I have a long way to go. If I know Carol Ann, she's made up a list, and organized around-the-clock watches. I'm sure someone will be here soon."

"Thanks Henry." Virginia hugged him goodbye. "I'm really glad you're here."

"Yeah thanks," Thomas said. "If it weren't for you, I know I wouldn't have a chance."

Henry had been right about Carol Ann. She set up a rotation so that someone was there every day for a week. Thomas got to meet several new people, including Jordan and Joshua, Virginia's two sons. Joshua, the younger son, was talkative and gregarious. His brown eyes sparkled with humor and life. Jordan had inherited his mother's pale blue eyes, but his disposition appeared to be as dark as his hair, which was nearly black.

Joshua had a wife and baby. His farm was up the valley, and he had inherited his father's green thumb. He grew a large variety of fruit, vegetables and grain, providing food for the community as well as for his little family.

Jordan was a hunter. He hunted and trapped, ranging far over the neighboring mountains. A couple of times a week, Virginia would find meat, maybe a shoulder of venison or a dressed-out rabbit or squirrel, hanging from the porch rafters. That would be his calling card. He seldom came inside. Thomas didn't trust him. He was brooding and sullen, and smelled like blood.

Martin and V. dropped by on their way back from burial detail. They looked tired, and didn't stick around long. Thomas wanted to talk to Martin alone, but decided that it could wait until he was on his feet again.

Every evening, Virginia would place a game board on the floor next to the bed, and they would talk and laugh, and play chess, or checkers, or backgammon. Checkers became their favorite, possibly because it required the least amount of thought and attention. It was the part of the day that Thomas most looked forward to. He would be thinking about something else, or talking to whoever happened to be on watch, and a picture would come into his mind. In this vision, Virginia would be sitting, Indian style, on the floor. The oil lamp would be burning brightly beside her, highlighting her hair and her smile, and he would be lying on his stomach, with his arm over the side of the bed. Suddenly, he would become too tired for company.

It was their sixteenth evening together. Thomas had been keeping track of the days, and noting the signs of his gradual recovery. The lamp and checkerboard were in place, and they had been joking about something or other. There came a moment of silence, and Thomas said, "So, tell me about your life. What did you do after I left?"

Virginia frowned a little. "Well, at first, like everyone else, I just wondered where you were. When I realized you weren't coming back, I cried. I really thought that we were on our way toward something, and then you were gone, and I didn't know what to think about it for a while. At first I was sad, and then I was mad for a long time, and then life just filled in around me and I got on with it."

"I've felt this horrible guilt about walking away, ever since the day I left," he said. "I justified it by telling myself that you'd have a better life without me. After all, I was just a bum with no job and no prospects. I knew that you wanted a home and family, and everything that goes with that, and I knew I wasn't ready to face that kind of responsibility. In the end, I realized I was just scared to death that I would let you down, that I wasn't worthy of your trust and the faith you seemed to have in me."

"You could've told me. I would have waited." She put a checker on the floor and stared at it. "After you left I went kind of crazy. I started drinking too much and living too fast. I met Carl, and he was nice, and then I got pregnant with Jordan, so we got married. I always felt guilty because I couldn't love him the way he loved me, but we made it work, and I think we were happy together. I think that's what made him do what he did. He thought that if he had a lot of money, maybe he could buy nice things that would make me happy, make me love him more or something." She looked up from the checker and into his eyes. "I think it's your move."

"There's a lot to consider here," he said. "The wrong move could put me in a really vulnerable position." Those incredible blue eyes were looking right through him. He looked down at the board. "If I move here, you'll jump me. And I'm not strong enough down here to survive that kind of attack right now." He gestured toward his defensive row.

She was smiling. "But it's your turn. You have to do something. You have a lot of men on the board, and a lot of different options. Besides, if I jump you, that doesn't mean you lose the game."

"To me, it looks like everything depends upon this one move. If I choose wisely, I win. If I choose foolishly, I lose. Is that it?" He looked up into those eyes again.

"Not necessarily," she said. She picked up the remaining pieces, placing them in the box, along with the board.

"Hey!" he said, "what about our game?"

"Oh, don't worry, we'll play again real soon." She closed the box and stood up. "Goodnight, Galahad," she said. Then she leaned over and kissed him on the mouth.

Fallen Idyll

"Try to get some sleep now. We have to get you well."

"I thought you said it was my move."

As she walked out the door, she said, "You think too much, Sir Knight. A girl can't wait forever."

He didn't fall asleep for a very long time.

15 RECOVERY

When she came downstairs the next morning, he was sitting up in bed. There were beads of perspiration on his forehead, and he looked a little pale and tired, but he was sitting up. He even managed a smile.

"What have you done now?" she asked. "You lie back down and behave yourself! You're not supposed to try anything like this without talking to Henry."

"Henry wasn't here. I just got real sick of being a lump. And besides, it wasn't all that big of a deal. It didn't even hurt much."

"Liar," she said. "I'm serious. Lie back down and let me check that wound. You're probably bleeding again." But he wasn't.

Henry came by in the afternoon. When he removed the bandage, he said, "This looks great! You should be able to start sitting up any time now. Before you know it, you'll be back on your feet again, but don't rush things too much. As I said before, the pain will tell you when to stop. A little bit is to be expected, but if something really hurts, don't do it."

Thomas and Virginia shared a hopeful look.

"Hey! What's going on, here?" Henry asked.

Still looking at each other, they both said, "Nothing."

"You kids are up to something," he said. "And whatever it is, just make sure nobody gets hurt."

"Okay dad," said Thomas. "We'll be careful."

"I see." He began putting things back into his satchel. "Well, it looks like everything is progressing nicely here. I'll be back next week sometime, but by then you'll probably be up and around."

That night, the checker game only lasted for three moves. Virginia moved first, and Thomas countered. As she was in the process of making her second move, she said, "Remember that day at the river when we were kids?"

There had probably been many days at the river, but he knew exactly which day she meant. "Of course I do," he said. "That's one of those things you never forget."

"Well, so do I. Do you remember your promise?"

"We were just kids, poised on the edge of life," he said. "Everything looked so simple. What were we, twelve or thirteen? I think that may have been the last time I saw things that way. It was my first kiss. I would have conquered the world for you."

"It was my first kiss, too. But you're changing the subject. What about your promise?"

Thomas closed his eyes. They had gone to the river with somebody's parents. Six or seven kids sat on the floor in the back of a pick-up, while the adults rode in the cab. He and Virginia had walked upstream, and were sitting on a rock, with their bare feet in the water. There was another, larger rock just downstream, which shielded them from the rest of the group. His memory was as crystal clear as the summer air. He could even feel the texture of the rough, granite stone beneath them.

"You're stalling, "she said.

"I'm remembering. What a great time to be alive. The future was big and frightening, but maybe for the last time, the present was natural and safe. We were holding hands, staring into that big, scary life that lay just ahead." He opened his eyes and looked into hers. "I said, 'No matter what happens, I will always take care of you. I love you, Virginia."

"Oh, so you do remember," she laughed.

"Every word. But, as long as we're remembering things, do you recall what you said back to me?"

"I don't know," she said, "probably something romantic."

"Yeah, right.' You said, 'Oh Tommy, you're such a sap!' And you jumped up and ran back to the picnic.

"Oh, really?"

"Really."

"Damn." Her blue eyes sparkled with life. She hesitated for a moment, and then she said, "So what? A promise is a promise, and I'm going to hold you to it!"

"Oh Virginia, you're such a sap!"

And then she jumped him.

"Ow!" he said.

"Oh, don't worry Galahad, I'm not going to do anything crazy. Although, it is tempting, with you lying there so helpless and all." She tried to look scary, leaning forward until their faces were just inches apart. "And there's nobody around to hear you scream!"

He put his arms around her and kissed her. It was a long, hungry kind of kiss; a thirty years apart when you should've been together kind of kiss. It was a kiss filled with passion and hope and regret.

With his eyes closed, and his forehead touching hers, he said, "My god, Virginia, what are we doing?"

"Obviously, not what I'd like to do, I don't think you're well enough yet." She pulled away, just a little, and lay beside him, with her head resting on her hand, smiling a mischievous smile.

"That's not what I mean," he said. "I mean, after tonight. How will your boys react to our being together? It's so soon, it doesn't seem right."

She lay back on the bed and sighed. "You always think too much. What do we do now? We live happily ever after, that's what. The boys will just have to understand, and I think they will. Out here, we're not bound by convention. Society makes arbitrary rules, but always leaves loopholes that are big enough to justify almost anything. For thirty years, the world has been turned upside down. Just now, I felt it turn right side up again, didn't you?"

"I'm sorry," he said. "You're right, of course. I do think way too much. Now, where were we?"

She rolled over, facing him again. "Right here."

The night passed like any other night. The earth whirled through the universe, and the stars danced and reeled through the heavens. But on the south slope of a mountain near the Mad River, in a cabin in the woods, the world turned right side up.

"Good morning. Galahad."

"Good morrow Princess." Thomas grimaced just a little as he sat up. Swinging his legs over the side of the bed hurt quite a bit, but not as much as he had expected. He didn't pass out. He did sit there for a long moment, collecting his thoughts and gathering his strength and courage.

"What the hell are you doing?" Virginia laid a hand on his arm. She looked really frightened.

"I figure it's time I stopped being a lump," he said. "And I have promises to keep."

"And miles to go before you sleep, I know. But don't do anything stupid. If you're trying to impress me, it won't work." She could read what was on his mind. He was about to stand up.

He concentrated on using only the muscles on his good side. If he could get his right leg to do all the work, he thought he could keep the muscles around his left hip from straining. "Maybe if you'll help me a little, I can pull this off."

As she got up and came around to his side of the bed, she said, "This is silly. You're not ready."

"We'll see." He braced his right hand on her shoulder and stood up. It worked. He was able to keep from using the muscles in his injured hip, but it still hurt like hell. A wave of dizziness passed over him and, for a moment there, he was afraid he was going to fall down. "Thanks," he said. "I'm alright now. Do you think you can bring me a broom, or something to use as a cane?" He transferred his hand, and his weight, to the night table. "I think I'd like to take a walk."

"You're insane." She ran to the kitchen and brought back a broom.

Thomas turned the broom upside down, and placed the straw part under his left arm. He found that, if he kept his hip and leg lined up, it wasn't too bad. The pain was only unbearable when he swung his leg in a natural walking motion. He did that only once.

He hobbled once around the room, and out onto the porch. The morning was a little chilly, but still, it was great to be outside again. "Virginia," he said. Would you mind doing me a favor?"

She was standing behind him with her hands out, as if she still expected him to fall. "Just name it."

"In my backpack upstairs, you'll find a grey, hooded sweatshirt."

"Don't move," she said. "I'll get it."

As soon as she went inside, he clumped over to the side of the porch and relieved himself on a bush. His timing was perfect. After he had finished, and was turning around, she appeared in the doorway and handed him the sweatshirt.

"I heard that."

"Of all the things I've had to put up with because of this," he gestured toward his hip. "I think I hate that stupid chamber pot the most. 'Sorry about your plants, but I don't feel quite up to tackling the steps just yet."

"I'll take care of that with a bucket of water. In the meantime, let's get you back into bed so I can get my morning chores done."

The pain in his hip had been steadily increasing, and it was beginning to burn. Suddenly, he felt tired. "Okay," he said. "That's probably enough excitement for now."

Virginia helped him get back into bed. She gave him a kiss, and said, "I'll be back in a few minutes. You just rest. You look a little worn out after all that exercise."

His hip was tingling, and the fire in it had turned to ice. After she left, he bent his head around as far as he could, and was relieved to see that the bandage was still white. He had expected it to be pink, or even worse, red with blood. He really was getting better.

The next day, he was stronger. The day after that, he successfully negotiated the porch steps. He was relieved to find, after the torture of descending them, that coming back up was much easier.

16 THE RUNAWAY

Most of the time, he was in Heaven. It was as if the world really had turned right side up. With Virginia, it was as if the past thirty years were just the wink of an eye. They laughed, and talked, and flirted together, and he was as happy as he could ever remember being. There were other times, though.

It was during one of those other times that Martin showed up. Thomas was leaning against one of the porch posts, trying to recall the events leading up to, and following his injury. A flash of red caught his attention. Someone was coming up the trail.

The red turned out to be a buffalo plaid wool jacket, and the someone turned out to be Martin. He quickened his pace when he saw Thomas on the porch, and was nearly running when he reached the steps. "Tommy!" he said, almost shouting. "God it's good to see you up and around! How the hell are you?" He leaped up the steps and grabbed Thomas by the hand.

"I've felt better. I've been shot, you know. But I'm glad you're here. We need to talk."

"Sure, Tom." Martin was still beaming. "Anything you say. Just look at you! You're going to be just fine!

For a while there I was afraid you weren't going to make it, but here you are, good as new!"

"I think it'll be a long time before I'm good as new. Right now I'm going inside to lie down. Come on, Virginia is up at the barn, and we can talk about what happened." Thomas grabbed the broom, and hobbled through the door, with Martin close behind. Martin closed the door.

"Marty, what we did was wrong. We crossed a line that people in society can't be allowed to cross." Thomas eased himself onto the bed. "We acted as police, judges and executioners. Somehow, we have to…"

"Hold on a minute, Tom. It sounds like you've been looking at this thing all wrong. What we did was necessary. It was necessary for the safety of everyone here." Martin slid a wooden chair over to the bed, and sat down. "I've been thinking about this quite a lot, and this is the way I see it. My old friend, Carl, got into a nest of rattlesnakes and got himself killed. You, me, and V. D. found the nest and killed the snakes. End of story."

"Is it really the end of the story? Those guys were alive and now they're not. Somebody, somewhere will probably miss them, then what? Suppose someone comes poking around up here looking for them?"

"They won't find anything. We buried those rattlesnakes about a mile apart, and transplanted bushes and other plants over the holes. Even if I ever had a reason to, I couldn't find them myself."

"What about the jeep?"

"Well according to the registration, that jeep belonged to Carl. I drove it out to the coast and left it by the road. When the cops find it there, they'll tow it to the impound lot, and send a letter to Carl's last known address, telling him where it is. When he doesn't show up to claim it, they'll auction it off. Don't worry so much. Everything has been taken care of. We emptied out the cabin, and we planted stuff in the trail they took to Baker creek. Nobody will ever know they were there."

"Okay, suppose somebody already knew they were up here. There's still a chance that they'll be missed."

"There are a couple of important things you're forgetting, Tom. One, these were lowlifes. They were the kind of people who move around a lot and don't leave forwarding addresses. Two, they shot first. You, of all people should know that we were acting in self-defense. Hell, that bastard shot you! You had to take him out."

"Wait a minute. You're saying I shot one of those guys?" Thomas was horrified. This was really bad news.

"Yeah, I thought you knew. When that ponytail wearing asshole shot you, you fired the twenty-two one handed and put a bullet right in his eye. It was the finest shot I ever saw."

Until that moment, Thomas hadn't even remembered firing the gun. Suddenly, the whole scene came to his mind, and he knew that Martin was telling the truth. He felt sick. "My god," he said. "What have I done?"

"You killed a rattlesnake," Martin said. "End of story."

They heard the front door open as Virginia came inside. She walked over to the bedroom doorway, carrying two large buckets of apples. "Looky what I found!" She held the buckets up for inspection.

She was radiant. Her long hair was tied back, and a few strands had come loose. She tried, unsuccessfully, to blow them back out of her face. Her blue eyes sparkled. Standing there in the bedroom doorway in her jeans and cotton shirt, everything about her glowed with life and joy. The men just stared, enraptured at the sight of her. "Oh, hello Martin," she said. The light faded, just a little. "What are you boys up to?"

"I just dropped by for a minute, to check on this guy and see how you were getting along. Looking at the two of you, I can see there's nothing to worry about. You both look great." Martin stood up. "Tom, think about what I said. You just remember how lucky you are to be alive. The future will take care of itself. There's no sense cluttering up the present with what might have been, or what might happen tomorrow. Today is all we really get, so let's enjoy it."

Virginia had taken the apples into the kitchen, and lifted them onto the table. Martin gave her a goodbye hug. "Thanks for all you're doing for him," he said. "He seems to be doing fine. With any luck, we'll have him out of here in a few days, and you can have your house back."

"You really are a piece of work, Martin. Always figuring the angles. You're like a sheep dog, circling and nipping at the flock, always trying to worry them in one direction or another. Well, since the boys have been gone, and with Carl always off doing whatever it was that he was doing, I've been pretty much taking care of everything around here for myself. If you don't mind, I think I'll pick my own pastures for a while. From what I've seen of Tom, I think he's capable of making his own choices, too. You're a good friend, I owe you a lot, and I love you to death. But a conversation with you is like a fencing match. Sometimes all that lunging and parrying just wears me out."

"Fair enough," Martin said, heading for the door. He smiled and shook his head. "Ginny, you are one hell of a woman. I hope whatever pasture you choose turns out to be filled with clover." He was still smiling as he sauntered down the trail.

"Oooh, he can be infuriating!" Virginia said, turning around. Thomas was leaning against the bedroom doorpost. "I know he brought you here, thinking that I'd fall in love with you all over again. And I just hate it when he's right. He's always so damn smug about it."

"He thinks in straight lines and acts in circles," Thomas observed. "Me, I think in circles and act in straight lines." He chose to pass over what she had just said, but inside, bells were ringing, lights were flashing, and fireworks arced across the starry sky. She loved him.

"Apple pie," she said. "That's what I'm thinking about. Are you feeling well enough to peel some of these?"

"For apple pie, I could do just about anything." He walked over to a chair near the table and carefully sat down. She handed him a paring knife, and he began to peel, core, and slice the apples into a large bowl. Most of the apples had worms at the core. Thomas simply cut away the affected parts, and threw them away with the parings.

"Well, that seemed awfully serious." From various shelves and cupboards, Virginia began taking out flour, sugar and the other ingredients for making the crust. "What's Martin up to now?"

"Oh, you know how he is."

She frowned a little, disappointed at his evasive answer. "Yeah, I know." She sighed and paused for a long moment. "But who cares about him anyway? We're gonna make a pie!"

They ended up making two pies. Soon the cabin was filled with the delicious aromas that wafted from the oven of the old wood stove. Thomas was preoccupied, mulling over his conversation with Martin. Virginia tried several times to pull him into a little light conversation, but finally gave up. In the end, they sat at the table, staring into space.

When the pies were done, Virginia pulled them from the oven, covering each with a clean, cotton cloth. "Do you mind if I leave you all alone for a little while?" she asked. "I think I'll take one of these to Carol Ann. She's been so much help these last few days, and it'll give me a chance to say thank you."

"That's a great idea. When you see her, I wish you'd thank her for me, too. I owe her a lot." Thomas actually felt a bit relieved, and looked forward to a couple of hours by himself.

"This other one should be cool by the time I get back," she said. "You be a good boy and don't go snitching any of it. It's for dessert, and I don't want you to spoil your dinner."

He smiled at her mock concern. "Yes ma'am."

After she left, he got up and, now using the broom more as a cane than a crutch, went outside to take a walk. A light breeze was blowing, and the air was a little chilly. It suited his mood.

His uncertain steps carried him to the gravesite on the hill. Someone had carved a marker from a slab of wood. It read, "Carl Woodrow Wilson, 1946-2003, A Good Man." Beside the marker someone, probably Virginia, had placed a vase of Brown-eyed-Susans. Thomas stared at them for a long time. Suddenly, he had the feeling that he didn't belong there at all.

Martin had been right. Women were more practical than men. His feelings for Virginia were too strong. They clouded his thinking, and thinking clearly was imperative in his situation. He had killed a man. There would be consequences. He should turn himself in to the authorities and explain everything. He had been shot, and firing his gun had been nothing more than a reflex. Facing up to his actions now would mean that he could at least choose the time and place for whatever confrontation lay ahead. It would be the responsible thing to do. It would also mean the end of everything here.

Martin and V. would be implicated and, since this wilderness property was purchased with proceeds from the sale of drugs, it would be confiscated. Henry, Virginia, and the rest would have to reintegrate into a society that they considered polluted and corrupt. Some would be incarcerated, and the rest would just be lost. He wanted to run away. Now there's something he was good at.

In nineteen seventy-three, when things got too complicated, he ran away back East. When Helen got sick, and he found out she wouldn't get well again, he ran away into his work. Then, when his life became too boring and lonely too stand anymore, he ran back here again. Running away had been the motivation behind every major decision he had ever made.

He was still staring at the flowers. Maybe the grave is the only really peaceful place there is, the ultimate destination for runaways. "Okay, that's enough," he thought. "This is getting me nowhere." He forced himself out of the quagmire of morbidity he had stumbled into, and back to reality.

17 DRAFT HORSES

Two things he wanted: a simple, elemental life, and Virginia. Everything else would work out one day, one challenge at a time. First, he needed to get well. After that, who knew? One thing he did know, it was time to stop being the whipping boy of circumstance, and to take control of his own life and destiny. Carl was beyond the cares of this world, but he was also beyond its richness and joy. Thomas still had options and opportunities.

Suddenly, Thomas saw himself at the center of a large circle. The circle was divided into degrees, and each event, or circumstance, occupied a number of these segments. He saw that he could only see a few of these segments at a time, and when he was facing one event, the other three hundred and fifty-odd degrees still existed, undiminished. It was a simple choice. In his mind, he could concentrate on any of these circumstances, whether positive or negative, earth-shatteringly important, or mind-numbingly trivial.

Certain situations require decisive action at certain times. Some others need to work themselves out. Still others have to wait until you can gather more information, or until other, related circumstances provide the proper background and timing for decisive action. If you think about it long enough, even a simple decision can become incredibly complicated and difficult to make. Hence the urge to run away. As he limped back toward the cabin, Thomas decided to think about the incredible beauty of the forest and the growing pain in his hip. Maybe he should have stayed closer to the house.

He also tried to think more clearly about his life here. He began to take a mental inventory of the circumstances that occupied some of the other degrees of his circle. He had his life. That was quite a gift, considering how close he had come to losing it. He had the simplicity and manageability that he had been seeking when he came out here. He had Virginia. She loved him. Who knew where that could lead? As he entered the door of the cabin, he thought, "And, most importantly of all, I have fresh apple pie!" He hobbled into the bedroom and lay down. What a relief that was. In a few moments, he was sleeping.

He was awakened by a kiss. "Come on, lazy bones." Virginia was kneeling by the bed. "I made us some dinner. Are you hungry?"

Thomas grunted as he opened his eyes. He blinked a few times, trying to clear his vision and his mind. "Come to think of it," he said, "I'm starving!"

In the kitchen, she ladled vegetable soup into two crockery bowls. A plate of bread and a crock of butter were already on the table. The soup was aromatic and spicy, and the bread was a necessary part of the meal. It was the fire extinguisher.

Virginia was looking at him, shaking her head.
"What?"

She pursed her lips and thought for a moment. "You boys had quite an adventure, didn't you?"

"Ah," he said, "I wondered if you'd find out somehow. I couldn't figure out a way to tell you."

"And I'll bet you've been beating yourself up about

it all this time, haven't you? When are you going to learn to let go of things?"

"It's not something you should have to deal with." He was spreading butter on a piece of bread, taking his time. "I wish you still didn't know."

"You are such a blockhead sometimes. It's been thirty years, and you haven't changed a bit. I was crazy about you all the time we were growing up, but you were always so bottled up that you couldn't see it. You think everything to death. Sometimes I think the world inside your head is bigger than the one we live in."

Thomas finished buttering the slice of bread and sat, staring at it.

"The people who care about you deserve, not only the good stuff, not just the smiley face button you put on, but also the not-so-good stuff. When you share a burden, it's not so heavy and hard to carry."

"Okay," he said. "What about the fine line between sharing a burden, and being a burden?"

"You can't be a burden to the ones who love you. I've seen the way you look at me. From the first, I could tell that you still have feelings for me, right?"

"Right."

"Good. So let's suppose something is bothering me. Wouldn't you want me to tell you about it so you could help me deal with it?"

"Of course I would."

"Well, there you go."

They continued eating in silence, each one deep in thought. Finally, Virginia said, "We're like draft horses."

Thomas smiled. "Draft horses?"

"Yeah. There's a guy who built a sawmill down near the mouth of Baker Creek. He had a team of horses that he used for dragging logs out of the woods. He told me that, when he started out, he only had one horse, and that he was always getting into situations where the logs would get jammed up. When he got the second horse, he thought it would be a lot easier, but it took them a long time to learn to pull together. He had to work with the new horse separately for a while, until it learned about pulling logs. Then he still had to work with them together for a long time before they finally settled down and began to work as a team. He said that, once they learned to work together, there wasn't a log ever cut that they couldn't pull. People have a lot in common with draft horses."

Thomas said, "Whoa now. Easy, girl."

Virginia whinnied and snorted, and they laughed together.

She was right. From her perspective, people were meant to pull in harness. He had always seen himself as free and alone. For most of his life, the last thing he ever wanted to be was a draft horse. Even now, the very idea made him feel like running away. As he and the beautiful Virginia laughed and talked and flirted with each other there in the light of the oil lamps, Thomas was thinking about draft horses. And he tried very hard not to think about the sadness in the eyes of a bobcat he once saw. It was pacing, continually back and forth, wearing a path in the concrete floor of its cage in a zoo.

Every day, he grew stronger. He and Virginia canned applesauce, tomato sauce and green beans. When it came to cutting and carrying firewood however, he was not much help. He couldn't swing an axe, and he could only carry one or two pieces of wood at a time. Still, he pushed himself as far as the lessening pain in his hip would allow.

When he wasn't helping with the seemingly endless number of chores associated with wilderness life, he walked. Sometimes Virginia would come along, and then the walk would become a picnic, or have some purpose other than just hiking. This would require preparation, and the hike would become something of an event, a big production. But when he walked alone, he would simply let his feet carry him into the unknown.

And then it rained. Some of the leaves on the higher ridges were beginning to turn yellow, but the weather was still quite warm. It must have been late September, or maybe early October. It came as a shock to Thomas when he realized he didn't know which, and that he didn't even care.

The storm came up during the night. Thomas was awakened by the soft creaking of the cabin as the west wind began to rise. It came in strong gusts at first, and then it rose into a fairly steady gale. He began to hear leaves and twigs being blown against the walls. Virginia woke up. "Oh, listen!" she said. "We're getting a storm! Let's go outside!"

By the time they were dressed and out the door, the wind was shrieking through the orchard and they had to yell in order to be heard above it. "Isn't this great?" Virginia shouted. "I love the wind!"

Thomas was surprised by the fact that the moon and stars were still out. Cottony clouds raced across the sky in patches, forming and swirling as they flew. It seemed as if he could reach up and touch them, maybe tear off a piece of cloud. He and Virginia ran into the field to watch them pass.

The earth was still warm from the heat of the day. He lay on the grass, feeling her energy beside him. She was so alive! It was as if every nerve of her body was vibrating in harmony with the gusting wind.

He wasn't thinking about draft horses. For the next hour, draft horses never entered his mind. There was only Virginia, and the wind, and the clouds, and the night. It was a whirling, swirling roller coaster ride that ended just as the first few drops of rain began to fall.

The raindrops were so big that, when the first one hit him, Thomas thought he felt it splash. The clouds had gathered together, blocking out the night sky. Dawn was only a few hours away, and it was suddenly so dark that the only thing visible was the lamplight from the cabin window. First one raindrop, then another, then another and another and, it began to pour.

They jumped up and made for the cabin, but by the time they climbed to the porch, they were soaked to the skin. Virginia was laughing.

Thomas went straight to the bedroom, grabbed a towel and his biodegradable soap, and dashed back into the living room. Virginia stood near the door, soaking wet, with her hands on her hips. She had a twinkle in her eye. "What are you up to now?"

"I'm tired of sponge baths," he said. "And I haven't had a shower in months!"

He moved past her and out onto the porch. Tossing his towel to one side, and his clothes to the other, he dashed back out to the field.

It was a great shower-a little cool maybe, but great. He was singing "Figaro" when Virginia joined him. His hair was lathered up and he was waiting, eyes closed, for the rain to wash the suds away. When he opened his eyes, there she stood, wet and glistening in the grey light of the stormy dawn. She simply said, "My turn."

As with their hikes, Virginia's presence turned a simple activity, like showering in the rain, into something more, a lot more. They made love gleefully, hungrily, passionately.

Much later, back in the bedroom, she looked up into his eyes, and said, "I've never felt so alive!"

"I know," he said. "I can't believe we spent all those years apart. It's as if there was this path we were supposed to take, and we missed it. But now that…"

"You mean to say that you missed it. You're the one who moved away."

"Fine. I think we all know where to put the blame." He leaned over and placed his forehead against hers, with an expression of mock severity, and then he kissed her. "But, as I was about to say, now that we're here together, everything seems to make sense again."

"So, Mister Galahad, what does all of this mean? What, exactly, are we doing here? Are you going to jump back on your trusty steed and ride off into another sunset, or do we live happily ever after?" Her tone was light, but her expression was serious.

"I like the second one, the happily ever after thing." Thomas lay back, looking up at the ceiling, with his fingers laced behind his head. "I've been thinking though. There are a few things that I need to take care of in Michigan. If I'm really going to stay here, I should go back out there and put the house up for sale. Then there's my construction business. I'll have to pay off the last two months of the lease contract for the office, and I should probably give Janice some kind of severance package; maybe two months salary. But, once again, I'll need to go out there to make it happen."

"Ah, so you're planning to leave me after all. Once you get back there, you'll probably just fall back into your old life and forget all about me again."

"Not a chance," he said. "I'm not letting you out of my sight. You'll just have to come with me."

"Really?"

"Yeah, really."

Virginia was thoughtful. "Hmmm…" she said. "An adventure."

"What do you say?" Thomas turned to face her. "We could make it a real holiday!"

"Let's see. We'll have to stop by and let V. and Carol Ann know we're leaving. They can tell Joshua that we've gone. That way the stock will be taken care of…"

"We won't need to pack much," said Thomas. "I have some money saved up, and we can buy whatever we need along the way. Besides, when I sell my house, I'll have more money than I can ever spend, living up here."

"Trust me, honey. Money will never be a problem."

"Oh, I see." Suddenly, Thomas knew what the three men at the cabin had been after. "You have the money that started all the trouble, don't you? Is there a lot of it?"

"I don't know. I think so. There's a big bag of it up at the barn."

"Well then, what are we waiting for?" Thomas jumped out of bed and began getting dressed. "We're all showered and ready to go. Let's pack a few things and hit the trail for parts unknown!"

18 PARTS UNKNOWN

They left a note on the table that read, "To whoever finds this note: We're on an adventure. Back in a few days. Make yourself at home. You're welcome."

It took them only a few minutes to pack the things they would need for the trail. Thomas had his backpack, and he gave his smaller daypack to Virginia.

They went up to the barn and gave an extra measure of feed to the stock, then pulled the heavy moneybag out from its hiding place and started off. Thomas thought it was good that his pack was light. It made slinging the strap of the bag over his shoulder that much easier.

When they arrived at the Day's cabin, it was about mid-morning. Carol Ann was in the kitchen, slicing strips of venison flank to be smoked into jerky. V. was at the woodshed, chopping and stacking the last of the Winter wood supply.

"Well I'll be damned!" V. exclaimed when he saw them approaching. He came over and gave each of them one of his signature bear hugs. "Come on down to the house. Carol Ann'l want to fix you some lunch or somethin'.

"Oh, she doesn't need to do that," Thomas said.

"We really just dropped by to let you know that we're leaving for a few days."

"We're going on an adventure." There was excitement in Virginia's voice.

"I see. If I was a bettin' man, I'd say you were goin' to get hitched."

Thomas and Virginia gave each other a significant look.

"Hey Carol Ann!" the big man yelled as they neared the cabin. "Look what I found!"

She appeared in the doorway, wiping her hands on her once-white apron. "Well hello there, you two. What are you up to? You look like the cat that ate the mouse." She peeled off the apron and hurried out to meet them, whereupon the hugging ritual was repeated. "Why don't you take off those packs and come inside? I'll fix us something to eat."

"Thanks a lot," said Thomas. "But we probably aught to keep moving. We have a long way to go."

"We were hoping you wouldn't mind keeping an eye on the place while we're gone," Virginia said. "Or maybe let Joshua know we've left, so he can take care of the stock."

Carol Ann turned to her husband. "Valentine, why don't you just bring the animals down here? We can just put them in with ours."

"Yeah," he said. "That'd prob'ly be best." And to Virginia, he said, "That way, if you don't get back for a while, you won't have to worry about 'em."

"That would be just great." Thomas shifted the moneybag from one shoulder to the other. "Thank you. We'll have to find a present for you while we're out."

" 'Ain't necessary," the big man said. "Just bein' neighbors."

"Speaking of presents," Carol Ann took Virginia by the arm. "I've got something for you." They started toward the house.

Fallen Idyll

It was different from the other cabins. There was only one level, and the roof was pitched lower. It had six-paned windows with flower boxes on either side of the small, gabled porch. Everything was neat, tidy, and organized. There was even a stone path leading up to the steps.

Inside, it was just as organized. And in the kitchen, there was a minor miracle. Indoor plumbing!

About fifty yards up the hill from the house, there was a spring. V. had run a pipe from it down into the kitchen, and valved it off at the sink. Before the valve, he had teed off another pipe that led through the firebox of the woodstove, and into a big steel tank. They even had hot water!

Carol Ann had just brought a batch of jerky up from the smokehouse, and had been busy preparing the next batch. While she bagged up a couple of pounds for Virginia, V. took Thomas to the other end of the house, and opened a narrow door. A bathroom! He had a bathroom! There was a toilet, and a sink, and an old clawfoot tub.

"Well, what do you know?" Thomas was impressed. "Does Virginia know about this?"

The big man laughed. "The fact is, I was lookin' at the creek that flows by your place, and I think we could rig up the same thing there."

"Your place?" Thomas was quick to catch the fact that V. already assumed that he was a permanent resident, and that he and Virginia were together. He let it pass. "Let's check it out when I get back."

Virginia was thanking Carol Ann for the jerky, which had been stowed away in the daypack. She turned toward the men. "I'm afraid we ought to get started. Are you ready, Tom?"

"Yeah, I'm ready." To V. he said, "Thanks for everything. We shouldn't be gone more than a couple of weeks. I just need to take care of a few things back East, but you know how it goes. We may have to be gone for a month or more."

"It don't matter," said V. "We'll be right here, whenever."

There was more hugging then, and good wishes all around. Just before he and Virginia disappeared into the forest, Thomas looked back. What he saw became a mental snapshot, etched in his mind. Carol Ann and V. were standing on the stone path, arm in arm. When they saw him look back, they waved a last goodbye; the gentle giant and his plump wife, both dressed in overalls, with the late morning sun creating halos over their graying hair. "Halos?"

"Did you say something?" Virginia took his arm.

"Halos. I said, 'Halos.'"

She looked puzzled for a moment, and then she said, "You're right. They're just angels, aren't they?"

Thomas smiled to himself and pushed on.

From the Day's cabin, they traveled west, crossing two ridges before turning south toward the river. They had debated whether or not to take the main trail through the village, but had decided to cut across country instead. At the village, they would have run into more of their friends, and that would have delayed their progress even more. "Progress toward what?" thought Thomas.

That first night, they slept at Thomas' old campsite. Martin and Henry had done a good cleaning job. The only evidence that anyone had ever been there was the stroller Thomas had hidden away. He thought about using it again, but this time they weren't carrying all that much. And besides, with the wheel all bent out of shape, it would have been more trouble than it was worth. And Thomas still hated it.

He woke up just before dawn. The sky was turning from black to grey, and there was just enough light to make out the details of Virginia's contented expression as she slept.

As he lay there beside her, Thomas was struck by the irony of the fact that, the last time he had been here, he had been seriously considering life as a hermit. He had actually been looking forward to a solitary, contemplative existence. Now, with Virginia, warm and full of life, sleeping beside him, he felt a renewed connection with the world. Well, maybe not with the world, exactly. It was more of a spiritual connection with… what? History? The force? Mother Earth? Whatever it was, it felt right.

He tried not to disturb her as he extricated himself from the sleeping bag, but as he was about to stand up, she stretched and said, "Good morning, Galahad."

"Good morning, my princess. Why don't you try to get some more sleep? We had a big day yesterday. I'll build up the fire and make some coffee."

"I've had enough sleep. When you're finished, why don't you just come back to bed? I think we need to have some 'warm-up' exercise before we hit the trail again. You wouldn't want me to get a cramp, would you?"

He struck a dramatic pose. "As you wish, Highness. I am but your faithful knight. My sword is at your service."

"Never mind," she said.

Progress that morning was slow. The climb up from the river was steep and difficult, but Thomas wanted to reach an elevation that would get them beyond the cliffs without having to climb too much later on, when they would be tired.

In the end, it probably didn't really make all that much difference. They walked all that day and most of the next.

They reached the ravine that marked "the boundary line of the civilized world" in the afternoon. Thomas wasn't sure how they could fit two people, two backpacks, and the big nylon bag on the bicycle, but he was confident that he could figure out a way to do it. He hadn't told Virginia about the bike. He wanted to surprise her.

They removed their packs, and he said, "Come on, there's something I want to show you."

"Up there?"

"Yeah. It's not far, come on."

She looked skeptical, but followed along into the brush, and up the hill. The camo tarp looked like it had been there forever. It was all wrinkled and decorated with leaves and debris. When she saw it, she became a little more animated. "What's this?"

He pulled back the tarp.

"Ooh," she said. "A bicycle!" Her excited expression lasted only for a moment. Thomas followed her gaze to the bike, and found that the tires and the seat were in shreds.

"Porcupines!" Thomas couldn't believe it. "They ruined my surprise!"

Virginia was laughing. "Oh, I think you were surprised, alright! I wish you could've seen the look on your face."

"Oh sure, laugh it up." Thomas really was disappointed. "This just means you'll have to walk all the way to town."

"Walking won't bother me," she said. "I like it. What this really means is that we can take our time and enjoy the trip."

"Did you hear that?"

"Hear what?"

"I thought I heard voices." Thomas was silent for a moment, listening. Sure enough, they heard what sounded like complaining in the distance.

"Oh my god! The money!"

They scrambled down the bank and out onto the dirt road. The packs and the moneybag were there by the ravine, exactly as they had left them. Thomas sighed deeply. "That was close," he said. I'll have to be more careful."

"It's only money," said Virginia. "It doesn't really

matter."

The voices were getting closer. There was someone coming up the ravine. At first, it was impossible to make out what they were saying, but gradually, they became clearer. "...the last time I ever go fishin' with you! You're nuts!" Silence. Seconds pass. "My legs hurt! Let's stop for a minute!" Silence. "You're lost, aren't you? You don't know where the hell we are! Slow down!"

"Will you please shut up?" The other man had obviously had enough. "You haven't stopped whining since we left the river! And by the way, you're right. This is the last time you go fishin' with me. Here's the road."

"Thank god!"

Thomas and Virginia had shouldered their packs, and were waiting when the first of the two men appeared. He was tall and dark, and carried a fishing pole and about a dozen pan-sized trout, suspended on a forked stick. He was walking easily, and smiled when he looked up and saw them standing above him on the road. He simply said, "Hello." He stopped and waited for his friend.

A few seconds later, the other man appeared. He was skinny and blond, and carried only a fishing pole. "What are you waiting for?" he said. "Let's get the truck and get the hell out of here!" He glanced at Virginia and Thomas, but didn't speak.

"Having fun?" Thomas asked.

The taller man smiled and shrugged. "A bad day of fishing is better than a good day of working." He strode forward to shake hands, then hesitated. "I'm sorry. My hand probably smells like fish guts. I'm Glen, and this poor, worn-out fellow is Johnny."

Johnny brightened a little. "He said we were going fishing. He didn't say anything about mountain climbing, or hiking around in circles all day in the woods."

Thomas shook the hand anyway. These were just boys, really; probably eighteen or nineteen years old. "I'm Thomas, and this is Virginia. Glad to know you both."

They all started down the road together. You folks look like you've been up here quite a while," Glen observed. "On vacation?"

Thomas looked at Virginia. "You might say that."

"Boy! I wish I could spend more time up here. Sometimes I get to take a three-day weekend, but that's about all. I work for my dad, and since it's just him and me, I don't get much time off."

Virginia had been holding on to Thomas' arm as if it was a life preserver and she was afraid she might drown. She was obviously not used to meeting strangers, but she finally spoke. "What does your dad do?"

"Oh, we just have a gas station. I was going to start school this fall, but I didn't get registered in time. I think I'll sign up for the winter."

Around a bend from the ravine, they came to a red, four-wheel-drive Chevy pick-up. It was a little dusty, but looked new. The boys laid their fishing poles in the back, and Glen opened a plastic cooler, and slid the fish into it, then threw the forked stick into the woods. "Well," he said. "Good luck." He pushed a button on his key chain, and the truck lights flashed twice. Then it started, all by itself.

Thomas was watching Virginia's face. She was impressed. He realized that a lot had changed in the ten years she had been away from the world.

The boys climbed into the truck and Glen backed it around, and then pulled up beside the two "backpackers." He pushed a button and his window rolled down. "Say, would you folks like a ride into town?"

"That would be great, thanks!" Thomas was relieved. He hadn't been looking forward to two or three more days of walking. He had been prepared for it. He had been resigned to it. But this would be much better.

"Hey Johnny, why don't you jump in the back?" Glen was a nice kid.

Virginia said, "No, no. We'll be fine. I like the

open air."

They sat with their backs against the cab, and watched the scenery retreat and disappear behind them. The wind was cold, and Thomas wrapped a sleeping bag around them. In what seemed like the blink of an eye, they had gone up and over the mountain, and Glen pulled over to the side of the road.

He got out, and came around to the back of the truck. "I hate to ask this," he said. "But, if a cop sees you back here, I'll get a ticket. I wouldn't mind so much, but if I get one more, I lose my license. Would you guys mind lying down? I don't think anyone will see you if you lie down."

"We can get out right here," Thomas said. "I can't tell you how much we appreciate the ride. After all, you saved us at least two days of walking, and I'd hate to cause you any trouble."

They said goodbye then, and Glen received a few more enthusiastic good wishes. The red pick-up drove out of sight, and Virginia and Thomas started walking into town.

They had gone about a mile, with several more to go, when Thomas felt something hit him, hard, in the back. A dark green sedan was passing them from behind, and someone had thrown what was left of a large coke out the window. There was apparently a lot left. The cup exploded against his backpack, splattering both of them with ice and brown, sticky cola. The carload of teenagers accelerated and disappeared around a corner.

Thomas stood for a long moment, watching the spot where the car had disappeared. Then he looked up at the sky with a "what was that?" expression.

Virginia said, "Can we go home now?"

"Not now," said Thomas. "If someone will just throw me a burger and fries, I'll have a happy meal. Can you believe this?"

"It makes me glad I live in the woods."

As they walked along, wet and sticky, rumpled and disheveled from their ride in the pickup, Thomas thought about what they must look like to passers-by. Here he was, a successful businessman, a pillar of his community. Virginia was a landowner, and, judging by the weight of this bag, quite well off. But to the people driving past, they must appear to be societal outcasts, homeless and unwanted. In a way, he found that liberating. But in another way, he found it embarrassing. He was surprised by that. He was surprised to find that he cared so much about appearances.

A Chevy pickup was coming. They could just make out the bright red color in the gathering twilight. It sped past, made a u-turn and pulled up beside them. The passenger window slid open. The driver said, "What happened to you guys?"

"Someone was kind enough to airmail us a soft drink." Thomas was trying to keep a sense of humor. "Where's Johnny?"

"I dropped him off at his house. He was still whining when I left. Hop in. I'll take you to the gas station and you can clean up."

"That's okay, we don't want to mess up your nice truck," said Virginia.

"Don't worry about that. I need to clean it anyway. Come on."

"Just a second." Thomas took the sleeping bag from his pack, opened the door, and spread the bag out on the seat. "Thanks a lot, Glen, we owe you."

"No problem. You guys seem like nice people."

Glen's father looked like a much older version of his son. When introductions had been made, he said, "There's a shower stall in the back. I used to do a lot more mechanic work back there, and Glen's mom would have a fit if I came home all greasy, so I had one put in. There's towels over there on the shelf. You folks are welcome to use anything you need."

After showering and changing into their "town" clothes, Virginia and Thomas looked and felt a little bit less like hobos. They offered to pay Glen and his father for their trouble, but were refused.

The fluorescent lights of the gas station almost hurt their eyes. They were used to candles and oil lamps. It was as if they had been riding in a time machine instead of a Chevy pickup. They still felt a little out of place.

Their faces must have showed their hesitation, because Glen's father asked, "Are you folks okay?" Virginia answered that they were fine.

Thomas asked Glen and his dad about restaurants and hotels and, after getting some directions, took Virginia by the hand. "Are you sure we can't pay you for your kindness?" he asked Glen. "If it weren't for you and your dad, we'd still be out there in the woods, huddled around a campfire."

Glen smiled. "That doesn't sound like such a bad thing, to me."

Virginia smiled back. "Me neither."

Eureka is a small town, but to Thomas and Virginia, it might as well have been New York City. The downtown area boasts wide streets and is extremely well lit. Cars whizzed by and lighted signs flashed and blared their messages about stores and bars and even churches. It was all pretty overwhelming.

19 PASSING THROUGH

They walked the entire length of the town before they found what they were looking for. It was a small, tired but friendly looking motel; the "E-Z Rest." It had one level, and was sided with white clapboards.

The woman at the front desk was in her sixties, plump and pleasant. When they came in the door she was watching a small television. She got up immediately and greeted them. Then she turned back toward the T.V. and held up a pudgy finger. "Just a second," she said. "I have to watch this part!"

On the screen, William Wallace was being disemboweled. With his last shred of energy, he screamed the word, "Freedom!" His impassioned face faded into the face of a dog. It wanted a certain brand of dogfood. "Woof."

She turned back to face them, as the commercial continued. There were tears welling up in her eyes. "I'm sorry, folks." She wiped her eyes with her fingers. "That part really gets to me." She looked at her hands, now smudged with cheap mascara. "Damn!" she said. I must look like a raccoon!" And she did.

They paid the raccoon in cash. In his wallet, Thomas had set aside about fifteen hundred dollars for his return trip.

It occurred to him that they still had no idea how much money was in the duffel bag. When they entered the clean, but shabby room, he immediately unzipped it and dumped it out on the gold bedspread.

On the surface, there had been a covering of loose bills: fives, tens, twenties, and even a few ones. Underneath that top layer, there were bundles of hundreds, bound by rubber bands. They were about a half-inch thick, and contained a hundred bills each. He began placing them on the night table, in stacks of ten. Virginia whistled.

Together, they counted out eleven stacks, with four bundles left over. "My god!" said Thomas. "There's over a million dollars here!"

"Wow!" Virginia was as surprised as he was. "He must have been saving this stuff for years." She shook her head sadly. "Look at it. It's just paper."

"Yeah, but this kind of paper is something people will kill for."

"What are we going to do with all this? Shouldn't we put it in the bank or something?"

It was Thomas' turn to shake his head. "We can't do that. If we put this much in the bank, we'd have Federal agents knocking on our door and asking where we got it. Banks have to report deposits this big."

"But we didn't do anything wrong. We just found it."

"Maybe so, but we know it was payment for drug deals, which means it belongs to Uncle Sam."

"So what do we do with it?"

Thomas thought for a moment. "Tomorrow morning, we're going to buy some new shoes." He began putting the money back in the bag.

"Yeah," said Virginia. "Real expensive shoes." She looked puzzled.

They did buy expensive shoes. They each got a pair of

cross-trainers that cradled their feet in "pillow soft comfort." Virginia had been wearing hiking boots in the winter, and had mostly gone barefoot all summer. She thought the new shoes were "Wonderful!" As a matter of fact, she thought everything was wonderful.

Thomas stacked the money in the shoeboxes. Half a block from the shoe store, there was a Bank of America. They left the shoeboxes in a safety deposit box at the bank.

It was a big relief not to be carrying around all that loot. They still had a little over fifteen thousand dollars left' and Thomas wasn't sure how much cash Americans are allowed to carry these days, but fifteen thousand would be easier to explain than a million. Besides, he had a plan.

His first thought had been to buy a Harley and cruise out to Michigan in leather pants, with the free wind blowing through their hair, and the open road stretching out into the distance in all directions. But then he remembered that most states now have helmet laws. The other problem was Virginia. The idea of a cross-country motorcycle trip made her think of rednecks in old pickups, and shotguns in rifle racks.

They bought a used Chevy "Silverado" pickup for nine thousand dollars cash. Virginia liked the name. She thought it smacked of adventure. Her driver's license had expired, so they bought it under Thomas' name. He was a little bit concerned about the complications of a Michigan resident purchasing a car in California, but everything went smoothly enough. They were issued a temporary, paper license that they could use until they got to Michigan, where they would get a permanent plate and registration. It occurred to him that the system was set up to make sure he didn't get out of paying sales tax.

Thomas was also a bit concerned about Virginia. She had spent ten years in a place where the only thing that ever changed was the weather. She seemed okay most of the time, but there were moments when she seemed elated and filled with wonder, and others when he thought he detected a hint of panic in her striking blue eyes. They had paid for the room, and were leaving town, heading south to pick up interstate eighty, which they would take all the way to Chicago. How are you holding up, Highness?"

She was sitting in the middle of the bench seat, with her head on his shoulder. Still looking at the road ahead, she said, "Oh, I'm okay." She snuggled even closer. "I guess it's kind of like a dream. Sometimes it feels like I'm flying, and sometimes I feel like I'm falling."

"Well, if there's anything you need, or anything you want to talk about, even if you think it's silly or unimportant, I'm here."

"Thanks, Galahad."

Thomas put his arm around her and held her close. He realized that people used to drive that way a lot, but now they always seem to sit on opposite sides of the car. Seatbelt laws. That was the reason. "Maybe you should wear your seatbelt. I don't know what the fine is in California, but in Michigan, I think the ticket and court costs come to about a hundred dollars. Plus, it puts points on your license. It can even cause your insurance rates to go up."

"All that for not wearing a seatbelt?" She picked up the belt and buckle on her right, and fished around between them until she found the left one, then clicked them together.

"That's right. They make laws now to protect us from ourselves."

"But what kind of country charges its citizens for taking personal risks?"

"This kind."

"But that doesn't make any sense."

"It doesn't make sense to you, because you've been out of circulation for so long. You still remember when people believed that government passed laws to regulate certain, specified things, and everything else was considered free choice. Now, with the merits of every new law being tried in the courts, every one of our "free choices" has to be protected and regulated. The choices are being made for us, with the idea that we aren't capable of making them for ourselves."

"But that's tyranny."

"De Toqueville called it 'the tyranny of the majority.'"

"My god," she said. "We sound like Martin." She snuggled closer again, putting a strain on her seatbelt.

Yeah, she was right. Martin's idea was that, the less you accepted technological and material excesses, the less regulation and intrusion you had to endure. But, if you want to drive a car across the country at sixty miles per hour, instead of walking across the country at four miles per hour, you're going to have to put up with speed laws, road taxes, licensing regulations, insurance costs, all the peripheral baggage that comes with the convenience of making the trip in five days instead of three months. It's the tyranny of convenience.

Thomas was reminded of the conflicts that had arisen between him and his son. It had been the final battle in a long and bitter war. Looking back, he realized that he had given Tyler too much in the way of material things, trying to make up for not spending real quality time with the boy. But everything that he had given had borne a price tag. As long as Tyler was living in Thomas' house, eating his food, and accepting the fruits of Thomas' labor, he was expected to follow Thomas' rules. This was a concept that made perfect sense to Thomas, but one which gradually became a source of anger, frustration, and bitterness for his son. In the end, Tyler had stormed out of the house in a fit of rage, and simply driven away. That had been almost two years ago.

"Where are you?"

"I'm storming out of the house in a fit of rage."

"What?"

"I'm driving across the bridge between Rio Dell and

Scotia, California. I'm on the third planet from a mediocre little star, in the Milky Way galaxy, somewhere in the infinite, ordered chaos of space, which exists on such a tremendous scale that we humans cannot possibly comprehend it."

"Oh."

"In other words, I have no idea where the hell I am."

Virginia patted him on the knee. "I know exactly where you are, now."

"And where is that?"

"You're here with me, silly boy."

And that, Thomas realized, was the heart and soul of their relationship. He could think things to death. He would start with a simple observation or idea, and think it into incomprehensibility. Virginia, on the other hand, had a mind like Robin Hood's arrow. She could take a complicated situation, ignore all the peripheral mumbo-jumbo, and go straight to the causative center every time.

It was as if they occupied the extreme opposite ends of the perceptual spectrum. They provided much needed balance for each other. It was as if he was poised on one end of a seesaw. Without that balance, he was just sitting on the ground... He was gone again. She let him go.

20 REDWOODS

They left the freeway at a little town called Weott, and took the scenic route, which snaked around the tremendous columns of ancient redwood trees. Some of the huge trunks rose up right next to the road, and bore the scars of their battle with progress. They had tested the metal of Model "T" Fords, Peterbilt trucks, Sports cars, pickups, motorcycles, everything the mechanized world could throw at them. There they stood, scarred and victorious.

Finally, man surrendered. Freeways were built around this valley and the war has all but ended. But, even though the peace has been negotiated, every now and again some reckless, or inattentive driver will challenge the right of these trees to exist so close to the pavement. The people always lose. Once again, tow trucks and ambulances are called in to haul away the wreckage and the wounded. Sirens break the peace of the forest. Colored lights dance and flicker around the great trunks, only to retreat slowly down the twisted road. And the big trees never move.

Thomas broke a long silence. "Do you want to hear a story?"

"That depends; is it a comedy, or a romance, or an

adventure?"

"I guess you could say it's an adventure."

"Okay, adventures can be fun. Is there a princess?"

"No."

"How about a knight in shining armor?"

"No."

"Now you're going to tell me there aren't any dragons."

"Nope, no dragons either."

"Well," Virginia sighed. "I don't know how you can have much of an adventure without dragons, but go ahead. I'm listening."

"Okay. Once upon a time, there were two friends. We'll call them Thomas and Martin."

"Hey! I thought you said there was no knight in shining armor. I happen to know that Thomas is really Sir Galahad in disguise. I bet there's a princess, too."

"No, the princess was away at school."

"A dragon, then?"

"Look, do you want to hear the story or not?"

"Geez, what a temperamental storyteller. You're lucky I love you so much."

"Yeah, I am." Thomas gave her a squeeze as he drove on.

"Well?"

"Well what?"

"Well, weren't you telling me a story?"

"I was trying to."

"So, go ahead. I'll be good."

"Promise?"

"Promise."

"Okay then. Martin and Thomas were having quite a Sunday. It was nineteen seventy-three, and they were twenty-one years old and full of piss and vinegar. They had come down here with four cases of beer, a pint of vodka, and a couple of ounces of pot, and they were determined to go through all of it before Monday morning."

"They sound like ambitious boys."

"They were. Anyhow, Martin had this old 'brush buggy.' That's a Volkswagen with the front and back chopped off. It was evening, and the boys had achieved their ambition. Since Martin was driving, Thomas had taken it upon himself to drink most of the beer, and the vodka, but Martin was pretty lit up too.

There's a fairly common phenomenon that occurs when young men have been drinking and getting high all day. Unless they have fallen asleep, which is also quite common, there is a kind of momentum that makes them want to continue all night. This was the case in our story. In any case, these boys decided to visit a tavern that was way off the beaten path. Now remember, this was in the seventies, and our story takes place in the mountains of northern California. There was no pot smoking allowed in the bar, so there was a big crowd outside.

Our heroes would smoke outside, then go in for a shot and a beer, then go back outside… You get the picture."

"I think those boys should stop right now and get some sleep."

"You're absolutely right, of course, but they didn't. Well, it was two a. m. and the bar was closing. Our inebriated friends decided to drive back to town. Now, this is where the story gets a little sketchy. From here on, it's based on hearsay instead of direct memory. My best guess is that they were driving down this twisted, redwood tree lined road, when they both passed out.

The Volkswagen became airborne, and both boys were thrown out. I don't know if they flew out the same side, or if both front doors miraculously opened, and they sailed out on opposite sides of the car. At any rate, the VW encountered one of our old friends…"

"Ah, a redwood tree. The Villain."

"Not necessarily. This is a true story, so heroes and villains aren't well defined. In true stories, the characters and the circumstances create situations that bring out heroism and villainy in everybody."

"Then how do you know who to love and who to hate?"

"In real life, it's not always that easy to tell. Hey, you said you were going to be good."

"Okay, but there ought to be a villain."

"If you'll let me finish, maybe we'll meet one."

"Sorry."

"So both boys were flying through the air. Somehow, Thomas' seat had come loose, and was also flying and tumbling through the air. The car encountered the tree, not with the front or the back, but with the top. Since the passenger seat had come out, the roof was smashed clear in to the floor."

"Those were lucky boys."

"Yeah, they were. Anyway, someone called for an ambulance and a tow truck. When they arrived, Martin seemed to be unhurt, but Thomas had disappeared. They found him down in the brush, still unconscious. When the ambulance guy woke him up, he came up swinging."

"Thomas?"

"Yeah. He probably had a severe concussion. Anyway, he punched the ambulance guy in the nose. Then the ambulance guy sedated him with a six-cell flashlight."

"Ouch!"

"When he woke up again, Thomas was incoherent. He was yelling and swearing and fighting mad. They took him to a small, local hospital and tried to examine him. He had no idea what was happening. Two orderlies tried to hold him down, but he had retreated into old brain or something, and was acting like a trapped animal. Finally, the doctor gave up, and told Martin to take him away."

"They never examined him?"

"Nope. The boys had this friend who lived a couple of blocks from the hospital, so they started walking toward his house. Thomas wanted to sleep, so he climbed into a car that was parked on the street, and told Martin to go on without him. Martin finally convinced him to go on, and they made it to the friend's house.

Thomas went in to use the bathroom, and didn't come out again. They found him passed out on the floor, and carried him out and put him to bed. The next day, the friend drove Thomas back up north to his mom's house, where he slept off-and-on for three days. After that, it was another three days or so before Thomas was himself again. I guess he was a little loopy for a while."

"Maybe he still is."

"Maybe."

"Wow, that's quite a story. You could have sued the ambulance company, the hospital, the doctor, everybody. You could just about own that town."

"Probably, but somehow, that didn't occur to me at the time. I didn't realize until much later, that my actions were probably the result of injuries I sustained in the accident. Even though it's the only time in my life that I ever became violent, I assumed that it was the result of all the alcohol and pot in my system at the time. I just put together a backpack and took off."

"That's why you went to Michigan!"

"That's why I went to Michigan. I figured that the accident might be my last warning. When your life is on a negative, or self-destructive course, things usually start going wrong. At first, they'll be minor annoyances but, if you continue on in spite of them, the incidents get more and more severe. I was afraid that, if I didn't make some big life changes, my next warning would land me in jail or kill me."

"I never heard that story. All I knew was that, when I got back from summer term, you were gone. Even Martin didn't know where you went. I started waiting tables, making money and having fun, and I decided to take some time off from school. I started hanging out with Martin and his crowd, and I never went back."

The scenic route ended, and Thomas pulled onto the

freeway, heading south. "Isn't it funny how you can cruise along through life for a long time, maybe even for years, and nothing seems to change, and then one seemingly unimportant decision or chance occurrence can turn everything around."

"Tell me about it, Honey," said Virginia. "Hey, this next town is Leggett. That's where Dina went when she and Martin split up."

"Oh, you mean Dina Price, Marty's old girlfriend? I'd forgotten all about her. They were 'on-again-off-again' for years. They used to fight so much, I was sure they'd end up getting married."

"Yeah, they did. I think it was about a year after you left, maybe two. They weren't married long, only a couple of years, and then she kinda flipped out. She got real paranoid, and started accusing Martin of abusing her and cheating on her."

"Ah, beatin' and cheatin'. That sounds like a country song."

"Right. Well anyway, her folks had a little roadside coffee shop down here somewhere. Let's see if we can find it. I'm hungry."

Thomas pulled off the freeway and into the town of Leggett. There was a gas station, a liquor store, and "The Squirrel Hole Coffee Shop." It was all very picturesque. It was in a little bowl-shaped valley. Second growth redwood trees grew up to staggering heights among the few buildings, and everything was rustic, looking like a town from the 'fifties. A hand-lettered sign next to the parking area for the coffee shop even read, "Good Food!"

Thomas parked the pickup in front of the sign and got out. Virginia had flipped the sun visor down, and was tying her hair back and checking herself in the mirror, as he stretched and came around to open her door.

She said, "Oh mister Galahad, you're so gallahnt!" and offered him her hand, which he kissed and held onto as they walked toward the mossy old wooden building. They promenaded up the steps and through the door. A bell, which hung from the jamb, tinkled merrily, and a young girl, probably seventeen years old, came out from behind the counter to greet them. Thomas noticed that she checked the clock on the wall before she spoke.

"Good afternoon folks," she said. "You can hang your coats over here, and sit wherever you like. If you sit there by the window, you might get to see an eagle. There's a nest in the top of that tallest tree. Even though it's empty this time of year, sometimes they hang around. I saw the male just the other day. My name's Sarah and if you need anything, just yell, 'Hey Sarah,' and I'll come running. Now, can I get you some coffee?"

Thomas could see a strong resemblance to the woman he remembered. She had the same hair color, the same soft brown eyes, and the same bubbly personality. He hadn't known Dina well. Somehow, Martin hadn't brought her into the circle of his other friends. He used to hang out with Thomas and the others, and then excuse himself and go visit Dina. At the time, he'd just accepted it as one of Martin's idiosyncrasies, but looking at now, it seemed kind of strange.

"I'll bet you're Dina's daughter, aren't you?" Virginia asked. Robin Hood's arrow twanged across Thomas' mind again. "Is she here?"

"Yeah, she's in the back. I'll go get her." She disappeared through the door that led to the kitchen. Thomas heard her call, "Mom!" and then her voice dropped a little and she said, "There's a big guy and a pretty lady out there. They seem to know you."

Dina appeared in the doorway, wiping her hands on her once white apron. She was a little heavier than Thomas remembered, gone to grey, but still quite attractive. She fitted the atmosphere of the diner perfectly. "Ginny?" she said. "Is that you?" She hurried around the counter and toward the table. "My land girl, just look at you! You haven't changed a bit!"

Virginia stood and accepted an enthusiastic hug. Dina!" she said. It's so good to see you! You remember Tom?"

"Of course I remember Tom!" she said, shaking his hand. "This is a real treat; sort of a blast from the past. What brings you folks to Leggett, of all places?" Thomas and Virginia sat down in the booth, and Virginia scooted over to make room for Dina. She sat on the corner of the seat and said, "Sarah honey, why don't you bring us some coffee and some of those nice sweet rolls?"

"Sure, Mom."

As Sarah poured the coffee into heavy, ironstone cups, Dina looked expectantly at Virginia.

"Oh, we're on our way back East. Thomas has some business to take care of, and then we'll be coming back to our place up on the Mad River."

Dina frowned. "You're not living up on Marty's ranch, are you?"

"You know about the community up there?" Virginia was surprised.

"Sure I do. For years, Marty tried to get me to move up there so he could be closer to Sarah. He still comes by once or twice a year and brings her things, little presents. But we like it here, don't we honey?"

Sarah smiled. "I'll go back and finish up what you were doing in the kitchen. If you need anything, you know what to do."

"Yeah," said Thomas. "We'll yell 'Hey Sarah.'"

As Sarah headed for the kitchen, Thomas turned back to Dina. "She's a cute kid. You've done well."

"I can't take much credit for who she is. From the time she learned to talk, Sarah has been the adult in this family. She takes good care of me."

"So you're a single mom?" Virginia asked.

"Yeah, always have been. After Marty, marriage just didn't appeal to me anymore. He was such a control freak. I told myself that I'd never give anyone that much power over my life again."

"I know what you mean. Thomas says... what is it? Oh yes, he thinks in straight lines and acts in circles."

"You don't know the half of it. Behind that, 'I just want what's best for you' attitude, he's a very dangerous man. He keeps up this front that seems so normal and harmless, but he's always got this secret life going. He comes down here a couple of times a year to visit Sarah, and he usually sets up meetings with his 'associates'. They show up in big, fancy cars and wear expensive suits. Who wears suits around here?"

Virginia looked puzzled. "So, she said. Sarah is Martin's daughter."

"Yeah, I know. The math doesn't add up. For a long time after I left Marty, he'd come down here and try to convince me that he'd changed. I knew him well enough not to believe anything he said, but I was lonely. Then, eighteen years ago, he pulled out all the stops. He convinced me that he would never be happy with anyone but me, and that he was just sitting up there in the woods all alone, beating himself up for the way he'd treated me. He stayed here for about a week, but it didn't take longer than that to see that he would always be a self-serving, manipulating bastard. The one good thing I ever got from him was Sarah... What?"

Virginia had given Thomas a look that said something was amiss. "Oh, nothing," she said.

"If it's about Marty, it won't surprise me or disappoint me. He's an asshole and he'll always be an asshole."

"Well..." Virginia fingered the handle of her coffee cup.

"Come on Gin, out with it," Dina said.

"It's just that Martin and Maggie just celebrated their twentieth anniversary."

"I really hate that lying, manipulating, evil sonofabitch."

"I'm so sorry. Maybe we shouldn't have come."

"No, this is definitely not your fault. I'm glad you told

me. Knowing he was already married even makes it easier somehow. It just reinforces the fact that I made the right decision. Besides, it really is good to see someone from the old days. Marty and Carl are the only ones who ever come down here anymore."

Thomas heard the other shoe drop. Virginia tried to look disinterested as she said, "Carl?"

"Yeah, the last few times he's come, Marty has brought Carl Wilson with him. They've been meeting with some of the Suits, cooking up some sort of big deal. It's kind of sad to watch. Carl just follows Marty around like a puppy dog. I'm not sure what Marty is using him for, but I'm afraid Carl is going to get hurt before it's all over."

Virginia was turning pale in spite of herself. Thomas thought he should draw Dina's attention. "What do you mean?"

"Oh nothing. I could be wrong. It's just that, Marty has always lived two lives. He really is a Jeckyl and Hyde character. Carl knows too much. If he finds out the whole story, then Marty's cover is blown, and Marty will never let that happen." She looked from Thomas to Virginia, and back again. "Ah, I was right, wasn't I? Something has happened to Carl?"

Virginia reached for Thomas' hand. "He's dead."

It was Dina's turn to go pale. "Oh my god!" She stood up from the booth. "You'd better leave."

Virginia was recovering. "I don't see how Martin could have had anything to do with it."

"You never do." Dina walked over to the coat rack and brought their jackets. "Marty plays percentages. He sets people in motion and guides them like a sheep dog; a little nip here, a little push there. It's all very subtle. He never gets in a hurry, and in the end, he always gets what he wants. I've always figured that I was safe because of Sarah, but if he finds out you were here, we could all end up like Carl. Now go! And never come back."

Thomas and Virginia took the offered coats and walked

out of the little café. The sky was overcast and the surrounding trees gave it a green cast. They climbed into the truck and drove away. Thomas looked back to see Dina standing on the café steps and waving. She mouthed the words, "I'm sorry."

21 A HISTORY LESSON

"Well, that was bizarre," Thomas said.

"Yeah, either all that stuff about Martin is true, or she's a raving lunatic. All we have to do is figure out which."

"If she's wrong, there's no harm done. But if she's right, we really are in danger. That would mean that the money we took belongs to Martin."

"I don't see how that's possible," said Virginia. "I showed Martin that money weeks ago. If he wanted it, why wouldn't he have taken it then?"

"Maybe he thought it would be safe there. He didn't think you'd have any opportunity to spend it. You hadn't been to town in ten years."

"I don't think we can come up with any answers, driving down the highway. I'm just going to believe that Dina is crazy, and that everything else is fine."

Thomas nodded. "We might as well think the best. There's nothing we can do about any of it anyway." He drove on in silence.

The silence continued as each of them thought back to situations that might shed some light on Martin's character. After about fifteen minutes of this, they looked at each other. They had arrived at the same conclusion.

Virginia sighed. "My god, what do we do now?"

"We drive to Michigan. Maybe we'll just stay there."

"I can't do that. I have to think about my boys."

"Oh, that's right, your boys. Well, I don't think they're in any immediate danger. I just wish there was some way to communicate with them."

"But, suppose Dina is right. Suppose that money belongs to Martin. He'll know that we took it, and he might try to use Jordan and Josh to make us give it back."

"The hell of it is, we don't really know anything about anything," said Thomas. "Is Martin an idealist: an independent, freedom-loving dreamer? Or is he a deceptive, manipulating megalomaniac, who has enticed a group of people out into the woods so that he can control them and use them like game pieces? If he's as patient as Dina says, there's a good possibility that he'll bide his time and wait to see what happens next."

"Maybe you're right. Besides, how could he have had anything to do with what happened to Carl? By the way, what did happen to Carl?"

Thomas thought for a moment, trying to remember the details of the incident. "Well, it appeared as if he had some kind of business arrangement with those three guys. I assumed they were helping him grow marijuana. When the crop had been harvested and sold, they must have decided that they were entitled to more of the profits than whatever amount they received, so they tried to physically force him to give them all of the money. They went too far, and he died, so they tossed his body off a cliff. Henry found the body, and then Martin, V, and I tracked the bad guys to a shack in the woods. Everybody started shooting, and the bad guys were killed."

"Can you remember anything that might prove whether Martin had anything to do with them?"

"Come to think of it, when we had those guys cornered in the shack, he yelled to them that they should give themselves up. They didn't seem to recognize him or his voice. As a matter of fact, I remember they asked who we were and what we were doing there. But, on the other hand, there wasn't enough time to tell if they knew him or not. Everything happened too fast."

Virginia sighed. "I'm sure Dina was wrong. Martin had nothing to do with Carl's death."

"I hope you're right, but given the other things she told us; the meetings in Leggett, the existence of an illegitimate daughter and all, Martin has still been carrying on some sort of secret life. The problem now is that we might know more about him than we should. As long as he doesn't know that we went to Leggett, I'm sure everyone is safe enough. Even if Martin is a little Napoleon, he has a nice little kingdom up there, and if he stays true to form, he won't do anything to jeopardize that until he feels he has no other choices left."

"I just hate to be gone so long, with so much left up in the air, and so much at stake."

"I'll tell you what," said Thomas. "Let's just drive to San Francisco and take a plane to Michigan. We can be there tonight. It shouldn't take more than a day to do everything I have to do. I think I'll hang on to my house for a while, maybe rent it out through a property management company. Hopefully, I still have a business to check on. I've been away for a long time, and I really need to touch base with Janice."

"Good idea. That way we can get back to Mad River in a couple of days. I'm not too worried about Jordan. He can take care of himself, and nobody ever knows where he is. But Josh has the farm and the family."

"It's settled then. San Francisco here we come."

Four hours later, they crossed the Golden Gate Bridge. It seemed more like four days. In the meantime, they had been discussing and rehashing all of the past dealings that each of them had been involved in with Martin. In retrospect, it was obvious that he was a conniving manipulator, and they had both known that already, but neither of them could remember a time when he had been openly malicious. "Hey, wait a minute!" Thomas said. "He had Henry knock me on the head with a frying pan to keep me from leaving! That seems pretty damn malicious!"

"He what?"

"Henry knocked me on the head with a frying pan; one of those big cast iron jobs. I could have been killed! Then they blindfolded me and dragged me through the woods to the old pot-drying barn. Then I was a prisoner for two days while Martin figured out whether or not he could trust me enough to let me go."

"I didn't know that. I knew that he asked V. to show you around, but nobody said anything about you having been kidnapped." Virginia was smiling, almost laughing. "You put up with that? I can't believe you let them do that to you!"

"I was pretty sore at first, all right. But then you came along, and all of a sudden I had a reason to stay."

"Well, at least it was Henry. You were probably pretty safe. For a while in the old days, Martin tried his hand at managing a couple of boxers. V. was the trainer, and he hired Henry to act as ring doctor. I think Henry got caught up in the life a little too much; you know, the parties, the women, the gambling. That's about the time he got into trouble."

Thomas felt a light go on. "Isn't it strange that, everybody who gets close to Martin ends up doing something illegal or unethical? In my own case, I was put in a situation where I ended up shooting a guy, and getting myself shot in the process. Did Martin engineer that whole thing, playing on the percentages, setting me up to do something that he could use to control me later? 'Makes you wonder, doesn't it?"

"Yep, even if he never did anything else that was evil and despicable, he has found a way to cause everyone around him to become paranoid. He may not be psychotic himself, but he's definitely a carrier."

"Damn!"

"What?"

"I just realized that you can't fly to Michigan or anywhere else."

"Why not?"

"You don't have an I. D."

"Why would I need an I. D. to fly to Michigan? It's not like we're going to Europe or something."

"You don't understand. Since 911, all passengers are checked and rechecked to make sure they aren't hijackers or mad bombers. You'd need to show your I. D."

"911?"

"Yeah, some middle eastern terrorist wackos hijacked four airliners. They crashed two of them into the twin towers in New York and one into the Pentagon. I guess the passengers stopped them from doing any critical damage with the fourth one by causing it to crash before it reached its target. They all died."

"My god! That's terrible. Can I go back to the woods now?"

"It was terrible all right. It sparked a surge of patriotic fervour that got everybody pushing us toward world war three. It caused people to question their values and views. Personally, I have always believed that war kills all the wrong people, from innocent children to the cream of the crop of young men. The soldiers who die are the ones who have a clear idea of their duty, and are willing to risk their lives for it: the best and the brightest of the coming generation. But at the same time, I was incensed at what those zealots did to the innocent passengers on the planes and to the innocent people in the buildings. Something like that can't just be ignored."

"What a horrible mess."

"It's like what I told Tyler when he was in school. If a bully hits you, tell him to stop. If he tries to hit you again, make him stop. But on a national level, how do you sort out the good guys and the bad guys?"

"That's right. What do you do, just kill everybody who disagrees with you?"

Thomas shook his head sadly. "You'd be surprised how many people thought that was perfectly reasonable."

"Sooner or later, somebody is going to find a way to justify the use of nuclear weapons, aren't they?"

"The longer they exist, the greater the risk becomes. But nukes aren't getting the press they used to. The new bad boys are the biological weapons. Most countries have developed strains of untreatable viruses that can wipe out whole populations without firing a shot. On top of those, they have chemical weapons that can melt your face off."

"So what you're saying is, we're technologically evolving, but we're no more civilized than the cave men. We just carry bigger clubs."

"You get the picture, Ooga."

"That makes my life out in the woods a reasonable alternative; kind of a passive rebellion."

"Right again."

Thomas left Virginia in a suite at the "Regent" with plenty of cash and a promise to return in two days. The fourth floor rooms were nice, and it was close to downtown, shopping, and all the sights of the city. She could take a trolley car to the Wharf and spend the days loafing and sightseeing.

Before leaving the hotel, he made a couple of phone calls to Michigan. He tried calling his office, and got a recording that said the number was no longer in service. He tried calling his house, hoping to retrieve what must be a mountain of messages, and got the same recording. "That's strange," he said. "None of my phones seem to be working."

Virginia was going through her backpack, pulling things out and refolding them. Without looking up she said, "Maybe there's some kind of problem with the phone lines."

"Yeah, maybe that's it. I'll find out when I get there. Speaking of which, I'd better get going. Are you sure you'll be okay here by yourself? I hate to leave you like this."

"I'll be just fine," she said. "If I'm going to be living in the world, I need clothes, make-up, lots of stuff. Besides, I haven't really been shopping in years. "It'll be fun."

"Okay then. I'll be in touch with you through the front desk and let you know what's going on. In the meantime, just relax and loaf, or 'shop til you drop,' I should be back in a couple of days."

22 A DEAD MAN

It was raining. San Francisco looks good in the rain. As cities go, it is more colorful than most. The green and yellow trolley cars were teeming with people who carried brightly colored umbrellas. "Painted lady" Victorian mansions stand shoulder-to shoulder along the sloping streets. It is a city that calls you to see and explore---a carnival, even in the rain. Thomas resisted the urge to stay and play, and with wipers on fast-delay, drove to the airport. He left the pickup in the secure parking lot, placed the claim slip in his wallet, and dashed to the terminal.

After buying his ticket, and going through all the check-in routine, he barely made the eight-fifteen flight. There was a two-hour layover at O'hare, so it was almost six a.m. when he landed in Traverse City.

It was snowing. He had gotten a few hours of sleep on the plane, and felt surprisingly good. The passengers filed into the terminal, and most of them were hugged and greeted by friends and relatives. Happy chatter filled the room. Thomas realized with a shock, that it was holiday chatter. These people had mostly come home for Thanksgiving.

He thought about calling Janice to come pick him up,

but called a cab instead. It was too early and he thought it would be too much to ask.

The cabbie was a young woman. Thomas thought that driving a cab was a gutsy thing for a woman to do in this day and age. Society doesn't respect and revere women the way it used to.

She seemed confident and self-assured, even helping with his packs. "Where to?" she asked.

"Seven thirty-two Princeton Court."

"Oh, I know where that is. Do you have a good view of Lake Michigan?"

"It's not too bad in the winter. But in the summer, I have a bunch of maple trees that block all but a little sliver. I've thought about thinning them out, but I decided I'd rather have the privacy than the view."

"Good for you. Trees aren't like hair. They don't grow back in a few weeks, or even in a few years."

So she was working her way through school. All these kids were so environmentally conscious. Thomas had always though that nature didn't care how long it took to grow a tree. Only people were worried about that stuff. Nature exists outside our ideas of time and space. People break time into increments. In the natural world, time just flows. A thousand of our years, a million years pass. Things change. Some things survive, some things don't. He had always been glad that there were no Environmentalists around during the ice age. We'd have to live underground. He imagined Pterodactyls swooping down and snatching up school children.

It was seven-thirty when the cab pulled up in front of his garage. The snow was letting up. Trees and lawns had a thin coat of wet, sloppy snow, but the pavement was only wet. Streetlights still cast their eerie glow, and lights were on in most of the neighborhood homes. There were even lights on in Thomas's house. "Well that's weird," he said to the driver. "Somebody's been in my house."

"Do you want me to wait?"

"No, you can go on. I left a key with my neighbor and asked him to keep an eye on the place. Maybe he just turned some lights on so it would look occupied."

He paid her and cut across the lawn to the front porch. The wet snow stuck to his shoes, so he stomped his feet a few times and tried the key. As the door opened, he bent down to pick up his packs.

"Hey! What are you doing there?" said a voice. It was a woman's voice. Thomas looked up to see a stoutish, fortyish woman standing in the kitchen doorway. "Get out of my house!"

"Hold on a minute," said Thomas. "I'd like to know what you're doing in my house."

The woman seemed to be getting more frightened by the second, so Thomas put his packs down and let go of the doorknob. He noticed that she was holding a cordless phone.

"If you try to come in, I'm calling 911," she said. She was trying to be brave.

"That works for me," said Thomas. "By all means, call the police. My name is Thomas Graham, and this is my house."

"Oh my God!" The panic that had been motivating the woman began to fade. "You're dead!"

"No", said Thomas. "Dead is when you stop moving and turn blue. If I was dead, we probably wouldn't be having this conversation."

"No," said the woman. "Dead is when somebody buys your house from your son, who is selling off your estate."

From upstairs came the sound of children arguing, followed by a loud crash.

"Oh, I see." Thomas was suddenly very tired. "It would seem I have a problem here. Do you mind if I use your phone? I need to find a place to stay, while I figure all of this out."

"Sure, here you go." She crossed the room and handed him the cordless phone. "I'd better go and see what's going on up there." She turned and walked quickly up the stairs.

Thomas needed a phone book. The woman was upstairs and he didn't feel like waiting, so he punched the buttons for information, and got the number for the "Green Light Cab Company."

"Billy, get down from there! Look what you boys have done! You broke grandma's pitcher. Now clean up this mess and get dressed. The bus will be here any minute!"

By the time the woman returned, Thomas had made his call, and the cab was on its way. She still looked somewhat bewildered. "Don't worry," he said. "I was thinking about selling this place anyway. This just saves me the trouble."

"So I don't have to move again?"

"So you don't have to move again. If you don't mind my asking, how long have you been here?"

"Just a couple of weeks. I wanted to move in sooner, but I had to wait thirty days for the closing."

"Ah, I see. So I must have died in August, or early September. How did it happen? Was I sick?"

The woman smiled. "No, you were hiking with a friend in the mountains out west, and you fell off a cliff."

"Ouch. I'll bet my friend's name is Martin Tyler."

"I never heard. Oh, here comes your cab." The woman was looking past him and through the open door.

"Thomas handed her the telephone and picked up his packs. "Thanks for the use of the phone," he said.

"Thanks for letting me keep my house," she said. "I'm glad you're not dead."

The sun was up. There was even a trace of warmth in it. Thomas used the walkway this time, instead of cutting across the lawn. It wasn't his lawn anymore.

"Well, hello again," he said.

The young woman was standing beside the open trunk of the cab. "I had a feeling you'd need a ride back to town," she said.

Under his breath Thomas said, "Well it sure surprised

the hell out of me."

"What?"

"Oh, nothing. Do you get these hunches often?" He deposited his packs in the trunk.

"Yeah." She closed the trunk and got into the cab. "All the time. I'm a psychic."

"And I'm a dead man." Thomas slid into the back seat.

"No," she said. "I'm totally serious. I get like, these images of things that are going to happen, and a lot of the time they really do. It's like my apartment keys."

"How's that?"

"Well, my apartment door has two locks. There's one in the doorknob, and one above it that's in this round thingie."

"A deadbolt?"

"Yeah, that's it. Well anyway, there are two keys, and they both look the same. One works in one lock, and the other one works in the other lock. I always choose the right key for the right lock."

"Always?"

"It never fails," she said. "Well, sometimes I think about it too much before I decide, and sometimes I forget to think about it at all, but when I do it right, it always works."

"Why don't you just mark one of the keys, so you'll know which is which?"

"What would be the fun of that?"

"Good point," Thomas said.

The girl glanced at her watch. "Hey, are you hungry? My shift is over, and I want some breakfast. What do you say?"

"Sure, why not?" Thomas was still reeling from the news that he was dead. He needed to figure out what to do next, and it was still too early to do much of anything. "You pick the restaurant, and I'll buy."

"It's a deal." She reached over and shut off the meter. She caught Thomas' eye in the mirror and said, "It's on the other side of town."

Her name was Monique and she was twenty-two. She'd moved up to Traverse City from the Detroit area to go to school. Her major was marketing, and she wanted to open a clothing store someday. And yes, she really was a psychic.

Breakfast was good. Thomas sat facing the door. He looked up whenever anybody came in, expecting to see a familiar face or two. He thought maybe he should start spreading the word that his obituary had been exaggerated. Throughout the meal, people entered and left the coffee shop, but he didn't see one familiar face. He thought it was sad. He really had isolated himself from life for the past few years. There wasn't anybody here to care if he was alive or not.

As he watched Monique drive away in the rusty old green Impala that was her cab, he changed his mind. Being dead might not be such a bad thing.

Janice had probably moved easily into another job. She was a survivor. She had been the perfect office manager; smart, detail oriented, efficient, and without even a shred of personality to muck things up.

As for the rest of the people out here, he had a few friends, but he suddenly realized that it wouldn't bother him if he never saw any of them again. By now, they would've gotten used to the idea that he was worm food. Nobody had erected a Thomas Graham monument in the town square, or even in the middle of the mall, which is the modern version of a town square. There had been no marching bands, no flags at half-mast, no interruption of local television programming.

It's a little bit disturbing to realize how small the effect of your death has been. All you get is an inch or so in the back of the newspaper, and six feet of dirt. He wondered if anyone had even proposed a toast to "good ol' Thomas," or shed a single tear. Come to think of it, it was downright depressing! He was dead and gone, and it didn't seem to matter to anybody. Well, screw 'em all. He'd just stay dead.

Tyler would have to be told. He really wanted to sit down and have a long talk with the boy anyway. They needed to figure a few things out together, the most important of which would be how to repair the holes in their relationship.

The first thing he needed to do was call Barry. Barry Sly was Thomas's lawyer and friend. Barry always said that his parents chose his career when they gave him his name. How could a kid called Barry Sly grow up to be anything but a lawyer? On second thought, maybe he should drop by Barry's office. His news would probably be better delivered in person. Besides, the office was only a couple of blocks away. He shouldered his packs and set off.

23 RESURRECTION

It was good to be there, walking down that familiar street on a crisp November morning. It was good to be anywhere. The clouds were breaking up, and it had stopped snowing. People hurried here and there, all bundled up in their coats and hats. A few of the faces looked vaguely familiar, but most of the people he saw were just extras in a crowd scene.

Barry had a new secretary. Barry always had a new secretary. She was gorgeous. They were always gorgeous. According to the little sign on the desk, her name was Tiffany. She leaned forward to press the button on the intercom, straining the fabric on her low-cut blouse. "Mister Sly, there's a gentleman here to see you." She watched without a change of expression as Thomas placed his backpack in the corner, and stood his daypack up against it.

Through the machine, Barry's voice said, "Thanks Tif, send him in."

Tiffany stood, came around the desk, and escorted Thomas down the hall to an unmarked door. She pushed the door open, stood aside so that Thomas could enter, and then closed the door behind him. Barry was punching keys on a computer, facing away from the door.

"Just a second," he said. The keys chattered for a moment longer, and then, with a flourish, he hit the last key and spun around in his chair. "Now, what can I do for you?"

It started with his eyes. The twinkle disappeared, and they glazed over. Then the lids began to rise, and his cheeks began to fall. That was when his jaw dropped. He looked like a cartoon character. Thomas laughed.

Barry blinked. Barry blinked again. "You son of a bitch! You crazy bastard! You're alive. Hey, wait a minute! I just sold your house and everything you own!" Barry started laughing.

Now they were both laughing. Thomas because of tension released, and Barry out of nervousness.

While he was laughing, Barry's mind was racing. Finally, he said, "I'm going to have to do a little research about bringing you back to life. I don't even know where to look."

"How about the bible?"

"Very funny. Seriously, your son has inherited all of your effects, including the money from your bank accounts and the sale of your house. Oh hell! Then there's the insurance company. They paid out a half-million dollars for your accidental death! He'll have to pay that back."

"That's why I came to you first. I wondered if I could stay dead for awhile."

"Well I would have to advise you against committing fraud. That's pretty serious stuff. What have you gotten yourself into, Tom?"

"I'm not sure. I think I know who engineered my 'death' and I'd like to be free to look into it a bit before he finds out what's going on. Besides, there are other people involved, and I want to find out who knows what, and how deep this thing goes, before I rise from the grave."

"That would be a pretty dangerous game to play. If

somebody recognizes you, it's all over. You'd have to get out of town, and you'd want to contact Tyler, and try to stop him from spending any of the insurance money so that when you rise from the grave, he won't be implicated in anything illegal."

"That's all fine. I'll give him a call today, and let him know that I'm alright. Now, do you have a file I can look at, all the paperwork on my accident? I'd especially like to see a copy of the death certificate."

"Sure, I have it right here." Barry, scooted his chair over to a file cabinet, and pulled out a thick manila file. "All of this is in the computer, but I like to have the hard copies available. You're lucky. I've been meaning to put this in my inactive case file, but I never got around to it. Here you go." He stood and placed the file on his desk, opened it, and handed Thomas the death certificate. It was signed Dr. Henry Burns, MD." And witnessed by Martin Tyler.

"Damn!" said Thomas.

"What?"

"Oh, nothing. I'm just a little disappointed, is all. This was one of the things I wanted to know about."

"You know these guys?"

"Obviously not as well as I thought I did."

Barry came around the desk. He was short and muscular, a little younger than Thomas. He looked like somebody you'd want on your side in a bar fight, or in a courtroom. "There's some correspondence in here from this Martin Tyler. I also had several phone conversations with him. He seemed like a stand-up guy."

"Hey, you're talking about the man who killed me. If he's such a stand-up guy, why would had do that?"

"I don't know, it doesn't add up. How would he benefit from your death? He never received anything from your estate. Oh, wait a minute. We did reimburse him for the funeral costs. But, since he had you cremated, it came in at a little under two thousand dollars. That doesn't seem like enough to kill you for."

"You're right. But with Martin, it's always what you wouldn't expect. If he derived some benefit from this, it wouldn't be something up front, like an immediate payoff. Whatever it was, you'd never see it coming, and he would come out of it looking as if he hadn't done anything wrong."

"You make him sound like a lawyer. Has he ever thought about running for office?"

"Probably. No, on second thought, holding public office would put him too much in the spotlight. I think Martin would rather be in control of a senator than be one himself."

"I like him better and better."

"Everybody does."

Barry was shaking his head. "I can't believe you're alive." He took his jacket from a hook by the door, and started putting in on. "I'll tell you what. I have some errands that I can run. Why don't you use my phone to make your call? That way, if there are any difficulties with the law later on, it'll look like Tyler was talking to me."

"Wait a minute. I don't have his phone number."

"Really? You don't know your own son's phone number? There's a phone list in the inside front cover of the file. You should probably start with his work number. If I'm not back before you leave, good luck. I'll tell Tiffany you were never here." Barry walked out and closed the door.

Thomas punched in the numbers. It rang twice before someone answered.

"Good morning, Sunrise Property Management, how may I direct your call?"

"Hello, is there a Tyler Graham working there?"

"Yes, Mr. Graham is on another line. Would you like to hold, or should I connect you with Mr. Graham's voicemail?"

"I'll hold, thank you."

"Just a moment." This was followed by some kind of

generic, synthesized music. Then a soothing, almost whispered man's voice came on, talking about how much easier life can be when Sunrise Property Management is taking care of you, your house, your loved ones, your rental contracts, your maintenance issues, and just about everything else that could possibly affect your life. The voice was going through this schpiel for the fourth or fifth time, when the woman came back on the line. "Mr. Graham can speak to you now."

"Hello Barry. What can I do for you?"

"Hi Ty. This isn't Barry."

There was a long pause. "Who is this?"

"Are you sitting down?"

"Dad? My god Dad, is that you?" Tyler's voice broke.

"Yeah, son. It's me. There's been a misunderstanding. I'm fine." There was another long pause. "Are you there, son?"

Tyler's voice was still shaky. "Dad, I thought... well you know what I thought."

"I know. And I'm sorry. I don't know if this was some kind of sick joke or what, so I need you to keep quiet about me being alive for a while; at least until I have a chance to look into it. Can you do that?"

"Sure dad, whatever you say. Is there any way we can get together? There are some things I want to talk to you about. When I thought you were gone forever, it made me think about a lot of stuff, things I should've said and done, you know?"

"Yeah, I know. I've been thinking too. Right now though, I need to go back out west and sort this thing out. As soon as I do that, I can fly out and spend some time with you. I just wanted to let you know that I'm okay, and to warn you not to spend the insurance money."

"No problem. There's been so much red tape, I haven't even gotten anything yet. If it comes, I'll just put it in the bank until I hear from you."

"Good. I'll get back in touch with you as soon as I can, but it might be a month or more. I don't know what I'm going to run into out there. I love you."

"Be careful, Dad. I don't want to lose you again."

"Don't worry Son, I'll see you soon. Goodbye."

"Bye Dad. I love you."

It was the best conversation they'd had in years. Thomas was tempted to just go back to San Francisco, pick up Virginia and forget the whole thing. Why should he care what Martin was doing out there in the woods? He could come back here, resume his business, buy another house, and get on with his life. With Virginia by his side, everything would be different.

But the nagging questions remained. What had Martin been up to? Why should he have gone to all the trouble of faking Thomas' death? On the surface, it didn't make sense. But then, Martin never operated on the surface.

He pulled a slip of paper from his wallet and punched in the numbers for the Regent Hotel. A nasal voice came on the line.

"You have reached the Regent Hotel, San Francisco's premier vacation and business address. If you would like to make, or confirm a hotel reservation, press one, now. If you would like to make a restaurant reservation at the Regency Arms, press two, now. We are sorry. The Regency Café doesn't accept reservations. If you would like to speak with one of our guests, please enter the guestroom number. If you do not have the room number, please stay on the line, and an operator will assist you."

Thomas punched in the numbers: four-one-four. He counted off eight rings and gave up. She wasn't in. That was strange. It was ten o'clock in Michigan, so that would make it seven a.m. in San Francisco. Why would Virginia be out this early? He hung up the phone and walked out to the lobby, lost in thought.

"Excuse me?" Tiffany waved to get his attention.

"Mister Sly said to give you these." She handed Thomas a baseball cap and a pair of dark glasses.

"Thanks." He put them on, along with his jacket, shouldered his packs, and walked out into the cool Michigan morning. Before the door closed, he said "Bye."

Tiffany was already busy at her computer. Thomas had never been there.

He found a pay phone a couple of blocks away, and called the "Green Light" cab company. In a few minutes he was headed for the airport.

It looked like the same cab, but this time, the driver was a heavyset man about Thomas' age. Thomas thought about V. Seeing Henry's signature on the fake death certificate had been a big disappointment. Henry had given the impression of being an open, honest, decent man. V. had given the same impression. Thomas began going over their conversations in his mind, looking for a sinister undertone, something that would clarify this muddy mess. In V's favor was the fact that he hadn't tried to stop Thomas from leaving.

24 HOMELAND SECURITY

It's a small airport. Thomas stood in line for ten minutes or so, and checked his backpack through. Then he stood in line for another fifteen minutes, and emptied his pockets into a little silver plastic tray. He had started to pass through the metal detector, when the armed attendant said, "What's this?" He was holding up Thomas' Swiss Army knife. "You can't take this on an airplane, sir. I'm afraid you'll have to check it through with you bags."

"Oh hell, I forgot all about that nonsense," said Thomas. He backed up, and reached for the tray.

"Loudly, the attendants said, "There's no reason to use abusive language, sir. I'm just doing my job. Homeland security is serious business. Because of me, you don't have to wonder if the passenger sitting next to you has a weapon, or some means of commandeering the airplane and crashing it into a building."

Thomas scraped the contents of the tray onto his hand, and placed the items in his pockets: wallet to right rear, change to left front, keys and pocket knife to right front.

He removed his daypack from the conveyor belt and looped one of the straps over his shoulder. He thought about explaining to the attendant that he hadn't been the least bit abusive yet, and that the only abuse that had occurred was abuse of power. But he realized that the man had either been waiting all day for an opportunity to make that speech, or he made it several times every day. In either case, anything Thomas could have to say on the matter would only encourage the man.

The line to the ticket counter was even longer than it had been before. This time, when Thomas finally reached the front of the line, he asked the uniformed ticket agent if he could have his bag back for a moment, so that he could put his pocketknife in it.

"Can you describe the bag, sir?"

"I just checked it through a minute ago. It's a big, blue, frameless backpack."

"Just a moment, sir."

Thomas stood aside, so that the woman behind him could check through her bags. After a few moments, the agent returned, "I'm sorry, sir. Your bag has left the building."

"Well is there any way I can get to it? I've had this pocketknife for a long time, and I can't carry it on."

"I'm sorry sir, it would be out on the tarmac by now. There's nothing I can do."

Thomas pulled the Swiss Army knife from his pocket and held it up in the air for all to see. He walked deliberately toward the door. With his left hand, he pushed open the cover of a trashcan, and with his right hand, he slam-dunked the pocketknife. Then he deliberately walked back to the counter, picket up his daypack, and stalked to the back of the line that led to the metal detector. Two security guards appeared at his sides. One of them said, "Do we have a problem, sir?"

Thomas was dumbfounded. It felt like grammar school.

The other security guard said, "This would go a lot smoother if you would just make an effort to co-operate, sir. These are difficult times for all of us."

"There's no problem here," said Thomas. "As soon as I can get checked through, I'll go up to the lounge and have a cup of coffee or something. Soon I'll be out of your hair, and everything can get back to normal for you."

The first guard said, "May I see your ticket please, and some identification?"

Thomas laid his pack on the floor, reached for his inside coat pocket, pulled out the tickets, and handed them over. Then he pulled out his wallet, removed his driver's license, and handed that over, too. The office looked them over carefully. "Well, Mister ah...Gray-ham, it looks like everything is in order. According to this, you're a U.S. citizen. Like we said, these are difficult times. As a good citizen, you'll need to learn to control that temper and think about the good of your country." He handed Thomas the papers, and gave him a fake smile. "Can we count on you sir?"

This was a crucial moment. Thomas could say something sarcastic, and risk creating an even bigger scene. He had wanted to be invisible, and he had already caused a big mess. Cameras were probably trained on him right now. How long would it be before someone really checked his ID and found out he was a dead man? He said, "I'll be good."

"Thank you, sir. I'm sure everyone will appreciate that." The guards, moved away proudly, secure in the knowledge that they had saved the day once again, helping a misguided citizen discover the error of his ways.

Thomas felt sick. He felt like a caged animal. No, standing there in line, he felt like a sheep, being herded from pen to pen. He felt like a sheep that had a sneaking suspicion that the farmer might not really be his friend, after all.

This time, when he reached the metal detector, the attendant nodded, and an armed, uniformed, severe looking woman appeared, escorting Thomas into a side room. She said, "Please remove your hat and coat, and empty your pockets onto the table sir. And I'll need that backpack."

Thomas dutifully did as he was told. The woman dumped the contents of his pack out onto the table, and began to separate the items and search through them with her nightstick. She looked his toothbrush over carefully, shook his can of shaving cream, and then shot a dab of foam into a trashcan to make sure it was real, and threw his disposable razor into the trashcan. Then she went over his extra socks and underwear with a metal-detecting wand, and finally waved the thing over Thomas as well, At last she said, "Thank you for your co-operation, sir. You may now repack your bag and proceed to the boarding area."

He stuck his wallet back into his back pocket, and put the tickets back into the breast pocket of his jacket. Everything else, he scooped into the main compartment of the pack. Her eyes never left him. She didn't speak to him again, only stood where she was, feet apart and hands in the "at ease" position.

There was a lounge near the boarding area. Thomas sat at the bar, and ordered a shot of bourbon. He felt the need to do something manly. After the second shot, his outrage began to mellow, and he no longer felt the urge to become a terrorist. As he sat, thinking about the scene he'd just made in the ticket area, it occurred to him that this wasn't the first time that this sort of thing had happened. Maybe Martin was right. Maybe Thomas was like a prism. The incident with his pocketknife hadn't been enough to cause him to react as he did. He was angry with Martin. He was angry with himself for, once again, giving Martin an opportunity to meddle with his life. And now he was also angry with himself for acting like a child, and throwing away a perfectly good jackknife.

When the call came over the intercom that his flight was ready to board, Thomas scooped up the broken pieces of his dignity, shouldered his pack, and went out to stand in line again.

By the time he landed at San Francisco it was dark. The big jet circled once, making a pass high over the Golden Gate. Colored lights reflected on the smooth surface of the bay, a perfect postcard picture.

He found his truck, paid the parking lot attendant, and drove away from the airport with a feeling of tremendous relief. He was in the process of making a vow that he would never again fly anywhere for any reason, when he remembered his promise to Tyler that, when this was all over, he'd fly back to New Jersey and spend some time with the boy. Well, maybe at that point, he's just take a few extra days and drive out.

San Francisco at night really is like a big carnival. Flashing neon lights announce everything from "Fortunes Told" to "Fresh Fish" to "Girls, Girls, Girls." As he drove toward the hotel, Thomas was thinking about a little lamp-lit cabin, nestled deep in the heart of an endless, peaceful forest.

He parked the truck and hurried through the lobby to the elevators. It occurred to him that he should check at the desk for messages, but he decided instead to call down from the room. He hadn't been able to reach Virginia, and he had been fighting a nagging inner voice that kept telling him she was gone. In the elevator, the voice continued.

The key card was still in his wallet. He pulled it out and slid it through the reader at the door. The door opened with a click, and swung into the empty room. Thomas' heart sank. His inner voice said, "I told you so." He called out, "Virginia? Are you here?" But he knew she wasn't. His inner voice was never wrong.

The housekeeper must have left the bathroom light on. The fan was humming softly to itself. With a long sigh, he sat down on the perfectly made bed. A quick survey of the room showed him that nothing was out of place. The room had been thoroughly cleaned. The little coffee pot on the counter was wearing its cellophane jacket, the wastebasket by the door was empty, and the television remote control was in its place on top of the TV.

Suddenly, Thomas felt very tired. He lay back on the bed, placed his hands behind his head, and stared at the ceiling. He felt as if he'd just stepped down from the steel steps of a gigantic rollercoaster. He was a little bit dizzy and disoriented, and it felt like his connections with everything around him had just evaporated. He needed to think. He needed to plan. He needed to get up and turn off that damned annoying bathroom fan.

With a tremendous effort, he got up and made his way wearily toward the bathroom. He reached around the doorjamb and flipped the switch. Virginia screamed.

Thomas yelled. He switched the light back on and there she was, in the bathtub, reading a book. On the floor next to the tub, there was a portable disk player with a wire that led to the headphones she was wearing. With one swift motion, she ripped off the headphones, tossed the book to the floor, jumped out of the tub and into his arms.

Thomas' inner voice died instantly. He strangled it.

With his outer voice, he said, "Where's all our stuff? You scared me half to death! I thought you were gone."

"That makes us even, at least. Feel that." She took his hand and placed it on her wildly beating heart. "I didn't have anything to do, so I put everything away. And now, my love, let's get you out of these wet clothes." She grinned and winked at him.

They had a very late supper at the Regency Arms. Virginia had purchased several new outfits, one of which was a slinky black dress. For Thomas, she had gotten slacks, a turtleneck shirt and a nice wool sweater. Even with his hiking boots, he looked pretty sharp. She looked incredible.

The house specialty was a crab salad. They each ordered one. When the waitress walked away, Virginia said, "Just before you walked in and scared the hell out of me, I was thinking about something."

Thomas took her by the hand. "Oh yeah? And what was that?"

She put on her worried face. "You may not like it."

"Try me."

"Okay. I was thinking that I'm getting tired of sponge baths in the kitchen."

"Not a problem. I can pipe the creek and build you a full bathroom."

"But I'm tired of a lot of things. "I'm tired of working all summer to store up wood for the winter. I'm tired of stoking the fire in the smokehouse, and tending the cows, and no electricity. I'm tired of being a pioneer.

"I see. Two days in the big city and you're spoiled already."

"Something like that."

"Thomas put his free arm around her. "Well, the fact is, I don't care where we live or what we do. The important thing is, we're together.

"Good. Why don't we just forget about Martin and run away together."

"Oh, so that's where this is going. Well, that would be fine, but I can't just walk away. Martin has gone too far."

"What do you mean?"

"He killed me."

"What?"

"He killed me. He even sent my ashes to Tyler who, by the way, inherited everything I owned, along with a half-million dollars in life insurance."

"That doesn't make any sense. Why would Martin do that?"

"That's one of the things I have to find out."

"Ooh, this is spooky."

"Yeah, I know. Who can say what's going to happen when I confront Martin with all of this."

"No, I mean it's spooky that I'm having dinner with a

dead guy."

"Oh, very funny. Let's have a little more respect for the deceased, shall we?"

"I don't know, maybe you should think about joining the Marine Corpse."

"Okay, Darlin', you went too far. I'm in a grave situation here. I have to undertake a possibly dangerous journey tomorrow."

"Stop!" Virginia said. "You're too good at this. I quit. I don't have a ghost of a chance."

"You call that quitting? I can see right through you. But I'll be the bigger person here and let it rest in peace. I don't want this to become a bone of contention between us."

"No more, no more! You're killing me!"

The waitress appeared with their food, effectively ending a potentially deadly pun war. The salads were delicious, with crisp romaine and big chunks of Dungeness crab, slathered in a special house dressing that hinted of exotic spices and mysterious foreign shores. And they were huge.

When Thomas and Virginia had finished, given the waitress a generous tip, and had the bill added to their room charge, Thomas said "You know that you don't have to go back up there, right?"

"I've been thinking about that, and I think I do. I have Josh and Jordan to consider, and as for Martin and whatever he may, or may not have done, I owe him a chance to explain himself. I've always known he was a scheming, manipulating bastard, but until now, I always thought he meant well."

"I don't know. You have to remember that he wasn't above having me knocked on the head and kidnapping me when he thought I might pose a threat to his little kingdom up there. I think maybe you should stay, either down here or in Eureka, until I have a chance to look into things and get some answers. I'd like to make sure it's safe before you go back in."

"Oh, I can't believe he'd ever do anything to hurt me. We've known each other too long, and been through too much together. Sure, he may have killed you, but he didn't actually kill you, kill you. I'm sure I'll be alright."

"Whatever you say. Obviously, you know Martin better than I do. It's just that, if anything were to happen to you, I think it really would kill me."

"Ooh Galahad, I love it when you talk that way!"

When they got back to their room, Thomas made a phone call to Barry's home number. It was nine o'clock in San Francisco, so that would make it midnight in Michigan. "Hello Barry. I'm sorry to be calling so late, but I had a hunch that maybe Martin had called."

"No problem. Yeah, you're right. He called about an hour after you left. He is a slick son-of-a-bitch, isn't he?"

"Apparently. What did he have to say?"

"Well, he asked about Tyler, and he asked how things were going. He couldn't ask any direct questions about you, without revealing that you were alive, but I could tell that I needed to be real careful with my answers. Maybe I'm just paranoid, but it felt like he was studying everything I said, and if I didn't use the right tone of voice, or if I wasn't careful, he could trap me into giving you away."

"So, how'd you do?"

"I think I did okay. I'm sure I didn't say anything to give you away. If he got any hints from my attitude, or voice patterns, I don't know. But I think it went alright."

"I guess I'll find out soon enough. We're headed back up there tomorrow, and I'll probably see him in a few days."

"Are you sure that's wise? After all, he tried to kill you off and you didn't stay dead. What if he tries to make it a permanent condition?"

"I don't know. I suppose that's a possibility. But his position up there depends on his maintaining an

appearance of benevolence. If he loses that, he loses the power to keep everybody there. He'd have people skipping out all over the place."
"I hope you're right."
"Me too. See ya."
"I sure hope so. Keep me posted."

25 THE FOREST

By noon the next day, they were back in Eureka. On their way north they discussed stopping in Leggett to see if Martin had been down there, looking for them, but they decided it didn't matter. Thomas had a feeling that Dina wouldn't say anything about their having dropped in. She had seemed to be really frightened of what Martin might do if he knew.

They tossed around the idea of spending the night in a motel, and continuing on in the morning, but decided that it would be better to get started on their hike. It was two o'clock or so when Thomas parked the pick-up at the ravine. There was a light dusting of snow on the ground

It was cold; and not the dry, single digit, Michigan kind of cold that Thomas had become used to. This was a wet, penetrating, Northern California, Thirty-three degree kind of cold. Thomas pulled his hat down low over his eyes. "Are you sure you don't want me to take you back to Eureka?" He looked at the bleak, grey and white landscape.

"Nah," said Virginia. "I'm a tough gal, remember? Where you go, I go Kemosabe."

They had brought just enough provisions for a two-day trip. Their packs were light, so they made good progress. Thomas didn't miss his stroller at all.

"Everything feels different." It was getting too dark to go on. Virginia was taking off her pack.

"What do you mean?"

"I mean that, after being in the city, I kind of feel like a stranger here. I don't know. I don't feel connected anymore. Does that make sense, or am I just being silly?"

"I don't think it's silly at all." Thomas began setting up their tent. "In your mind, everything out here is connected to Martin. It seems that he's betrayed your trust, so there is a natural tendency to distance yourself from everything you associate with him. Maybe when we get you home, you'll feel differently."

"I don't know. I feel like Rip Van Winkle. It's like I was asleep up here in the
woods for twenty years, and then I woke up. I think I like being awake."

"Well, as I said before, I don't really care much where we live, as long as we're together. I've always had this romantic notion of living off the land, getting away from the excesses of technology and the insanity of an overpopulated, over-regulated society. Maybe when this is all over, we can find some sort of middle ground."

Soon, they had the camp all set up, complete with a crackling fire a few feet from the open flap of the tent. They lay on their stomachs, talking and staring into the fire, watching visions of their future together in the dancing flames. Virginia sighed. "You know Galahad, I just might still be a country girl after all."

By sunrise, the fire had burned down to a bed of hot coals. Thomas had gotten up to replenish it twice in the night, but the wood he had gathered was all burned up. They were snug and warm in their sleeping bag, and the temperature had dropped below freezing during the night.

"I wish I'd brought a coffee pot," Thomas said, wistfully.

"I wish I'd stayed in a motel."

"Let's get up, on 'three.' One, two…three!"

Neither of them moved a muscle.

"Why didn't you get up?"

"Why didn't you?"

Thomas reached for his clothes.

"Hey! You're letting all the heat out!"

He quickly pulled his arm back under the cover and sealed up the draft. "Okay," he said. What do we do now, wait for spring?"

Virginia snuggled closer. "What a great idea."

"But we'll starve."

Virginia purred, "We can live on love."

"I hate to run the risk of being too realistic here, but we'll still need food and water, if we're going to survive."

"Really?"

"Really."

Virginia had been stealthily unzipping her side of the sleeping bag. Now she threw it open. "Then let's get up!"

The shock of cold air took their breath away. They instantly dove for their respective piles of clothing, and went from totally naked to totally clothed, in record time. Thomas began rolling up the sleeping bag. "That was a mean, evil thing to do," he said. "I didn't know you had a dark side."

"Bwah ha ha!" said Virginia. "If I hadn't gotten us up, we would've starved. You said so yourself."

"I guess you're right. That means you saved my life. Now I'm forever in your debt."

Virginia said, "Bwah ha ha" again.

They decided to travel north, over the hills, and try to come in on the back end of Joshua's farm. That would mean skirting around Henry's place. After seeing Henry's signature on his death certificate, Thomas no longer trusted the good doctor to be the open, guileless fellow he appeared to be.

The higher they climbed up the side of the mountain,

the more snow they encountered. By afternoon, they were tracking through four inches or more. The temperature continued to drop, and it began to snow; first a light, mealy sleet, and then great, heavy flakes.

Their pace was slow and easy. They still had a lot of Carol Ann's venison jerky left, so the thought of spending another night in the woods didn't bother them at all.

"Isn't it beautiful?" Virginia was holding on to Thomas' arm.

"It seems awfully early for snow," he said. "What's the date?"

"Let's see, I think it's almost December. In the city, everyone was gearing up for Thanksgiving."

"Well, I'll be damned! Said Thomas.

"If ya don't quit cussin', said Virginia.

"Happy Thanksgiving."

"Aw, is it really?"

"What's wrong?"

"Oh, nothing. It's just that Thanksgiving is my favorite holiday. I usually work all week, baking and preparing for the big feast. The house is always snug and warm and filled with such great smells... pies and sweetbreads, the whole Thanksgiving thing. Then the boys would show up and we'd be a family. We'd play games.

We'd all sit around the table and Carl would say grace, always the same prayer; about how thankful we were to be together. Jordan would spend the night in his old room upstairs, Joshua and Suzy would be in his room, and we'd all get up and have a big breakfast before they all went home. I just can't believe the day is here and everything has changed so much."

"Do you miss him?"

"Carl? Sometimes." Virginia wrinkled her brow. "Like I told you, we didn't have the greatest relationship. We never had what you and I have together. But we had good times. We made it work. I think it's just that, with the Holidays coming, I'm remembering all the old familiar feelings.

"We'll have lots of holidays together. Maybe when we get this mess all straightened out, we'll get a place near here and establish some new family traditions."

"Yeah, I suppose you're right. I'm just being silly." A tear squeezed out of her eye.

"I'm sorry honey," Thomas said, stopping and embracing her. "This must be awful for you. For all these years, everything stayed pretty much the same. You had a comfortable, established routine. It must feel like a bomb dropped on your house and blew it all apart."

They stood together for a moment. Surrounded by the falling snow. Thomas felt Virginia's body stiffen a little as she took control of herself. "But now I have you. And whatever happens, we'll be okay, right?"

"Right," he said.

After walking for another couple of hours, they picked up the trail to Josh's place. Half an hour later, there it was.

When they first saw the house, it looked like a picture, framed by the surrounding trees. It was an old, white farmhouse, probably abandoned years before, and now filled with life once again. There was a large, unpainted barn, and there was even a windmill, turning slowly above it all. Lamplight flickered from the windows of the house. Viewed through the falling snow, it looked like the cover of a Christmas card. Thomas and Virginia stood for a moment of appreciation before going on. Thomas said, "Wow."

Virginia didn't say anything. Thomas had the feeling she was a little choked up.

26 THANKSGIVING

They strode up onto the covered porch, opened the wooden storm door, and knocked. A dog started barking inside. A woman's voice said, "Hush up now, Blackie!" And they heard soft footsteps padding toward the door.

A blast of warm air accompanied the opening of the door, and there was Joshua. "Mom?"

"Happy Thanksgiving Joshie," Virginia managed to say.

At the far end of the room, Jordan was sitting in a big, well-worn easy chair by the glowing fireplace. He stood and with three long, hunter's strides, joined the group at the door. Suzy too, hurried over to greet the travelers.

Thomas removed his pack and helped Virginia with hers, then leaned both of them against the wall. There followed much hugging and handshaking. When he shook the hand of Jordan, Thomas felt the piercing power of those pale blue eyes. He also felt the power of the young man's iron grip.

It started as a simple handshake, but as he felt the pressure begin to increase, Thomas returned the favor. Gradually, the tension mounted until their hands were like two vises, locked together. It only lasted for a moment, but it was long enough that each man felt the strength of the other. In the end, Jordan's icy stare melted into a smile. Thomas smiled too. An understanding had been reached.

Virginia looked around the room. "Where's Rebecca:"

"I put her down for a nap about an hour ago," said Suzy. "This promises to be a big night, and I wanted her to be rested up so she doesn't get cranky later."

"My sweet little granddaughter, get cranky? Never!"

"Oh yes she does! And now that she's mobile, she's quite a handful."

"She's walking?"

"Yep," said Joshua. "For a couple of days now. It's like she's been doing it all her life. And she only has one speed. We blink and she's off getting into some kind of mischief."

"I just can't wait to see her. Let's wake her up!"

Suzy and Joshua exchanged a wink. Suzy said, "I just have a few more things to do, and dinner will be ready. Then we can bring her in."

Virginia sighed. "Okay. How can I help?"

"Well, the goose is about done, and everything else is just about ready. I guess you can mash the potatoes."

"Great!" Virginia disappeared into the kitchen, leaving Thomas alone with Jordan and Josh. Thomas stood in front of the fireplace, and the boys returned to their easy chairs. "This is a beautiful place you have here, Thomas began.

"Thanks," said Joshua.

"When we first saw it, through the trees, with the snow coming down, it looked just like a Christmas card."

"Yeah, we like it." Then, after a long, uncomfortable pause, during which they could hear the women chattering in the kitchen, Josh said, "How was your trip?"

"Fine."

Jordan had been silent, watching. After another uncomfortable period, he said, "So what's going on with you and our mother?"

Fallen Idyll

Robin Hood's arrow twanged across the room and stuck Thomas right in the heart. He forced a smile and thought for a moment. Finally, he said, "I guess it started in second, or third grade. Your mother and I were best friends. As we got older, the friendship grew. You know how kids are. There were times when we were closer than others, but I think we both always felt that we would end up together.

After high school, your mom went away to college, and I stayed up here. I made some bad choices, and ended up moving back east to get some perspective and a fresh start. I tried to dissociate myself completely from my old life here, and that included getting married out there, and having a son.

My wife died a few years ago, after a long illness, and I came back out here hoping to make sense of my life: past, present, and future. I stumbled on this place entirely by accident. Then your dad was killed, and I was injured. Your mom was kind enough to help me get well again, and in the process of that, we both realized that we still belong together.

I don't want to try to be your father, and I'm certainly not here to take your mother away from you. I'm looking forward to getting to know both of you, and I hope we can all get along and be friends. But the fact is, I hope Virginia and I will be together for the rest of our lives."

Jordan spoke again. "That sounds fair enough. Do you think you can make her happy?"

"That's going to be the central purpose of my life from here on."

Joshua looked relieved. "Well, I think you can understand why we've been concerned. We don't know you, and things have been happening awfully fast between you two. A few months ago, we had a father and a mother. Now it feels like we've suddenly lost them both."

"Well, I'm hoping that, rather than losing your

mother, you've gained a friend," Thomas said.

"We'll see", said Jordan. But his blue eyes were thoughtful. The fire and ice had not returned.

"Hey!" said Suzy from the kitchen doorway. "Why is it that you boys get to sit by the fire and relax, while mom and I do all the work? How about you drag your lazy bones in here and help bring the food out?"

"Yes Ma'am!" Joshua said, laughing. All three men obeyed instantly.

Thomas was surprised at the abundance of delicious-looking, aromatic food. There were mashed potatoes, stuffing, Hubbard squash, green beans, cornbread, and the goose. There was zucchini, fried with egg. There were various kinds of pickles. There were pies, pumpkin and apple. Suzy and Joshua must have been working for days.

They all filed in from the kitchen and deposited their various kettles, plates and platters on the table. As they were preparing to sit down, Suzy looked significantly at Virginia and said, "Oh, I almost forgot, there's one more thing I need to do."

"Ooh I can't wait," said Virginia, brightening up even more.

Suzy disappeared into an adjoining room, and Virginia brought an old, wooden high chair over from its place by the wall. When Suzy reappeared, she was carrying a small, golden haired bundle. "She was wide awake in there, listening," she said.

Rebecca said, "Bamma!" and held out here arms.

Virginia was beaming. "May I?"

"Of course," said Suzy, handing over the wriggling bundle.

Thomas felt his eyes begin to well up, as he watched the child, gleefully hugging her grandmother.

Virginia's voice broke a little when she said, "Good morning, Bright Eyes. Happy Thanksgiving, Are you really, really hungry?"

Rebecca said, "Yep." She sat up then, and surveyed

the room. Her eyes were deep blue.

Virginia placed her in the high chair, and Suzy pivoted the wooden tray into place. Suzy took a chair on one side, and Virginia sat on the other. Finally, the men sat, too. For a long moment, everyone just sat in a silence that became uncomfortable. It seemed as if nobody knew what to do next. In the end, it was Thomas who spoke. "Do you mind if I say something?"

Nobody minded.

"I know this must be hard for all of you. I didn't get a chance to meet Carl Wilson, and being here with all of you, I regret that even more. I came back out here because my life was empty. I felt like I was just 'going through the motions'. I'd get up in the morning and go to work, come home in the evening, have a couple of drinks, and go to sleep; only to repeat it all the next day, and the next. I knew something was terribly wrong. I knew something was missing, but I didn't know what it was; not until this moment.

I was living, but I wasn't really alive. I was disconnected." He had been staring into space, as if he were staring in to the past. Now he looked up, into the faces around him. "This is what's important, these connections that you have. If Carl had anything to do with the sense of family and love that I see here, in all of you, then I know he was a good man, and a great loss to the everyone who knew him."

Virginia said, "Thank you, Thomas, Now, would any one like to say grace?" She gave Joshua a look and a nod of her head.

He looked a little embarrassed. "Mom! I think Jordan should have to do it. He's older."

"I'll tell you what, Buddy." The boys were playing. "When we have Thanksgiving dinner at my house, I'll say the grace."

"That won't work," said Joshua. "You don't have a house!"

"Boys, come on," said their mother. "The food's getting cold."

"I know," Jordan said. "Since this is our house, Suzy and I will start. But then we'll each take a turn, and everyone will get a chance to say what we're thankful for."

"As long as we get to eat soon," said Jordan.

"Okay then. Honey, would you like to start?"

Suzy's expression said, "No, thank you" and, "Hurry up," at the same time.

"Alright," Joshua relented. "Here goes…" They all bowed their heads, except Rebecca, who was decimating a piece of cornbread. "Lord, You've been good to us this year. We had a big yield, and got enough food, not only for ourselves, but enough to share. The cellar is full, the house is warm, and we're all together. Thanks for my home, and my family."

Suzy was next. "I don't know where to begin. I'm so thankful for so many things. Right now, I feel like I have everything I want and need. I think that, if I had to choose, that's what I'm most thankful for; this feeling of contentment." She picked a piece of cornbread up from Rebecca's lap, and placed it on the tray of the high chair.

Everybody looked at Rebecca, as if it was her turn to speak. She giggled.

Virginia sighed. "A couple of hours ago, we were hiking through the woods, with the snow falling around us. We were walking slowly, taking our time, talking about this and that, when we suddenly realized what day it is. For just a moment there I felt, I don't know, lonesome. No, that's not it. I felt isolated. I felt that we were just two small specks in that great, white, silent world. Then, when we saw this house, all glowing and warm, I realized that, no matter where we go, or what we do, we have each other.

The ties that bind us together are stronger than distance, stronger than time, and in the case of your father, even stronger than death. I think that's what I'm most thankful for, that and Thomas. It may be hard for you boys to understand, but I'm thankful that he's here with us, that he's joined our little circle." She gave Thomas' hand a squeeze.

Thomas wasn't sure what to say. He'd just finished giving two long speeches, and he'd pretty much exhausted his oratorical repertory. He hesitated just a moment, and then said, "I'm thankful that, after two days of hiking, beef jerky and gorp, we've arrived at this bountiful feast."

Jordan was ready. "I'm thankful for the mountains, the rivers, the game trails, the sun, the stars and the wind. Now let's eat."

The food was every bit as delicious as the tempting aromas had promised. Conversation revolved around the wonderful food, the early snow, and Rebecca. Everyone ate enough to be just a little bit uncomfortable, and then the pies were served.

Dinner was over, the mountain of dishes had been washed, and they had retired to the living room. Conversation was intermittent, separated by long, contented pauses, which were punctuated with sleepy sighs. Joshua laid a fresh log on the fire. He stretched and said, Well, I'd better go out to the barn and check on the stock. I have a feeling it's going to be a cold one tonight." He went to the hall closet and pulled out a heavy wool jacket and a pair of gloves, sat on a nearby bench and began pulling on his boots.

Thomas was sitting on the couch with Virginia. He stood and said, "Mind if I come along?"

"Not at all."

From the closet shelf, Joshua produced what looked like, and probably was, an old green-painted railroad lantern. He carried it over to the fireplace. He chose a thin piece of kindling from a metal box on the hearth, held it in the flames until the end was burning well, and then used it to light the lantern.

Joshua led the way through the kitchen, where he

grabbed a shiny silver bucket, and out the back door. It had stopped snowing. Patches of stars showed among the retreating clouds, and he's been right about the cold. The only sound was the soft crunching of their boots on the snow, which had piled up to a depth of about six inches.

The barn was old. It had a single, high gable, under which the hay was stored, and lean-to additions on either side where the animals were kept. On one side there were two milk cows, one with a Hereford calf. On the other side, there were a few Suffolk sheep. A sorrel horse occupied a stall at the far end, and chickens roosted in the rafters.

Joshua hung the lantern on a peg, grabbed a pitchfork, and laid forkfuls of hay into the mangers of the horse and the cows. He ladled grain onto another manger in the sheep's area, and took a one-legged milking stool down from its peg near the stanchion where the cows were already contently munching their hay. After levering the stanchion bars over against the necks of the cows, trapping their heads while they munched, he sat on the stool and began milking.

Thomas looked around. "What a great barn," he said. It seemed older than the house, being supported on massive, hand-hewn beams that showed the marks of the broad-axe and adze that he been used to make them square. They were mortised together and pinned with wooden pegs. The stanchion bars were simply peeled poles, dark and shiny with countless years of use. "Do you have any idea how old it is?"

"I'm not sure, but I know it's pretty old. Over on the east end, there's a stone arrowhead embedded in the outside wall".

"It makes you wonder how many generations of men have sat where you're sitting, and done what you're doing."

Joshua continued squirting the milk into the bucket. "Yeah, I figure it must've been built in the eighteen forties or fifties. Living here feels right. It's like I'm connected somehow with those generations, like I'm carrying on an important tradition. It's a tradition of hardworking, plain-speaking, honest men of the soil. What's on your mind, Tom?"

"Martin Tyler."

"Ah, Jordan's the expert on Martin. I don't really know anything about him, other than to say that I try to steer clear of him as much as I can. According to my agreement with Martin, I have one more year to prove up on this place, and it will be mine. Until then, unless things get really crazy, I'd rather not know too much."

"I see. And what if things did happen to get crazy?"

"Well, then I'd have to make a decision, wouldn't I? If I felt that I couldn't be involved with him anymore, I guess I'd have to give up this place and move my family out of here. But I'll tell you right now, that would take a lot of craziness." The rhythm continued, as the foaming white milk rose gradually in the bucket.

"I don't blame you a bit," Thomas said. "You seem to have a good life here. I envy you."

"Thanks. You know that feeling I was talking about, how I feel connected to the generations that have been here before?"

"Yeah?"

"Well, I can see that connection becoming a long line, running through the generations that'll follow after me... What I mean is, I'm the link that connects it all together. Does that make sense to you?"

"It sounds like you've thought about this a lot."

"Yeah, I have. I don't know if I ever put it into words before. It probably sounds silly." Joshua finished milking and stood up. He released the cows and hung the stool on its peg.

"There's nothing silly about it," said Thomas. "It's a rare and exceptional man who understands his place in history."

"Being a farmer teaches a man to be patient. Seasons

pass, and everything is in a gradual, continual state of change. Some years, you can spend the spring planting, tending, and anticipating, only to have a late storm come along and ruin everything. Other years, things can look bad, and then perfect weather will come along at just the right time, and bless you with a bumper crop. It's only natural that, as I see the connected flow of the seasons and the years, that I can project that into the generations as well."

"Hey, you sound pretty well educated for a country boy."

"I read a lot. Mom taught Jordan and me as we were growing up. We had school for four hours a day, five days a week. It wasn't so bad in the winter, but in the spring and fall, we wanted to be outside, doing other things." He picked up the brim-full bucket, and started toward the door. "When we get back inside, there's something I want to show you."

27 JORDAN SPEAKS

In the kitchen, Joshua pulled a couple of large glass jars out of a pantry cupboard. He placed a clean cloth over the mouth of one of these, and slowly poured milk through the cloth until the jar was full. Then he repeated the process with the other jar, emptying the bucket. He screwed on the metal lids, and placed the jars out on the enclosed back stoop. "Come on," he said, "Let's go upstairs." With a lamp from the kitchen counter, he led the way.

The stairs were worn and narrow. With Joshua carrying the lamp ahead of him, it seemed to Thomas as if he were following Quasi-modo up some kind of secret passageway. At the top of the stairs, there was a long, narrow hall, with doors lining both sides. Behind one of these doors was the library.

Joshua opened the door, and Thomas felt a blast of cooler air from the unheated room. There was another lamp on a table. His shadowy host lit this second lamp, and the room sprang into focus. Bookshelves lined the walls from floor to ceiling. It was a small room, but it must have held a thousand old books. All of the classics were there. History books, science books, classic literature, how-to books, books about philosophy, mechanics, farming... anything and everything was represented there.

Thomas was surprised and impressed. He said, "Wow. Where did you get all of these?"

"I always got books as gifts for birthdays and Christmas, and then Jordan brings more in from time to time. He gets out more than the rest of us."

"Don't be giving away all my secrets." It was Jordan. Thomas hadn't heard him come up the stairs, even though the old steps creaked and groaned.

Joshua said, "Don't worry Jord, Thomas is okay. We've been talking, and I think we can trust him."

"We'll see." Jordan turned to face Thomas. "Aren't you a good friend of Martin's?"

"The truth is," Thomas said. "I was kind of hoping you might be able to answer a few questions about my old buddy."

"Oh? Like what?"

"Like, how crooked is he, really?"

"He's as crooked as it gets. If Martin Tyler tells you anything, you can bet it's a lie. If Martin is being nice to you, it's because he wants something from you. And if he wants something from you, he'll never ask for it. Instead, he'll figure out a way to trick you out of it. He's the scum of the earth."

Joshua said, "Jordan."

"Well, you said we could trust him. I'm just telling it like it is."

"It's okay, fellas," said Thomas. Some issues have come up that make me want to know more about him and his activities. Another thing I've been wondering is, how many people have 'proved up' on their properties, and gotten the deed transfers they were promised."

"Yeah," said Jordan. "I've wondered that, too. I know dad did, and Mister Day, and probably Henry. It's hard to say about the others. Martin keeps trying to get me to pick out a place of my own. I think it bothers him to have me floating around out there, unattached. He never knows where I'll turn up."

"Jordan thinks he's double-oh-seven. He's always sneaking around in the woods, spying on everybody."

Thomas sighed. "I wish you'd have seen what happened last fall when I got myself shot."

"Maybe I did," said Jordan.

"You're kidding." Thomas placed the copy of 'Lillith' he'd been looking over, back into its slot on the shelf. "Then you saw it all? You saw what we did?"

"Well, after that first shot, when those guys came boiling out of the cabin, I ducked down behind a log, but I could still see everything. Martin was as cold as ice until it was all over. His first shot took out Tony, and the second one took Ben out. Then he fired again and killed Mike."

"Wait a minute. You're saying that it was Martin who shot the first one?"

"Yep, blew a big hole out of the back of his head."

"What about V.D?"

"He was firing the shotgun over their heads."

"That son-of-a-bitch!"

"Who?"

"Martin. He told me that I killed one of them. Even complimented me on my shot."

"That's classic Martin, alright. He can't hide the fact that he's a type-A egomaniac, so he uses flattery to bring down your guard, to keep you off balance."

"Wait a minute," Thomas said. "It sounds like you knew those guys,"

"Tony and Mike and Ben? Yeah, they worked for our dad, who was working for Martin. The canyon on the other side of that cabin had pot plants salted all over it. Tony lived in the cabin, and helped take care of them. There was even a gravity-fed watering system that snaked all over the canyon. It was always having problems, so Tony took care of that, too. There must be miles of plastic tubing out there, and he used to check all of it, every day. When harvest time came, Tony brought in

Mike and Ben."

"Why didn't you say anything before?"

"Dad made me promise not to, and besides, who would I tell? I thought you were somebody Martin brought in, maybe to help with the operation. I guess I could've told Mister Day, but I've never been able to figure out how much he knows about Martin and his dealings."

"Jordan kept quiet because of me," said Joshua. "He was afraid that, if he blew the whistle on Martin, I'd lose this place and everything I've worked for."

"You see," Jordan said. "If Martin got busted, all of his property would be confiscated by the Federal government, including Josh's farm. Since dad was involved, mom's place would go, too. I don't see how I could be the one to destroy so many lives, and still live with myself."

"Dad used to call this place 'The Hole-in-the-Wall' because it's like an outlaw hide-out from the old west. Just about everyone here is wanted for something, somewhere, and they're all trying to start over, to build decent lives for themselves. Martin is like a snake in the henhouse. He doesn't keep the hens from laying eggs, but he gets one here and there."

Jordan chuckled. "I think you've been a farmer too long, Josh. I mean really, hens and a snake?"

"Hey, it works. I can see Martin, slithering around from nest to nest, swallowing a few eggs... Oh shut up. It's not that funny."

Thomas started toward the door. "We'd probably better head downstairs. Everyone will be wondering what happened to us."

"Just a minute," Joshua said. "You're not a cop, are you?"

"No," said Thomas. I'm just a guy who wants to know the truth about what's going on here."

Jordan said, "While you guys were out at the barn, I

asked mom and she told me all about him. If she trusts him, so do I."

Joshua crossed to the library table, blew out the lamp, picked up the one he had brought, and led the others down the narrow stairs. Virginia looked up when they entered the living room and said, "What have you boys been up to?"

"Joshua was showing me his library," Thomas replied. "Very impressive."

"I see. Well, Suzy and I are feeling pretty neglected. The kitchen is all cleaned up, and Rebecca is back in her crib, sleeping. How are you boys going to entertain us?"

"Funny you should ask," said Thomas. "While we were upstairs, we worked out this little dance number. Hit it, boys!" He shuffled awkwardly across the floor. Jordan and Joshua didn't move.

Virginia and Suzy clapped their hands. "Oh yes, very entertaining!" laughed Virginia. "No wonder you were gone so long. I only have one, tiny little suggestion that might improve it just a little."

"What's that?"

"Give it up, and don't ever do that again."

"Aw... And a glorious career on the stage flickers and dies." Thomas walked dejectedly to the couch where she was sitting.

"That's okay, maybe your talents lie elsewhere. You play a mean game of checkers."

"Of course! You're absolutely right! I'll go on tour! Thomas Graham, the world famous checker player! I'll hobnob with the snobbish elite! Kings and Rock Stars will genuflect as I walk by! Supermarket tabloids will chronicle my escapades! Fans will hound me wherever I go! I'll be on television, endorsing a wide variety of personal hygiene products! My life will become a whirlwind of hotel rooms, fast food, and shallow, meaningless relationships with people who just want to reach out and touch the hem of real power! Bwah ha ha!"

"Sit down," said Virginia. "You're scaring me."

"I have a better idea," said Joshua. "Let's see what you can do in the kitchen."

"Whatever you say. But I think I should warn you that I'm almost as good at cooking as I am at dancing."

"That's okay, you can be in charge of the stirring part."

With a big serving spoon, Joshua skimmed the cream from one of the jars of fresh milk, and left it in a crock on the back porch. Then he emptied the milk into a large, ironstone bowl. He and Thomas added a half-dozen eggs, honey and vanilla. He grated cinnamon sticks and nutmeg, and added them to the mix. Handing the big spoon to Thomas, he said, "It's all yours."

Thomas stirred. When he was finished, he laid the spoon on a cloth napkin. Joshua said, "More." This happened three times. The eggnog was now thick, frothy and creamy. Josh took a taste and said, "Perfect."

"Not quite," said Thomas. From his pack in the living room, he produced a bottle of rare, single malt scotch whiskey. "I don't think this is the correct compliment for eggnog, but we could try it."

"Why not?" said his host.

They poured the eggnog into heavy, ironstone mugs, and added the whiskey to taste.

"Okay," said Virginia, after sampling the masterpiece. "Forget checkers. Maybe you should join the Olympic eggnog-making team."

After an hour or so of light conversation, Joshua built up the fire for the night. He offered Virginia and Thomas a room upstairs, but since it was one that Jordan usually used, and was comfortable with, they declined, and chose instead to roll their sleeping bags and mattress pads out in front of the fire.

They woke up when Joshua brought in the morning milk. It occurred to Thomas that, although this life was filled with rich rewards, it was filled with hard work, as well.

28 PORCUPINES

The sun was out. During the night, the wind had changed. It was now blowing from the south, and the temperature was rising. Much of the snow had already melted by the time Thomas and Virginia had said their goodbyes, shouldered their packs, and started down the trail. Jordan had insisted upon joining them.

He moved like a cat. He seemed totally relaxed, and yet Thomas had the feeling that he was holding himself back. If the young man had been alone, his pace would have been much faster. Thomas had always considered himself to be a woodsman. Growing up near the forest, it was the place he felt most comfortable. But this young man moved more like an animal than a human. There was no wasted motion. It was a spiritual oneness with his environment and with himself, as if he were a Kung Fu master, or some kind of Eastern Mystic.

"I'll tell you what," the young man said. "Why don't I just meet you at the house?" Virginia said that would be fine, and he was gone. He left the trail and disappeared among the trees.

Thomas said, "He's a good man."

Virginia said, "I know."

The spot where the trail they'd been following joined the main trail was familiar. Thomas recognized a hollow, twisted Tan Oak that housed a family of porcupines.

You can always smell a porcupine nest, long before you come upon it. They're not very good housekeepers.

When Thomas was a young man, he built a tiny shelter of plywood and two-by-fours at the top of a cliff near his parent's home. From that cliff, he could see clear out to the coast, about fifteen miles away, where the blue ocean swept out to the far horizon and beyond. He had planned to spend many a summer night up there, staring into his campfire and dreaming, even before he slept.

During his first night in this lean-to shelter, he awoke to the sound of crunching and munching. A little frightened, he pulled on his boots, and crawled out to investigate. Three porcupines were making a meal of his house. He could see them quite clearly in the moonlight. He yelled at them and banged on the roof with a stick, until they slowly ambled off into the woods that ended at the cliff.

A few minutes later, they were back, crunching and munching. Now he was more angry than frightened, and he grabbed his camp shovel. He crawled out once again, only this time, instead of frightening them away, he bashed their heads in.

In the morning, he pushed their prickly bodies off the cliff. He could still picture them, bouncing down the face of the rock, and landing, lifeless at the bottom.

He had tried sleeping up there a few more times, but his heart was no longer in it. Finally, he dismantled the shelter and hauled it away. And he had been especially nice to porcupines every since.

It's one thing to kill an animal for food, or if it's particularly dangerous, as in the case of hydrophobia or whatever, but he'd killed those porcupines because they were inconvenient, and he'd never really forgiven himself for it.

"What are you thinking so hard about?" asked Virginia.

"Porcupines."

"You're a funny, funny man."

As they walked along, he told her the story. In the end he said, "I killed those porcupines, simply because I could. Their only defense was their ability to flip over and slap a predator with their quills. I used my advantage and destroyed what was weaker. I'm, not sure, exactly, how to explain it, but I guess, in my mind, it showed a lack of character. The strong should be champions of the weak, not their destroyers."

"I don't think you have to worry about a lack of character, Thomas. A lot of people, most of them in fact, believe that they have the right to press their advantages to the limit, that in the natural order of things, the strong survive, and the weak are simply tools, to be used to facilitate that survival."

"Martin?"

"Martin."

"So that would make me a porcupine."

"Something like that."

"Well, I hope he doesn't have a shovel."

The snow was melting fast. By the time they reached Virginia's cabin, there were only a few white patches left, under the trees. Their shoes were all muddy, and mud had splashed and spattered, almost to their knees. They removed their packs, and then sat on the porch steps and removed their boots as well.

Inside, everything was just as they had left it. Virginia's note was still on the table. Jordan had not yet arrived. Virginia shivered. "Brrr, it's cold in here! Why don't you turn up the thermostat?"

"Good idea," said Thomas. He went to the wood stove and, using crumpled paper and kindling, built a fire. Picking up an empty bucket, he said, "I'll turn the water on, too. I could use a cup of coffee." With that, he went outside, slipped his boots back on without tying the laces, and headed for the stream. He dipped the bucket in the icy water, and was turning around, when Jordan emerged from the forest.

Thomas said, "Hello there. I thought you'd get here ahead of us. Did you get lost?"

"I stopped by the Day place. I didn't tell them you were back. I asked them if they'd heard anything about where you went, or when you would be coming home. They didn't seem to be too concerned."

"Yeah, they seemed to think we were eloping or something. I'm about to make a pot of coffee. "You want some?"

"Sure. But I'll only stay for a minute. I've got some things I want to check out."

"Oh yeah? What's that?"

"I'll let you know. I'm just naturally the curious type." Jordan smiled.

It was still pretty cold in the house. Thomas set the bucket down and added a few sticks of wood to the fire.

By the time the coffee was ready, the kitchen had warmed up, and the heat was spreading slowly to the rest of the house. Virginia said, "I'm a little bit surprised at how good it feels to be home. Don't get me wrong, I loved San Francisco, but here I feel… I don't know… peace."

"I know what you mean," said Thomas. "I think it's what led me here in the first place. If you choose to accept all of the convenience and information that the world has to offer, you are choosing to accept the regulation and responsibility that comes with that choice.

You couldn't fly to Michigan with me because your driver's license expired twelve years ago, and you don't have any identification. Here, you don't have to prove you exist, you just do. You don't have to deal with taxes, insurance, Social Security, interest rates, any of it. But besides air travel, you also don't have showers, or shopping, or electric lights, music, automatic heat, or a thousand other things that the world takes for granted."

"Can't we have both worlds?" Virginia wondered.

"That would be nice, but I really don't see how. I don't think it's possible to reap the benefits of technology and the modern world without becoming a victim of its darker aspects. If you accept a coin from the world, you get both the head and the tail. There's no separating the two sides."

Jordan said, "Render unto Caesar that which is Caesar's, and give me what is mine."

"Something like that."

"So what are you planning to do next?"

Once again, Thomas was impressed with Jordan's direct approach. The young man seemed to have a clear idea of who he was, and the feeling that he was equal to whatever situation arose. "Well, I figured I might pay a visit to my friend V.D. I want to find out how deeply he's involved in all of this. "In his favor is the fact that Dina didn't mention him in connection with Martin's 'business trips'."

Virginia said, "Come to think of it, you're right. Dina implied that Martin always went down there alone, and then at some point, started taking Carl with him. She didn't mention anyone else."

"I think that's a good place to start," said Jordan. "He's always seemed to be a straight shooter. He might even be able to give you some information that will be helpful when you confront Mister Tyler." He placed his empty cup on the table, and stood up. "I guess I'd better get going. It'll be dark in a few hours, and like I said, there's something I need to do. See Ya." And he was gone.

Thomas stood and said, "I'd better get going, too. Do you want to come along?"

"Are you kidding? I'm as curious as you are. I should probably stay here and dust or something, but I want to find out what's going on, too. Besides, I have a present for Carol Ann."

29 VALENTINE DAY

The snow had all melted away, and the predominant colors of the forest were, once again, brown and green. The air was cool enough to bring a rose to Virginia's cheek, but not really cold. In just over half an hour, they reach the Day's cabin.

Inside, Carol Ann was slicing fresh carrots into a big pot of stew, and the big man was seated at the table, drawing up some kind of plan on a large sheet of newsprint. Virginia knocked lightly on the door.

V. said, "Now who can that be?" and stood up. When he saw who it was, he said, "Well I'll be damned!"

"… If you don't quit cussin'," said Thomas, wearing a big grin and holding out his hand.

"Hey Carol Ann, look what the cat dragged in!" said V. And to Thomas and Virginia, he said, "Damn, it's good to see you folks. I was afraid you weren't comin' back. Honey! Come on out here and say hello!"

"Oh, hold your horses Valentine, you big galoot!" Carol Ann came from the kitchen, wiping her hands, and with a look of mock perturbation on her face. When she saw Virginia, she said, "Welcome home, Honey," and gave her a big hug.

V. said, "Come over here and see what I've been workin' on."

On the table was a complicated drawing of what looked like an oil drum, with the bottom third of its height buried in the ground. A steel cap came down over the top of it, leaving a space in between. It was rather like a jar lid that was too large to fit the jar. Two pipes protruded from the barrel at ground level, a short one bending upward at ninety degrees, and a long one, a little lower, pointing down at a slight angle, and away. "Ya know what this is?" the big man asked.

"Not a clue."

"It's the water tank for your indoor plumbing. You see, we set this drum in the creek, buried up to here. The water comes in around the lid, so any floatin' debris stays out. This long pipe goes down the hill to your kitchen sink, where we'll have a faucet. A branch line'll 'T' off and run over to your new bathroom. What do you think?"

"I don't know what to say." Said Thomas.

Virginia said, "Does this really mean we can have indoor plumbing?"

"And take a look at this," said V., rolling up the paper to reveal another sheet, underneath. It was a drawing of a water wheel. "I've been wantin' to try this for a long time. I've got a couple of old car alternators down at the shop, and I figure if I use an overshot wheel, I can create enough rpms to make 'em charge. If we can scare up a battery or two and a converter, you can have free electricity!"

"Now hold on there. Thanks a lot for thinking about it, but what would electricity do for us besides saving a little bit of lamp oil?" Thomas was concerned about he changes that electricity might bring to this simple place.

"Well, I've got a big steel box up there in the pool that feeds my kitchen, where I keep food in the summer. I guess it works well enough, but I've always thought that a refrigerator'd be a real nice thing to have; or even a freezer. If we could freeze our vegetables, it'd be a lot easier, and take less time, than cannin'. Not only that, but they'd taste better, too."

Thomas laughed. "You sound like a T.V. commercial. Refrigerators, eh? I don't know... Do you think it'd be worth all the trouble of hauling them in here?"

"I don't see how that's such a big problem. Randy could fly in a couple of small ones. Even if he had to bring 'em in one at a time, we could prob'ly get up enough juice to power even three or four of 'em."

"I know! why don't you just use the creek down at your shop? I'm sure you could find a lot of uses for power around there."

"I looked into it. Down there, the creek bed is too flat. There's not enough slope to make room for an overshot wheel like this." He pointed to the drawing. "See, if the water comes down over the wheel, it turns fast enough to make it work. An undershot wheel, where the water turns the wheel from underneath, would turn too slow."

Virginia and Carol Ann had moved into the kitchen, and were talking and laughing about something or other. Whatever Carol Ann had said, it ended with, "…little boys."

Thomas thought it was time to change the subject. "V," he said. "I really appreciate all of this. I don't know how to thank you for all you've done already, let alone all the stuff you're planning here. But I need to talk to you about something."

"Sure, Tom. Shoot."

"What can you tell me about Martin?"

The expression on the big man's face showed that he had been expecting this. "Well," he said. "That's a little bit complicated."

"Why doesn't that surprise me?"

"Tom, you have to understand where we all came from, down here. This little nest of people you stumbled into started out as kind of an outlaw hideout. We used to call it the Hole-in-the-Wall. In the old days, we were like the Youngers, or the James gang. And Martin was Jesse James.

We started out in those fancy treehouses you saw down by the creek. We thought we were folk heroes. In the beginning, we were squattin' up here. That's why we lived in the trees. We were trespassin'.

Carl was a genius at growin' weed. He had little bunches of plants all over the place, and after a couple of good seasons we were makin' so much money, we couldn't spend it all. I think that's what started all the trouble. We had too much money, and no place to spend it.

Martin started thinkin' he was king of the world." The big man leaned back in his chair, and gazed off into the past. "He definitely had it by the tail. We were all livin' fast. Life was just one long party.

After a while, things just got too easy. Martin kind'a got bored with it all. He started gettin' into all kinds of stuff. Randy lived up here then. Groups of us started flyin' to Reno, and hangin' out in the casinos there. The money flowed like water.

Anyhow, he got in with some of the high-rollers, and they convinced him that he could make big money in the fight game. We built a boxin' ring, and started trainin' fighters down here. There was this old fella by the name of Newman, who acted as ring doctor. I never knew his first name. Everybody always just called him Doc.

We ended up bringin' in these three middleweights. Doc and me handled 'em, and Martin took care of bookin' the fights, through these guys he met in Reno. Now, what Martin didn't know, is that these fighters weren't supposed to win. Two of 'em were past their prime, and the third one, a kid named Kenny Haywood, wasn't expected to go anywhere, 'cause he didn't have any fire. He was okay as long as he was on top, but he didn't like gettin' hit. Instead of makin' him mad like it should, one good shot would make him give up. He'd go on the defense, and the fight was over.

Well, livin' up here, away from everything, the kid was able to get things in focus. He stopped losin'. He won four fights in a row. Martin was startin' to feel like god himself. It seemed like he had some kind of magic touch. He was rubbin' shoulders with these Nevada big shots. They were buyin' everything Carl could grow, and now he was beatin' 'em in the fight game.

Then came the fight with Robby Biggs. Biggs was tryin' to get a title shot, but it wasn't happenin' and he needed work. It had all the makin's of a real Cinderella story. We all figured that Kenny was ready. We were all set for him to win that fight.

You remember Biggs. They called him 'The Razor' because he had this wicked twist at the end of his jab that'd cut you to shreds. Doc used a lot of Vaseline on Kenny's face, but it was so hot in the arena that, by the end of each round, it was all melted off.

Well, the first round was dead even. Kenny was in great shape, and his shots, especially his left hand, had a lot behind 'em. He took the second round, but in the third, he started slowin' down. We knew what kind of shape he was in, and it didn't make sense, but he was fadin' fast. He started droppin' his left, and Biggs started getting' his jab through.

It ended up bein' an eleven round slaughter. Kenny ended up gettin' all cut up, but the kid was game. He wouldn't give it up until the ref stopped the fight with a t.k.o.

When Kenny was tested after the fight, they found secanol in his blood. It turned out that somebody had put it in the water. Doc was put on suspension, and Martin was banned from the ring.

We flew back up here, and Kenny climbed the stairs to Martin's tree house and dove over the porch rail. Martin got really upset. We packed up the body, flew it out to Reno, and left it in the alley behind the Hotel that was run by the guys that had set us up. Martin called 911 from a pay phone and gave the cops the address. He told them that he'd just seen a bunch of guys in suits throw somebody out of an upstairs window. Then he came back here and told everyone that we were gonna quit growin' pot and start livin' the good life.

We started buildin' houses on the ground. He said it was time we evolved out of the trees. He gave up drinkin'. We sold off our last crop, and started growin' food for ourselves instead. We had meetings all the time where Martin would talk for hours about how we'd gone too far down the wrong path. And then he'd talk about freedom and responsibility. It became our new religion.

We were all pretty wore out by that time. When you're young, you look for adventure. But when you get a little older, adventure gets to be too much work, and you start lookin' for a place to rest. For me, and probably for everyone else up here, this looked like a pretty good place to rest."

"Do you think Martin threw the fight?" Thomas had already decided that he probably did.

"Well, at the time I would've said 'no way.' But over the years, I've asked myself that same question, and the answer is, I don't know. Everything is a game to him, and the object of a game is to win. I've seen too many situations where, even though it might look like he lost, Martin won."

"You're not exactly giving me a clear picture here."

"I don't think it's possible to get a clear picture of Martin. I have a good life here, and I guess I've been content to go along without askin' too many questions. I'm not dumb enough to think he wouldn't sell me out if he thought it was necessary, but I've always tried to keep it from bein' necessary. I try to stay out of his games as much as I can. It's like havin' a pet wildcat. If you don't want to get bit, stay out of the cage."

"Wait a minute," said Thomas. "Weren't you involving yourself in his game by standing guard when I was locked in the barn? And what about that vigilante stunt we pulled?"

"Well, down at the barn, at first I was curious about what was goin' on. When I met you, I found out you were okay, and from then on, I just wanted to make sure nothin' happened to you. As far as the other thing is concerned, I guess curiosity got the best of me again. By that time, I figured you'd be safe enough, but I wanted to see how the whole thing would play out. It looked like somebody had killed one of us, and that was hittin' too close to home.

In the end, I screwed up. I was standin' there, tryin' to figure a way out of there, when those three poor bastards came boilin' out of the cabin. When you got shot, I just reacted, I guess I'm getting' old. Time was, I might've been able to keep things from getting' out of hand."

From the kitchen, Carol Ann called, "Come and get it, boys!"

"I guess what I'm looking for is some kind of handle." Thomas slid back his chair and stood up. "I can't make up my mind whether Martin is really the benevolent manipulator that he appears to be, or if his purposes are more sinister. He talks about a moral code, but I can't make up my mind whether it's something he lives by, or if it's just something he expects everyone else to live by, while he operates outside of it."

The big man placed his massive hands on the table and stood up too. "That's really the question, isn't it? And whatever the answer to that question is, he's able to keep playin' his parlor tricks with everybody, 'cause no one ever calls him on it. Whatever he's doin' behind the scenes, he's a likeable fella, and we all want to believe that he is who we hope he is. We don't want to look too close, maybe 'cause we're scared of what we might find if we do."

Virginia was standing in the kitchen doorway, hands on hips, in that familiar, sassy, little-girl pose that Thomas found so endearing. She squinted her eyes up, and in a low, "Dirty Harry" voice, she said, "Now we can do this the easy way, or we can do this the hard way. Are you fellas comin' in to supper or not?"

Picking her up, Thomas said, "Let's do it the easy way." He carried her to the table and deposited her gently into a chair.

The meal was delicious and the conversation was light and lively. Thomas was relieved that any doubts he'd had about his friends had been unfounded and unnecessary. They were indeed, the salt-of-the-Earth couple he had thought them to be. In the end Carol Ann said, "Why don't you kids stay here tonight? We have the extra room. We can play cards or something and make a nice evening of it."

Thomas and Virginia looked at each other, and he said, "We'd like that, but I have a lot to do tomorrow, and we should be getting back. I banked the fire before we left, but I don't want the house to get too cold. It'll take too long to get it heated up again."

"Yeah," said V. "I figure she's gonna be a cold one tonight. The clouds've all broke up, and it'll prob'ly stay clear. We can get together agin when we've had more time to plan things out."

30 HEAVEN OR HELL

The sun was already behind the mountain when they started home. A frigid breeze was makings its way up the canyon, and everything around them had a somber cast. It suited Thomas' mood perfectly. He and Virginia walked in silence, arm-in-arm, while he tried to plan his next move.

In his mind, he rehearsed his future meeting with Martin. Should he play dumb at first, letting Martin set the tone? Should he act as if he knew more than he did, putting Martin on the defensive right away? Should he play the wounded friend, or the outraged antagonist?

"Ow," said Virginia.

"Oh, I'm sorry," said Thomas, releasing his death-grip on her arm. "I was so deep in thought that I didn't realize what I was doing. Are you okay?"

The twinkle in her eye showed that she was. "Sure," she said. "I still have one good arm. What were you thinking about, so hard?"

"I was trying to figure a way out of this complicated mess with Martin. He's built a big house of cards here, and I'm involved now. If I don't handle this just right, I could end up destroying it. There's a lot up here that is good, and some things that appear to be not so good. Martin's relationship with all of you is none of my business, but his manipulation and control of my own situation, is. I'm just wondering if I can remove a card from the house without causing the whole thing to come crashing down."

"Wow," she said. "You're giving yourself a lot of extra responsibility here. If Martin has done things that are evil, and if he's taking advantage of everyone up here for his own, greedy little ends, then any negative consequences are his responsibility, and not yours." Virginia stopped and turned to face him.

"Let's say you walk into a dark room and turn on the light. You can't take responsibility for what you see there. It already existed in the darkness. You didn't create it, you just turned the light on."

"Yeah, I suppose you could be right. But it feels more like I'm carrying a flashlight, than that I'm about to flip a light switch. In life, we only get to see whatever is directly in front of us, and even then our vision can be dim, or distorted."

"You used to talk a lot about the dangers of too much...what did you call it? ...linear thinking? You said we get too caught up in causes and effects, and that we follow a chain of events into our imaginary future, which just adds unneeded stress to the present."

The light came on. "You're absolutely right!" he said. "I've fallen into the same old trap that I always fall into! If I could just be content to enjoy the present moment, a flashlight would be good enough. Here I am, walking along with an incredible woman, in a beautiful place, and all I can think about are the problems of the past, and how they relate to the imaginary future.

In fact, the past is a line that extends backward from where we are to where we were. But at the present moment, the line frays out into an almost infinite number of choices, with each choice fraying out into even more. And it is both the blessing and the curse of the human condition, that we live entirely and always within that moment of choice. We live out our lives, poised at the brink of more or less violent change, always standing at the edge of a bottomless cliff. We can't go back, and we can't jump ahead to see where any particular choice will lead."

"Oh look!" said Virginia.

They were standing in front of the hollow tree. A big, tattered-looking porcupine lumbered slowly over to the base of the massive trunk and began climbing. "Go in peace, my brother," said Thomas.

The porcupine stopped and looked at him, and then continued up into the tree. Virginia said, "I think that might have been your sister."

"I wonder how they tell the difference."

"I guess it takes one to know one."

"Let's go home."

"Thomas?"

"What?"

"Oh, nothing. I just love you, is all." She linked her arm in his, and they resumed their walking.

"That's not 'nothing' my love," he said. "That's everything."

"Why mister Galahad! That kind of talk could turn a girl's head!"

The next morning, Thomas and Virginia were in no particular hurry to get out of bed. They lay, talking about this and that. The house had cooled down during the night, but it was nice and warm under the blankets. Finally though, Thomas got up, built up the fire, and jumped back into bed.

It didn't seem to take long before the cabin was all warmed up. They got up, dressed, and made breakfast. Thomas had decided to let Martin come to him. He didn't have to wait very long.

"After we bring the stock back from V, and Carol Ann's, I think I'd like to check out the creek, and see if we can make V's power and water plans work." Thomas was drying the breakfast dishes. Virginia had finished washing them, and was wiping down the table, when there was a knock at the door.

Martin didn't wait for an answer. There was a rush of cold air as he opened the door and walked in. "Well, good morning, you two!" he said. "V. told me you were back. Damn! It's getting cold out there." He shook hands with Thomas, and didn't seem to notice that, when he hugged Virginia, she didn't hug back. "So, let me see the ring."

"What ring?" Thomas asked.

"I figured you two went off to get married."

"We thought about it, but we realized that we're already as married and committed as two people can be. We decided to just throw a party up here to let the world know that we are, and always will be together."

"Really? Then where'd you go?" Martin wasn't wasting any time.

"We went to San Francisco," said Virginia. "It was wonderful."

Martin was suddenly serious. "The reason I dropped by was; I need to talk to you, Tom. Can we go for a little walk?"

"Like I said, Marty, Virginia and I are together. Anything you need to say, you can say to the both of us."

"Fair enough. Mind if I sit down?"

"Not a bit. Have a seat. You want some coffee?"

"No thanks." Martin pulled a chair out from the kitchen table, and sat down. "Well, here's the deal. I've always tried to make sure that nobody knows about this place, and our life up here in the woods. This was a fresh start for a lot of us, and I'm sure there are outstanding warrants out for several, if not most of the people here."

"Marty, I know all of this. That's the reason you knocked me on the head and kidnapped me. Get to the point."

"Well, the fact is, I didn't just kidnap you, I killed you, too."

Thomas could feel the intensity of Martin's eyes upon him, watching for his reaction. "I know," he said.

Martin's eyes didn't move. "So, what are you going

to do?"

"I'm not sure."

"You could just stay up here and live a good life."

"Do I have a choice?"

"Not really."

So there it was. Martin sat there as cold as ice. His expression hadn't changed.

Thomas decided to go around the challenge. "How the hell did you pull it off?"

"How is not important. I do things. You have to realize, I used to be Jesse James. People owe me favors." Still, the cold stare. Still, the confidence of a cat with a cornered mouse.

"Suppose I call your bluff, and just leave?"

"That would be a mistake. And besides, I never bluff. Remember, you killed a man. Any life you might try to have out in the world would be, shall we say, complicated."

"So you say."

Martin's expression softened. "Hey, why are we getting so serious? You're safe here. You have life, and love, and everything you need. There's no reason that we can't just go on being friends, and enjoying all of this, is there?"

"Suppose I don't want to be dead?"

"If you're living up here, out of contact with the rest of the world, what difference does it make if they think you're alive or not? ...Look at it this way. You've died and gone to Heaven. Now that you're here, why can't you just relax, pull up a cloud, and learn to play the harp?"

"Okay, first of all, this may be a lot like Heaven, but there's one major difference, Marty. You're not God. You're just a lying, manipulating, two-bit hustler, and I want you out of this house. You may own everything up here in your little kingdom, but you sure as hell don't own me." Thomas walked over the opened the door. "Now get out!"

Martin gave Virginia a look that said, "Help me out here."

She looked away.

He placed his hands on the table, sighed and stood up. "You really don't want to go up against me on this, Tom. If you put me in a corner, all bets are off. I'll do whatever I have to do, to protect myself, and all the people who depend on me to keep them safe. You really aught to just go along to get along." He walked toward the open door.

"So what are you going to do, kill me for real?"

He walked past Thomas, toward the door. "You should keep one, very important thing in mind, old friend." For a split second, the intensity returned to his eyes. He said, "You're already dead."

At the door, he said, "So long, Ginny. Try talking some sense into this stubborn son-of-a-bitch."

31 FIRE

Thomas watched him walk away for a long moment, and then closed the door. "I think that went well, don't you?"

"Yeah, right," said Virginia. "You probably shouldn't have thrown him out."

"I just couldn't stand it anymore. I realized that, even if we'd talked all day, it wouldn't have changed anything. He made me mad."

"But Honey," she said. "That's what Martin does. The madder you get, the more he's able to control the situation."

"Exactly. That's why I had to throw him out."

"Ah, I see… I wonder what he'll do next."

"I don't know, and I don't think we should wait around to find out."

They repacked their backpacks and started out, pretty much as they had arrived a few hours before. The big difference was that now, Thomas was carrying Carl's old deer rifle. "I don't really think you're in any danger," he said. "But I'll feel better if you stay at Joshua's place until this is all over."

"Until what's all over? I thought we were leaving."

"Not just yet. I came back up here to get some answers, and I don't see how I can just walk away, and leave this thing unresolved. I've been running away from this kind of thing all my life, and I think it's time I made a stand."

"You're planning to shoot Martin?"

"Oh no." Thomas laughed. "This is just a prop," he said, indicating the rifle. "I just want to see if I can put him into a corner, and get him to tell me the truth, for once."

Virginia was doubtful. "That's a pretty dangerous game to play," she said. "Didn't we learn about this game a couple of months ago?"

"This time, it will be different." Thomas patted the rifle. "This time I'm in control."

"Is it loaded?"

"It has to be. If it isn't, Martin will be able to sense that he isn't in any real danger. I may have to shoot into the air or something to make my little drama more convincing. He needs to know that I have the power, if not the actual intent, to take him out."

"And you don't think all of this 'Wild West Show' stuff might be just a little bit childish?"

"I don't know what else to do. I really don't want to just walk away this time. You were right before, when you said that I'm like a porcupine. I just seem to bumble along, while people like Martin manipulate me, and set the rules and the direction of my life. When does the porcupine turn and fight? He waits until he senses that his life is about to be taken from him, and then he bristles up and fights back. Well, Martin is trying to take my life already, on paper at least. But this is more about my life as a man. It's about self-respect.

Inside every one of us, there's a core sense of self that exists apart from the world. It's where our strength and personal force come from. In others, as well as in ourselves, we see that force as either strong or weak, either passive or active, either dominant or submissive. It isn't pride, exactly. It's more of an energy source. It can burn hot or cold.

In some people, it burns so hot and bright that you can feel it from across a room. To see it in others, you have to peel off layers of self-protection, until you discover it, burning like a pilot light, before the burner ignites.

I don't know if this fire, this level of passion is established at birth, or if it grows and diminishes as a result of our experiences and our ultimate use of it. But it seems as if, living up here in the mountains, I can feel it burning hotter and brighter all the time. More and more, I'm feeling liberated, for lack of a better term, and more in charge of my own destiny.

It's like I've opened the damper on a stove, and brought in all this new combustion air. If I walk away from this, if I don't stay and face it down, I'm afraid the damper will close again. In that case, the fire would burn down. The flames would gradually suffocate, until it's just a pilot light again.

The fact is, I don't ever want to go back to a 'going through the motions' kind of existence. Martin may have reinforced the illusion of my death, but it started long before I came out here. I'd been dying for years."

Virginia stopped and looked up into his face. "Wow!" she said. "That was quite a speech! I can see why you think this is so important, even though I don't really agree with all of it. But now I'm left to decide whether to try to help you build up this fire of yours, and maybe lose your life in the process, or help you damper it down, and maybe lose your soul. Personally, I'd rather have you alive, with or without the fire. But that's not a decision that I'm prepared to make, so I'll have to leave it up to you. Just remember one thing, big guy. If you do end up losing your life over this schoolyard thing, don't come running to me. If that happens, you and I are through."

"I'll just have to make sure that it doesn't happen, then. If I lost both my life and you at the same time, I don't think I could stand it. I might never recover."

"Seriously," said Virginia. "Since we now know that Martin was the one who killed those three men at the shack, why don't we just go to the police, and let them handle it? I think most of the people up here would understand."

"Because, as I said before, this is as much about me, as it is about Martin. This is about me taking a personal stand, and seeing it through to the end. This is about me facing down my own demons of apathy and fear, no matter what the consequences are. It's really a simple question. Am I going to be the victim, or the victor here?"

"And to think I've been calling you 'Sir Galahad' all these years, when you're really 'Don Quixote'. Just remember, Sir Knight, if this is just a windmill you're fighting, it really doesn't matter who wins."

Suddenly, Jordan was walking beside them. Thomas was startled. "Where did you come from?"

"I've been with you ever since you passed that big maple back there. I stepped out from behind it."

"Maybe you really are double-oh-seven. You're good."

"You made it pretty easy. The two of you have been so preoccupied with your conversation, and with rehearsing the future in your minds, that you wouldn't have noticed me if I was a marching band. If you're going to be putting yourself in harm's way, you might want to let go of all that, and try to pay a little more attention to what's happening around you."

Jordan looked like Daniel Boone. He was dressed all in buckskins and was wearing moccasins instead of the hiking boots that Thomas had seen him wearing before. The semi-automatic rifle in his hands looked out of place. When he noticed Thomas staring at his attire, he said, "Theses are my hunting clothes. They help me blend in."

Virginia said, "Jordan Wilson. What have you been up to?"

"Oh, nothing much. I've just been out visiting a few

people. Martin's m. o. has always been to get other people involved in his little dramas, so that he can share the blame when it all goes wrong. I just had talks with Mister Day, and Henry, and a couple of others that I thought he might try to bring in, and for now, it looks like any problem between you and Martin will stay just between the two of you." The young man was smiling, and there was a twinkle in his eye. "As a matter of fact, I think they're all kind of hoping that ole' Martin gets a good ass whuppin' before this is all over."

"I don't know," said Thomas. "In the old days, Marty was quite the scrapper. He always seemed to be fighting with somebody, over something, and as I remember it, he usually won. As for me, I was always looking for ways and excuses to keep from fighting. Head-to-head, or I guess the expression is 'toe-to-toe' I don't know if I'd have much of a chance."

"Sure you would. I've seen you both, and the way you move. And besides, there's something else. Mister Day said he'd be glad to give you a few pointers. According to him, Martin doesn't stand a chance."

"Ah, you've got this all worked out then, don't you?"

"Not at all. I just thought maybe you would be interested in some different options." Jordan was still smiling. "This way, it stays between you and Martin, and it won't affect the rest of us, except maybe as a kind of entertainment."

"What's that supposed to mean?"

"A boxing match. Mister Day has all the old equipment, stored above his shop. We can put the ring back up, and you two can go at it!"

Now Virginia was smiling, too. "It's perfect!" she said. "Just look at you. You're so much bigger and stronger than he is. You must outweigh him by at least thirty pounds."

"Maybe so, but…"

"No buts," said Virginia. "A minute ago, you were

ready to risk your life over this. I think a boxing match poses a much more acceptable level of risk. You get to keep both your fire and your life. It's a win-win situation, even if you lose, which of course, you won't."

Jordan was really excited about the prospect of Martin's defeat in the ring. "You could come up with articles of war, that set out what it is that you stand to win or lose. In it, you could include a list of all the things the loser will be responsible for." He was grinning again. "With that tremendous ego of his, Martin will agree to anything. He'll just think there's no way that he can possibly lose."

They were almost to Joshua's house. "Well," Thomas sighed. "Why don't you two go ahead without me? I think I need a little 'time out.' He gave Virginia a kiss. "I'll be back for you as soon as I can." He turned away, and then turned back. "Jordan, take this damned thing with you. I won't be needing it." He handed over the rifle.

Virginia began to be concerned. "Thomas?"

"I won't be long," he said. "Maybe later today, or tomorrow at the latest." He turned quickly away, and stalked off, into the forest.

It was happening again. Thomas felt an almost irresistible urge to simply walk away. There was a sick feeling in the pit of his stomach that was hard to identify. Was it fear? Was it frustration, or even rage? He decided that it was rage.

He had come to this place because he thought that technology and a witless, consumption-based society had made modern life too complex. He had suddenly realized that life in a small, isolated society could be just as complicated. That political intrigues, played out on a small scale, are every bit as shallow and self-serving as the grand-scale power games he'd come up here to get away from. As the man lives, so lives the state. As the state thinks, so thinks the man.

Thomas' concept of time, and his perspective of society began to merge. As all of time: past, present, and future, are focused like sunlight through a magnifying glass, upon the moment of now, so all of humanity: here, there, and everywhere, are focused upon the actions of the individual member. The present moment, while critically important to the grand scheme, can have only a minute ripple effect. It's the same with individual actions. Taken separately, they are critically important, but seen against the backgrounds of society and culture, they become lost in the swirling fog.

Once again, Thomas felt like the misfit child in the schoolyard; the one that all the other children poke fun at. He felt the suppressed rage, the crippling impotence. And he saw that the anger that child feels, is directed, not at his tormentors for making fun, but rather at himself for being different, for being powerless to stop the abuse and humiliation.

The schoolyard gang is made up of the few who lead, and the many who follow. As a group, it is suspicious and intolerant of anyone who refuses to do either. The same is true of society as a whole. The truly independent thinker is interested, not in leading others to revolt against existing structures, but simply in being personally separate from them, and as far as possible, free of their influence and interference.

It was the interference part that had Thomas so pissed off. For the moment, he let go of everything but that. The action gave him a renewed feeling of power and energy. Suddenly he was moving toward something, rather than being buffeted by uncontrollable circumstances.

His walking pace was almost a run. Doom and salvation grappled together in his mind, and he raced forward to meet whichever one survived. He was surprised at how little time seemed to pass before he found himself standing in front of Martin's cabin.

32 THE PORCUPINE TURNS

He pushed open the door and walked in, unannounced. Maggie was relaxing in a window seat, reading something or other. She looked up from her book and started to speak, but Thomas said, "Where is he?"

She looked surprised, and then puzzled, but pointed to a door, which led to an office in the back. Thomas strode quickly across the room and through the open doorway.

Martin was seated at a massive wooden desk. He too, started to speak. He even scooted his chair back and prepared to stand up and shake hands, but Thomas said, "Sit." He said it with authority. Martin stayed where he was.

"I aught to kick your ass right now!" Thomas blurted out. "But I have a few things to say first." He was obviously agitated, almost shaking.

Martin leaned his chair back, and laced his fingers together behind his head. "By all means, old friend," he said. "What's on your mind?" He was totally relaxed; amused even; calm and in control.

"Whatever you did to fake my death, undo it."

"I can't do that. I'll admit that it was probably a mistake, but it seemed to make sense at the time, and it can't be undone."

"Do it anyway." Thomas was rising to a level of anger that he'd never allowed himself to reach before. "I flew out to Michigan. I talked with my lawyer. I know what you did to me. I've lost everything. Undo it."

Martin was unfazed. "I told you, I can't. I figured you'd get yourself all worked up and come here like this, so I've given it a lot of thought, and it can't be done. There's a little matter of insurance fraud." Martin placed his hands on the desk. "It started with a phone call. Then that lawyer, Barry What's-his-name got involved, and I had to come up with a death certificate. I even got an urn from a funeral parlor and shipped your 'ashes' out there. No, you're dead all right. And there's nothing I, or anybody else can do about it. If you resurface now, you'll be charged with all sorts of things, including the murder of one of those guys back at the cabin."

"But I didn't kill anybody! You shot them all!" Thomas noticed his hands were actually shaking. "You're such a hypocrite! You talk about freedom and responsibility, circles of influence and all of that, while you connive and manipulate, and destroy the lives of the people you pretend to care so much about!"

Martin stood, walked slowly around the desk, and softly closed the door. His upper lip twisted into a sneer. "Let me give you a little advice, my friend," he said. "You get that temper under control. We have a lot of history, or you might really be dead, right now. That night at your camp, I made the decision to let you live. I could just as easily have killed you on the spot. You said before that I'm not god. You were wrong. The lord Martin giveth, and the lord Martin can taketh away. You're alive right now by the grace of Martin Tyler."

Thomas had a powerful urge to punch Martin in the face. He resisted it because he wanted to see where this was going. He was seeing Martin, maybe for the first time, without the mask.

Martin continued. "All my life, I've wanted to be filthy rich. I worked my ass off. I invested here and there. I conned people. I begged, borrowed, and stole, until right now, even I don't know how much money I have."

"So what's your point?"

"My point is that, hiding out up here, I realized that, beyond providing this place, this 'world apart' money has very little value. I asked myself, 'If money, up here, is just worthless paper, what is real wealth, anyway?' The answer was 'people'. People are better than cash. The value of money is what it can do for you. The value of people is exactly the same.

I got all that money by exploiting the world's two big motivators: greed, commonly referred to as desire, and fear. About thirty seconds into a conversation, I can tell you what your motivators are.

Let's take you, for example. You're actually not that easy. Your greatest desire is to be left alone to live your life without complication or competition. Your greatest fear is of failure and confrontation. Look at you right now. You're sweating and shaking; almost powerless against your own emotions.

Your desire for simplicity makes you the perfect candidate for life up here in the woods, but your fear of failure keeps you from trying new things and taking chances. That's why I had to force you to stay. It was what you really wanted to do, but I could see you were trying to talk yourself out of it."

Thomas was mesmerized. Was this finally the real Martin? Or was this just another misdirection, more of the smoke-and-mirrors variety of deception that he always seemed to use?

Martin was on a roll. "You see," he said. "I just figure out what people really want, and then help them get it. If I receive some kind of benefit along the way, so much the better. It's a win-win situation, all the way."

What about Carl Wilson? What did he win?"

"Carl's big desire was for the love and admiration of his wife. His biggest fear was that he would end up just a useless old man, bitter and alone. He thought that, if he had a lot of money, it would make up for what he lacked in other areas. On the sly, I helped him bring in a couple of crops. It was what he needed to do. I figured it probably wouldn't work, but I had to help him try. Then that asshole, Tony got greedy."

Martin shook his head, sadly. "I should've seen that one coming, but I didn't. Then, when he came out shooting, I just reacted. I squeezed off three shots, and you know what happened. I was awful glad VD was there.

If I'd known we were going to run into that kind of trouble, I wouldn't have brought him along, though. His greatest desire is to grow old up here, tinkering with his little projects and making himself useful. His big fear is that he might revert back to the animal he once was."

So much for seeing the real Martin. After speaking with Jordan, Thomas knew that Martin had fired his gun carefully and deliberately. "What about Dina, and Sarah?"

Martin's face registered surprise, and then anger. "Dina and Sarah are none of your business!" he hissed. "And you'll stay away from them, if you know what's good for you."

With two long strides, Thomas was across the room, and in Martin's face. "How dare you try to tell me about my business? You've been in my business ever since I got here!"

Martin's left fist caught Thomas high on the right cheek. Thomas was surprised at how fast his old friend could move. He was even more surprised by the fact that it didn't hurt. Well, maybe it hurt just a little.

Thomas' right hand shot out and clamped around Martin's throat, as his right foot locked behind the smaller man's leg. He shoved hard, into Martin's adam's apple and drove him forcefully backward. He felt Martin's head bounce twice, when it hit the board floor.

Martin was dazed momentarily, and lay where he was, with Thomas' hand still clamped around his throat. His eyes didn't show any sign of clearing, until about the time Maggie opened the door and entered the room.

When she realized what was happening, her face turned pale, and her mouth dropped open. Still, she tried to sound commanding when she said, "Thomas! Get out of my house!"

Coming out of it, Martin began to struggle, a little at first, and then more vigorously. His knee came up in Thomas' back, whereupon Thomas raised him up and popped him one, hard in the eye. He released his hold, and Martin slumped back to the floor.

"I'm sorry, Maggie." Thomas stood, and made his way to the door, as Maggie ran to her fallen husband. "But he had it coming."

"Get out!" she hissed.

Thomas walked out into the open air. He felt as if he had just been struck by lightning. He tingled all over. His cheek began to burn, and his knuckles hurt, but he was incredibly energized. He felt intensely alive, more alive than he had ever been. A quick, mental inventory showed him that nothing had really been accomplished, but something was different. He decided that the difference lay in the intensity of the fire in his soul. He felt a warm glow as the flames danced and flared within him.

Of course there would be consequences. But for once in his life, Thomas didn't care what they might be. He felt almost weightless as he walked along the narrow path. The air around him was crystal clear, and he noticed the tiniest details in the bark and twigs of the trees that lined the trail. He had a sudden urge to climb one of them, pound his chest, and give vent to a Tarzan yodel.

Martin's eye would be turning to a beautiful, rich, plum color by now. That's one of the reasons Thomas had punched him, to leave a memento. He chuckled as he thought about it. He strode along, feeling on top of the world.

A sudden chill went through him like a winter wind, blowing through an open window. He actually felt his body shiver. He was walking through a low spot in the trail, where the ground was swampy, when he turned to look back. There, in the mud, were the clear tracks that his boots had been making.

Up ahead, the path rose out of the swamp, and up to the crest of a small hill. He quickened his pace, and at a place where the ground was harder and covered with a carpet of dead leaves, he carefully stepped off the trail, and made for a small stand of evergreens.

Sure enough, just as he slipped between the needled branches and out of sight, Martin appeared, coming around the bend in the trail, rifle in hand. His face was twisted in a look of rage, which was made even more grotesque by the presence of his swollen and discolored eye. He was walking fast, scanning the ground as he went. As he passed the grove where Thomas was hiding, his head wagged around, and he looked right at it. Thomas was sure that Martin would see him there, but Martin's expression didn't change. Returning his gaze to the trail ahead, he passed on, and out of sight over the hill.

In the split-second when they were face-to-face, Thomas was struck by the fierce look of hatred in Martin's eyes. Struck; that was the way he thought about it. It was as if that look had physical force.

Martin would be back. Even though he didn't appear to have seen him hiding in the trees, it wouldn't be long before he realized that Thomas had left the trail. The pines were the most obvious source of cover, and would probably be the first place he would check out.

Thomas slipped out of his hiding place and, choosing his footing carefully so as not to leave any obvious tracks, struck out in a line perpendicular to the trail. He proceeded in this direction for a few hundred yards, and then turned a few degrees to the west, back toward Martin's house. He continued in a wide half-circle that eventually brought him back around until he was traveling east again, a few ridges away from the trail. "My god," he thought. "Martin is insane."

Martin had always been mercurial and unpredictable. He'd always been an instigator, a manipulator of circumstances. But, even lately, Thomas had tried to remember that his old friend had always seemed to have a good heart. Something had happened in the intervening years. Maybe it was simply the incident with Tony and the others, but Thomas was finally waking up to the fact that Martin was a real danger, and that their lifelong friendship wouldn't be enough to protect him.

He was glad that Virginia wasn't waiting for him at home. Martin would probably go there first, which meant that Thomas should be able to reach Joshua's farm ahead of him, if he thought to go there at all.

Since he had been worried about leaving tracks, Thomas had been traveling at a careful pace. Now, he increased his speed, hiking quickly through the tangled underbrush, and jogging in the more open places. He had to make better time. Heavy clouds had gathered overhead, and the ones to the west were already touched with gold. Darkness would mean spending the night out in the forest. The wind was rising, and the temperature had been steadily dropping. He wondered if it was cold enough to snow. He thought that it probably was.

He began, unconsciously at first, to look for shelter. Darkness was coming on fast. There was no way to know how far he was from the farm, so he resigned himself to a cold night.

From the west, high in the distant trees, Thomas heard a familiar hissing noise. It gradually grew louder and louder, reaching a crescendo directly above him, before passing on. The sky opened up, and it began to hail. The hailstones were the large, hard, ear-stinging kind. His jacket had a light nylon hood, so he pulled it up over his head and continued on, in the gathering darkness.

Suddenly, there it was. A great Douglas fir had fallen, probably during the last thunderstorm. It had hung up in the branches of its neighbors, and was resting there, at about a forty-five degree angle to the ground. The wide, flat, root system had pulled loose, leaving a space underneath, which was big enough to allow a man to sit up.

The hail turned to snow; not the light, drifting snow of mid-winter, but the sloppy, heavy snow of December. Big, feathery flakes seemed to fall like rain, only faster.

Thomas scrambled into the space under the tree roots, and waited. Darkness closed in around his little shelter like a curtain coming down.

He dug his heels into the soft earth and, by kicking forward, was able to scoop out a fairly comfortable place to spend the night. He even got used to the musty smells of dirt, roots and fungus that, at first, had made him wrinkle his nose.

The problem was the cold. It crept into his legs, and through his thin, nylon hood. His jacket was almost warm enough. He kept his hands warm by shoving them into his pockets. In that way, he could sleep, curled up like a cat, for maybe an hour at a time. The cold kept waking him up.

The night seemed to go on forever. When the dark hour before dawn had come and gone, and the sky began to grey a little, he could see his breath. By then, even his jacket was insufficient to keep out the cold.

Thomas rolled out of his shelter, and into a winter wonderland. The wind had died out during the night, and the world was silent, still, and covered with a thick blanket of wet snow. He jumped around like an idiot for a few minutes, until he was breathing hard, and his blood had thawed out enough to carry a little warmth into his frozen limbs. He then made for the top of the slope, which was only a few yards away.

Even before he crested the hill, he saw Joshua's barn. He was approaching it from the back, and the farmhouse lay just beyond it. Smoke curled up from the chimney.

"Well I'll be damned!" He said it aloud. He'd just spent one of the most miserable nights of his life, freezing and trying to sleep in the dirt under a tree, when only a few feet away was a warm bed. Go figure.

33 PREPARATIONS

As he walked past the barn, he heard Joshua inside, busy with the morning milking routine. At least he hoped it was Joshua. What if Martin had anticipated his showing up here, and was waiting there for him? Thomas crept up and peered around the massive doorpost.

There was Joshua, in his usual place, with the big pail between his knees. The regular ringing sound made by the streams of milk, showed that he had just begun. The bucket was almost empty.

"Josh?"

The young man turned his head, looking over his shoulder at Thomas, without breaking the rhythm of his milking. He grinned and said, "My god, Thomas, where have you been? You look like hell!"

"I just spent a long night in a hole in the ground."

"Ah. Well, why don't you head on up to the house and get cleaned up? Mom's been worried about you."

"Thanks, I think I will." As he turned to leave, Thomas noticed a rifle, leaning against the wall of the stanchion. "Why the gun?"

"I thought there might be some rats out here in the hay." Joshua continued, methodically squirting milk into the bucket. "I hear the varmints are getting bolder these days."

Thomas walked back out into the biting cold of the

morning air.

The farmhouse was warm and cozy. Virginia and Suzy were in the kitchen, fixing breakfast, while Rebecca played with blocks on the floor nearby. The two women were chatting and obviously enjoying being together. When Thomas came through the back door, they didn't notice, thinking it would be Joshua, bringing in the morning milk.

He took off his filthy jacket, and placed it on a hook, near the door. Rebecca looked up, but Thomas put his finger to his lips, motioning for her to keep quiet. Then he snuck up behind Virginia, and placed an arm around her shoulder.

"Ew!" she said. "You smell bad! And look at you. What did you do, sleep with the wolves last night?"

It wasn't quite the reaction he'd been hoping for.

"Why don't you go change, and get cleaned up. Breakfast is almost ready." She wiped her hands on her apron, walked over to the counter, and handed him a basin of water, a bar of soap, a washcloth, and a towel. "Here," she said. "All of your stuff is upstairs."

Suzy was grinning at him, and Rebecca had gone back to arranging her blocks. He started to protest, but Virginia said, "...and take off those filthy boots! Just look at the mud you tracked in!"

Rebecca looked up at him and laughed. Thomas removed his boots and went upstairs. He took off his grimy clothes, and cleaned up with the washcloth. He really was a mess. Even though he'd been wearing the nylon hood, there were clumps of something-or-other in his hair. There must have been a lot of dust under that tree, because his face and hands were covered with it.

When he'd finished cleaning up, the water in the basin was dark brown, and there was a gritty residue on the bottom. He wrung out the washcloth for the last time, and laid it next to the bowl.

When he got back downstairs to the kitchen, Virginia

gave him a big hug, and said, "Thomas! So it really is you! I thought maybe a smelly old bear was wearing your clothes."

"Ha, ha, ha," said the bear.

Virginia placed a steaming platter of bacon on the table. "So?" she said. "Did you talk to Martin?"

"You could say that."

"Well... how did it go?"

"Not all that well. The last time I saw him, he had a rifle in his hand, and he was trying to figure out where I went."

"Oh Thomas, what have you done?" Virginia was starting to worry all over again.

"I simply explained things to him. He didn't take it well."

"That must be how you got that burn mark on your cheek."

Thomas touched the spot where Martin had punched him. "Oh, that's right," he said. "I guess Martin did some explaining of his own."

Joshua had returned from the barn, and sat down at the table. "Do you think he knows you came here?"

"Nah, I figure he probably took the trail up to the house, thinking I'd go there. Either that, or he went back home. It was getting pretty late, and the storm was coming."

"What's your plan?" Joshua began loading his plate with food.

"I don't really know yet." Thomas sat down as well, and began to follow suit. "I guess it depends on what Martin does. He might just cool off and realize there's nothing he can do. But, knowing how he is, I think he'll probably keep trying to figure out a way to get even. He's smart enough to realize that he can't just kill me without destroying his credibility, and losing the trust of the people up here. For once in my life, I wish I could think the way he does, but I've never been able to second-guess him.

One thing for sure, I'm not going to just wait around for him to find me."

Everyone was seated around the table by this time, and the warm, pleasant noises of forks and plates began filling the room. Virginia said, "Does that mean we're leaving?"

"Either that, or I'll have to go back and try talking to him some more. I'd like to have this thing over and done with so I can move on in peace, but I don't know if Martin would ever let that happen." Thomas picked a piece of homemade toast from the platter. "Something's happened to him. Something must have snapped. I think it was the tiny thread that used to tie him to the real world."

"Why don't you go have a talk with Mister Day?" Joshua offered. He probably knows Martin as well as anybody. And besides, I have a feeling he's resolved more than a few conflicts in his life."

"Good idea. I'll leave right after breakfast. But right now, let's eat!" Thomas' bravado seemed to fool everyone but Virginia. They shared a worried look, and then ate the meal in silence.

Maggie and V weren't home. Tracks in the snow showed that they'd left that morning, in one of V's hybrid buggies. Thomas thought, once again, about just walking away, but decided to follow the tracks, instead. They led him down to the village.

He walked quickly through the silent world. Only the soft crunch of the wet snow under his feet broke the stillness. The temperature had continued dropping, and the rolling grey clouds overhead promised more. As he passed among the ramshackle buildings that made up the little, isolated hamlet, he missed the hustle and bustle of summer. It felt as if, with the coming of snow, everyone had gone into hibernation.

He noted that the buggy had pulled up at one of the cabins, and Maggie had gone inside. After helping her down, V had continued on, and the wagon was parked in the shed next to his blacksmith shop.

As he crossed the covered porch, Thomas stomped the snow from his boots. He opened the door and walked in. The big man was bent over some kind of elaborate metal project, and without looking up, he said, "Mornin' Tom. I'll be right with you."

He finished clamping the odd-shaped pieces together and stood up' grinning. Reaching out to shake hands, he said, "That's quite a shiner you gave old Martin. And man, is he pissed!"

Thomas sighed and stuck his hand into the vise of V's grip. "That's what I came to talk to you about."

"I figured." The big man squeezed all the feeling out of Thomas' hand, pumping it up and down gleefully, several times, while his other great paw clamped around Thomas' shoulder. "Yessir, that shiner is a thing of beauty!" he said. "It's been a long time comin'."

Thomas walked over to look at some of the homemade tools that lined the cabin wall. "The question is, what do I do now?"

"Well, if it was anybody else you'd smacked, I'd say you aught to just lay low for a while, 'til he cools off. And that still ain't a bad idea, but this is Martin we're dealin' with. Coolin' off might take a really long time." V moved to another workbench, leaning against it before going on. "Ya see, him bein' the big chief around here, nobody ever stood up to him before. Right now, he's confused, and bein' confused makes him even madder. In his mind, he's fightin' for his life."

"But that's ridiculous. We just had a little argument."

"Yeah, maybe. But he prob'ly doesn't see it that way right now. You didn't finish anything. He hasn't had enough time to think about it yet. The way he's seein' it, you've just come along and challenged everything he cares about… everything he believes about the way his world is s'posed to work."

"Damn."

"Oh hell, don't worry. It ain't really your fault. I knew it had to happen some time. I just always figgered it'd be me who'd have to do it. A fellah like Martin, he'll just keep goin' 'til he runs into somethin'. In this case, he ran into you. This'll prob'ly end up bein' good for him."

"You mean, if he doesn't succeed in killing me, of course."

"Ah, I think you'll be okay. The only good thing about bein' knocked on your ass, is that you get a chance to sit there and look around for a minute, and maybe see what it was that put you there. I'm hopin' that's what Martin's doin' right now."

"Yeah right. What are the chances of that happening?"

"Oh, probly eighty-twenty against."

"Do you know where he is?"

"Haven't laid eyes on him since last night. He stopped by my place and pretended not to be lookin' for you." The big man stood for a moment, leaning against his workbench. Thomas thought it looked as though he was trying to peer through the heavy veil that hangs between the present and the future. Finally he said, "I'll tell you what. Let's go up to your place and pick up a few things. I don't guess Martin'll do anything dumb if I'm with you. Then you and Ginny can go on another little vacation 'til I get everything sorted out. What do you say?"

Are you sure you want to get involved in all of this? You have a lot to lose."

"Involved? I ain't getting' involved in anything. You and me are just goin' for a ride. Where's the harm in that?"

When they were seated in the wagon, V said, "You know, old Carl Wilson made a lot of mistakes in his life. I guess we all have. But, in spite of it all, somehow he and Ginny managed to raise up a fine pair of sons."

"Yeah," said Thomas. "They've sure impressed the

hell out of me."

"Jordan came by my place the other day and gave me a 'heads up' that somethin' was goin' on between you and Martin… 'Asked me to stay out of it."

"So he told me. He said something about you two cooking up some kind of boxing match."

"Oh, that was just idle talk. We was just playin' 'what if?' The thing is, I figure he hiked all over the valley, makin' sure that Martin couldn't put together any kind of posse to help him come after you. That's why I figgered it was you that gave Martin that black eye. Martin tried to feed me this made-up story about choppin' wood, and havin' a pine knot fly up and hit him in the face."

The forest closed in around them. The steady, muffled clip-clop of the old horse's lazy gate was soothing. If it hadn't been for the lurching progress of the wagon, Thomas could have drifted off to sleep.

He was a little surprised at how safe he felt, with his large, capable friend hunched over the reins, lost in his own thoughts, and clucking softly to the old horse from time to tome.

They were getting close to the Wilson place, when the big man pointed out the presence of footprints in the new snow. Someone had taken the path very late at night, or early in the morning. There were two sets, showing that whoever it was had gone out and back. Thomas guessed that it was Martin.

He was right. The tracks led up to the porch, and the door to the house was standing wide open. Inside, the cupboards had all been ransacked, and their contents strewn around. Martin had even dumped the flour bin out on the floor. It was difficult to tell whether he had been looking for something, or simply venting his rage upon the contents of the house.

"Damn!" said Thomas. "It looks like my old friend had quite a party here last night!"

"Yeah, this might be worse than I thought," said the

big man. "Was this full?" He picked up Thomas' bottle of scotch whiskey. It was empty, and had been left on the floor, under the table.

"Just about."

"I guess that explains this mess he made," said V, with a sweeping gesture that took in the destruction around them. "When Martin drinks whiskey, he gets crazy. I sure hope he doesn't get his hands on any more."

A quick tour of the house showed that Martin had visited every room. The mattresses had been pulled from the bed and slashed open. Dressers had been emptied, and clothing was everywhere. There were even a few broken windows, showing where objects had been thrown out into the back yard.

They gathered together a few necessary items and loaded them into the wagon. As they were starting out, the big man shook his head, sadly. "Martin can keep a drunk goin' for a long time," he said. "In the old days, he'd just keep on drinkin' and not sober up for weeks. Then he'd dry out for a few days, and go at it all over again. I sure hope he doesn't get his hands on another bottle. That could be real bad."

34 ARMAGEDDON

There were no footprints on the trail to Joshua's farm. There was just the clean, sparkling snow. The sun peeked through the clouds from time to time, bringing the winter landscape to dazzling life.

As Daisy or Maisy (Thomas wasn't sure which) plodded along, Thomas was thinking about the difference between the slow, easy pace of the wagon, and a seventy-mile-an-hour cruise on the highway.

Even though he had this crazy problem with Martin, he still felt contented on some level. He felt as if there was still a chance that everything was going to work itself out. He didn't have any feelings of panic, or even of urgency. This place, this life had worked a kind of subtle magic upon him.

The big man at the reins softly said, "Whoa there." The buggy rolled to a stop in front of the farmhouse. Virginia opened the door, and came out on the porch to greet them. "Well, here you are!" she said. "I've been so worried…" Thomas jumped down from the wagon. She hugged him and held on.

"Oh, he's just fine," said V, looping the reins over the brake handle before following Thomas up the steps. "We've just been takin' a little buggy ride through the forest, is all." The old horse stood motionless, its warm breath making ribbons of steam in the cold, December air.

Virginia continued to hold onto Thomas' arm, pulling

him toward the door. "Come on," she said. "I've made a decision."

Thomas allowed himself to be dragged inside, and the big man followed, closing the door behind them. As always, the house was warm and cozy. Flames danced and crackled in the fireplace. Suzy had just finished placing a fresh log on the fire, and stood up, dusting the sawdust and debris from her hands into the firebox. "Well hello there," she said. "Josh and Jord are out in the barn. Want me to go get them?"

"Don't bother," said Thomas. "We'll probably head out there in a minute." Virginia was still holding on to his arm. Looking into her eyes he said, "So what have you decided?"

"I think we should go away for a while. We could be gone for a few months, maybe even a year or so. By the time we got back, Martin would have gotten over all this craziness, and maybe we could either settle down here, or move on in peace. "What do you think?"

"Well, actually, the same thing occurred to me as we were driving up here," said Thomas. I was watching the big guy here, driving his buggy along, and I realized that it isn't right, getting him involved in all of this, let alone your boys, and Suzy and Rebecca. Maybe with me out of the picture, Martin will be able to deal with whatever it is that's causing him to act so irrationally."

"It's settled, then. I've already got everything packed up from here. There are a few more things I'd like to get from the house. What do you think, V?"

"Yeah, that's prob'ly the best way to handle it. Tom and me already packed up everything from the house that wasn't nailed down, so that part's all done. After you're gone, maybe I can sit down with Martin and talk sense to him.

The thing is, I've never seen him get this bad before; at least not since he quit drinkin'. It's like he's got this idea in his head, and he can't get past it. I'm thinkin' maybe what happened with them three fellas up there at the cabin must'a caused somethin' to go all haywire in his head. He don't seem to be thinkin' right.

I'm thinkin' maybe I'll swing around on my way home and invite Maggie over to see Carol Ann. They're both pretty level-headed, and maybe they can get this mess all figured out."

"In the meantime," said Thomas. "We're outta' here! V, why don't we run on out to the barn and see what the boys are up to?"

"Okay Tom, but let's make it quick. I think we better get started right away."

"We?" asked Virginia. "Are you going with us?"

"Yeah, if you don't mind. I got kind of an uneasy feelin' about Martin. I don't know where he is, or what kind of mischief he might be cookin' up. I'll just feel better if I tag along for a while; at least 'til we get you folks outta' the woods.

"Hmm," said Thomas, "An interesting choice of words." He stood and walked to the door. The big man followed.

Virginia started up the stairs. "I'll bring the packs down and get ready to go."

Thomas was feeling uneasy, too. As the two men walked around to the back of the house, and through the back yard toward the barn, he felt like they were being watched from the surrounding trees. He didn't actually see anything. He just felt something that made the hairs at the back of his neck stand up and tingle. "Thanks for doing all of this," he said to V. "I'm glad you're here."

"Oh hell," said the big man, peering into the forest. "I didn't have anything else goin' on today. If I wasn't out here with you, I'd prob'ly be back at the house, drivin' Carol Ann crazy."

In the barn, Joshua had been working, cleaning out the milking stall. He met the two men at the door. Jordan was seated on a timber, high in the peak of the barn, and keeping watch through a small opening in the plank siding. Quietly, he said, "They're here."

Thomas wasn't sure he heard. "What?"

"Martin. It looks like he brought some of those jackasses with him---I can't tell who. They came sneaking around that last bend, and fanned out into the woods. 'Must've been following the wagon tracks. There's four or five of them, and they're armed.

"Sonzabitches!" said the big man. "I was afraid of this. I better go have a talk with him before this gets outta' hand."

Thomas followed behind him. "I'll go too," he said. "This is my problem."

V placed a big hand on Thomas' arm. "Why don't you just stay here a minute?" I figger things might get complicated if you come along this time. If he tries any of his tricks on me, nobody'll feel safe here anymore, and he should be able to see that. Let me try to work some kind of a deal." He opened the heavy plank door, and stepped out into the cold December day.

Thomas moved forward and stood, holding the rough door and peering outside, as V walked around the corner of the barn, and to a spot that was within sight of the trail that ran up to the house and beyond.

The big man's voice boomed against the silent air. "Martin!" he yelled. Put that damn gun down and come here! We need to talk!"

A heavy rifle cracked. A puff of dust showed where the bullet passed through the plank siding, high on the barn wall. The sound echoed around the small valley and died away. The big man didn't move, but continued to stand, fearless and relaxed. "Why don't the rest of you men just go on home?" he shouted, ignoring the shot. "Whatever you think might be goin' on here, it ain't worth dyin' for!"

Nobody moved.

A second shot rang out. This time, the puff of dust was lower, narrowly missing the big man. "Okay," he yelled. "That's enough!" He began walking toward the spot where the shots had come from, looking a lot like a clothed, angry bear. "Martin, you're actin' crazy! And you really don't want to piss me off!"

As V neared the woods at the edge of the clearing, Martin stepped out from behind a small tree. "What the hell do you think you're doing VD? I know you brought him here. You better make sure you're on the right side of this thing."

"You don't look so good, Martin." V was still dangerously calm. "You been drinkin' haven't you?"

"That's none of your damn business, you Benedict Arnold turncoat sonofabitch!"

The big man was right. Martin's face was still swollen and his eyes were red and glazed over. He was unkempt, and looked as if he'd been sleeping in his clothes.

"Don't you see? That asshole's about to wreck everything! If we let him walk out of here, it's all over. The feds'll pick him up. They'll force him to spill his guts about you, and me, and everybody else up here. You want to give up all of this?" He swept his free arm around in an awkward gesture that almost made him lose his balance. His other hand still held the rifle, more or less trained on V. "You'll prob'ly spend the rest of your life in prison for what? For him?"

The big man stood, facing the gun, about ten yards away. "You know what Martin?" He sighed, and some of the anger seemed to go out of him. "I'm just a tired, old man. I did what I did a long time ago. I was young, and headstrong, and I did some stupid things. I think about it all the time. I've stopped wishin' I had it to do over again. We both know it ain't gonna happen. But you know what? I'm tired of hidin' out. I'm tired of wakin' up in the middle of the night, feelin' bad about somethin' I left unfinished, more that twenty years ago. Hell, Martin, like I said before, I'm just tired."

"Tired and stupid." Martin sneered at him. "Sure, you might be able to beat a murder charge, but what about the rest of us? We've been able to survive up here because we've stuck together." Standing suddenly seemed to take too much effort, and Martin sat down in the snow, with his rifle cradled in his lap

As if at a signal, the other men slowly emerged from their respective hiding places, some with muttered greetings for V. All were armed.

Martin continued. "We stick together, and we do what's good for the group, even if it hurts. That's the way it's always been, and that's what works, for all of us. Right men?"

A few of the others responded with grunts of assent. V dropped into a hunter's crouch, level with Martin. "Okay," he said. "I'll give you that much. But if we start killin' anyone who might give away our little secrets, where's it gonna end?

If you kill Thomas, do you think Ginny's gonna want to stay here? I doubt it. And then, when you kill her, you'll have to kill Josh and Jordan. And I'll tell you right now, that Jordan just might turn out to be more than any of us can handle."

"Thanks." Jordan's voice came from the trees behind Martin and his cohorts. The men looked around, and then at each other, with expressions of surprise, and maybe a little relief.

"Face it Martin," V was speaking as a friend. "You can't win this one. It was only a matter of time before somebody wanted to leave this place and go back to the world. And whether you stop 'em this time or not, it won't really make a tinker's dam worth of difference. It looks like it's either gonna be broken up from the outside, or the inside. That much is up to you. I been thinkin' about this for a long time, and it seems to me that we'll stand a better chance of gettin' through this if we just let 'em go. Hell, we been hidin' out here longer than any of us ever figured on, already. We've all known, for a long time now, that the time might come when we'll have to move on."

Martin sat, head bowed, dejectedly staring into space. He looked sad, tired, and beaten.

Softly, V said to the others, "Why don't you boys just go on home? 'Ain't nothin' gonna happen here."

One of them said, "Martin?"

Martin let out a long sigh, and nodded his head. The men turned to go. "I knew it," he said. "I knew that first night, when I brought Thomas in, that it would mean the end of everything. But I couldn't just let him go back and tell the world that there were people living up here. And I couldn't just shoot him, either."

"I appreciate that much, old friend." Thomas, Jordan, and Joshua appeared out of the woods, where they had been surrounding the group of would-be vigilantes.

"You!" said Martin. "I let you into my paradise, and now you're going to destroy it. Hell, you already have,"

V stood up. "Are you boys gonna be okay if we leave you alone together?"

Martin and Thomas both nodded.

"Martin?"

"Yeah, Yeah, what do I have to do, sign in blood? You're absolutely right, VD. I can't kill him, especially without this." He smiled a strange sort of grin and handed his rifle over to the big man. The gears were spinning in his mind again. Thomas could see it happening. The old finagler was fighting his way back to the surface, regaining control.

"Come on then, fellas." V motioned for Joshua and Jordan to follow him. "Let's go tell the ladies that everything's gonna be okay up here. I bet they're getting' kinda frantic by now."

"Not anymore." Virginia stepped out from behind a stand of young willow trees, rifle in hand. To Thomas, she said, "Did you really think I was going to let anything happen to you?"

"Well, I'll be damned!" said V. "It's like some kind of a convention up here. Is there anybody else hidin' in these woods?"

The forest was silent, once again. Only the wind answered, blowing softly among the snow-covered tops of the trees. "I guess that's everybody then," he said, turning to Thomas. "We'll be down at the house if you need anything. Come on down and join us when you're finished."

Virginia gave Thomas a big hug. Once again, he'd been surprised at how strong she was. She had actually been out there among the trees, with a rifle at the ready, in case he needed protecting. "Don't be long sweetie," she said. Then she followed after the big man and her two sons.

Thomas walked over and sat down next to Martin. "Sorry about the eye, old friend."

"Don't you dare patronize me, you two-faced, white-livered bastard. I can see what you've been up to. You've turned them all against me, haven't you? Well, I'll tell you right now, you won't get away with it."

"Martin, just listen to yourself. Think about what you're saying. I don't mean you any harm, and I certainly never turned anybody against you. Remember, it was you that brought me here, against my will."

"Uh huh. You're good, all right. With your passive, humble act, you almost had me fooled. But remember, asshole, you attacked me in my own house. I know the truth. I know what you're really after. Right now, it looks like you've won. But we're gonna wait a few more minutes, and then we're gonna take a little walk."

"Come on, Martin. You're not making any sense. Besides, in the mood you're in, what makes you think I'd go anywhere with you?"

"Because I've got this." Martin was sneering,

confident. Thomas looked down to see the barrel of a pistol protruding from his old friend's jacket pocket. Martin appreciated his look of surprise.

"That's right Tommy boy, you never really had a chance. Martin Tyler strikes again. Just when you think you've beaten him, he comes back strong, and you're dead."

"Martin, I'm not trying to beat you at anything, I just want my life back. Are you crazy?"

"Crazy like a fox. Did you really think you could come up here and take what you called my little kingdom away from me? Did you think I was just going to roll over and let you steal what I've spent all these years building up for myself? These people worshiped me. It was always, 'Yes sir Mister Tyler', or 'Can I help you Martin,' or 'Anything you say Mister Tyler." Now you've turned them against me. Now you've got VD and the Wilson boys taking your side against me."

"I'm not going anywhere. If you want to kill me, you'll have to do it right here."

"Oh you'll go, all right. You'll go or I'll kill them all. I'll torch the house and shoot them as they try to get out. With you gone, it won't take them long to fall back into line. I'll make it easy for them. With you out of the way, maybe they won't have to die. Now, let's go." Martin pulled an old snub-nosed thirty-eight special from his pocket.

"Not a chance. If you fire that thing, they'll all come running up here and take you down. You'll lose your little kingdom, and maybe even your life."

"Yeah, but you'll be dead, so it might just be worth it. Face it Tom, you lost. Now get up!"

"No." Thomas was remembering something that happened in the aftermath of the Kennedy assassination. He always wondered if it was true, or even possible.

"Have it your way, then. Everybody dies." Martin cocked the pistol, raised it up, and squeezed the trigger.

Thomas brought his right hand down, jamming the webbing of his thumb and forefinger between the hammer and the cylinder. At the same time, he brought his left fist up into Martin's grinning face. He wrapped his fingers around the gun and held on.

Martin kept firing: twice, three times.

Thomas was trying to wrestle the gun out of Martin's hand, while continuing to pummel his face. Both men were on their feet now, and with one final effort, Thomas landed a haymaker that staggered Martin, causing him to release his hold on the gun.

Thomas pressed his advantage, driving Martin to the ground with a rain of desperate blows. It wasn't anger, or hatred that fueled his attack. It was adrenaline.

Finally, Martin lay still. Thomas rolled off him, panting and worn out. Both men lay on their backs in the bloody snow. Thomas roared. It wasn't a roar of victory. It was a roar of anger and frustration, against Martin, against himself, against this situation. It was a roar of relief and pain. The flesh between his thumb and forefinger was torn to a bloody pulp. The knuckles of both hands were bleeding freely. He was surprised that his face hurt, and that his lip was swelling up. He had no memory of having been hit.

Martin groaned. He was waking up. His face was a puffy, bloody mess. Thomas hoped it looked worse than it actually was. His lips were smashed and bleeding, and his nose was probably broken. His left eye, swollen before, was a lot worse.

"What the hell happened up here?" It was Jordan. Thomas' roar had brought him running up the hill, followed by Josh, V, and Virginia.

"He had another gun." Thomas sat up, and stuck his hands into the snow. The cold would stop them from swelling, and slow down the bleeding.

"Damn it all to hell!" V ran up, a little out of breath. "I'm sorry, Tom. I should've figgered on that. I must be getting' sloppy in my old age." He looked Thomas over, and then turned to Martin, who was beginning to move around. "Hold still, you crazy bastard," he said. He placed a great hand on either side of Martin's nose, and squeezed them together. There was a crunching noise, and more blood.

The big man packed a snowball, and placed it in Martin's Hand. "Hold this on your nose 'til the bleeding stops." He shook his head. "You're lucky you didn't kill each other!"

While this was going on, Virginia had quietly sat down next to Thomas, and was speaking softly to him. "I'm so sorry," she said. "This has turned into such a mess… I'll understand if you want to just walk away. I can see why you'd want to get as far away from this place, and all of us, as you can get."

"Don't be silly," he said. "Things happen. I just might have an idea that will make everything work out."

Martin still hadn't spoken. He was sitting up, holding handfuls of snow against his face, and rocking just a little.

Thomas was holding his right hand together with his left, trying to keep the lacerations between his forefinger and thumb from bleeding too profusely. The firing pin of the pistol hammer had pierced it several times, and the struggle for the gun had torn it pretty badly. He held it out to V, who came over to take a closer look. "Can you do anything for this?"

"I think so. There's so much blood, it's hard to say. If Suzy's got a needle and thread I think I can stitch it together, but it all depends on what condition the muscles underneath are in. What the hell'd he do, bite you?"

"Nah, I tried a trick I heard about when I was a kid. I stuck it between the hammer and the bullet. I was kinda surprised when it worked."

"Oh yeah, that Oswald thing. Well I'll be damned!" V walked over and placed a big, gentle hand on Martin's shoulder, helping him to stand. Virginia helped Thomas to rise, and they all walked down the hill to the house, with Martin in tow, looking like a bleeding, angry child.

35 ESCAPE

From Suzy, V procured a bottle of peroxide, a needle, some black thread, and a few clean rags. He draped one of the rags over a section of the porch railing, and strapped Thomas' wrist to the rail with his belt. He said, "This is gonna hurt some."

Jordan handed Thomas a few strips of what appeared to be tree bark. "Chew on these for a minute," he said. "It'll help with the pain."

"What's this, some kind of Indian medicine?" Thomas wanted to know.

"That's right, paleface. It's willow bark. It tastes bad, but it works good. At least it should take the edge off."

Martin was sitting on the porch steps, leaning against a newel post, where Jordan had tied his hands. "Do you have any more of that stuff?" he asked. "I feel like I've been in a train wreck."

"Here you go," said Jordan, pulling more strips from a small leather bag that dangled from his belt. "I'll get some more in a minute. You two will probably need me to strip a whole tree, before this is all over."

"Come on V," said Thomas. "Let's get this thing done. I'm bleeding all over the porch."

"Just put some pressure on it with your other hand for a minute. This'll hurt enough, even when Jordan's voodoo medicine kicks in."

Jordan was keeping a close eye on Martin, who

seemed dejected and resigned to his loss, for the moment. While he waited, Thomas was wondering what kinds of sinister plots were hatching in his old friends twisted mind. He was also hatching plots of his own.

"Are you ready?" V got down on one knee, so that he could work on Thomas' mangled hand.

"Are you going to propose? Darling, this is so sudden!"

"Yeah, yeah," said the big man. "Go ahead and make jokes. But you might want to keep in mind, I'm the one with the needle."

It hurt. It hurt a lot. Through clenched teeth, Thomas said, "Jordan, bring me a tree."

V had obviously done this before. When he was finished, the ragged edges of Thomas' torn hand had been neatly sewn together with five perfect stitches. "It was pretty messed up," he said. "Even after it heals, it'll prob'ly be a while before it's much good to you." He released the belt from Thomas' wrist, and with a rag, wiped up the blood that had dripped onto the porch.

Joshua went into the house and came back with a bucket of water, which he poured on the stained boards. "Well," he said. "What do we do now?"

"I guess that might be up to you, Martin," said Thomas. "I've been thinking. If you could see your way to fulfill your promise to these people, and deed their properties over to them, they could go on living up here forever. You could still retain the lion's share. Maybe these folks wouldn't be your royal subjects any more, but I think they'd make pretty good neighbors."

"You really are a simple-minded bastard, aren't you Tom?" Martin said, through his swollen lips. "The joke's on all of you." He smiled a twisted, painful grin. "I don't own this land. I haven't for years." His expression changed again, becoming a ghastly sneer. "Game over. You lose."

The big man seemed to get even bigger. "Hold on a

minute, Martin. You mean I been basin' my whole future on a lie?" He stood, looming over Martin like a big, dark cloud. Even a hint of anger in his eyes was frightening.

Martin looked up at V, and decided to give them a straight answer. "I lost everything on Kenny Heywood."

"Well, I'll be damned." The big man leaned against a porch post.

"So, if you don't own it, who does?" Thomas was wishing he had some more of Jordan's willow bark. His hand was throbbing.

"Let's call it an 'association of business interests' in Nevada. I've been making payments to them, every six months, ever since. But I'm all done, now. You can all go straight to hell." He turned away, and sat, staring into the forest.

"All right, that does it. Let's go!" Thomas stood. "V, would you mind untying his hands from the post, and then driving us back to Martin's place?"

"Not a'tall, " said the big man. "What'cha got in mind?"

"I'll let you know when we get there"

They said their goodbyes then, loaded Martin into the wagon, and the three of them rolled off down the trail. With his hands still tied together, Martin was surly and silent. Thomas and V were thoughtful and silent.

The trip seemed to take forever. Each man, lost in his own thoughts, had the feeling that the forest was closing in around him. They were together in the buggy, but miles apart in their minds. With a soft word from the big man, the wagon creaked to a stop in front of Martin's cabin.

Maggie hurried out to greet them. When she saw Martin's tied hands, and swollen face she said, "My god V, what happened?"

Climbing down from his seat seemed to take a lot of effort. The big man looked tired. "Oh," he said. "Nothin' to worry about. These two boys just butted heads again. I think they're all done, now."

To Martin she said, "So, you've really done it now, haven't you?"

Martin slouched down from his seat on the buggy, and his one good eye glared at her. The other eye was completely swelled shut. His lips were swollen and split, and there was still a trace of dried blood at one nostril. When the big man had finished untying the rope that bound his hands, Martin walked over to her. "Now what?" he said. "Are you going to turn on me, too?"

"Get a grip, honey." She placed a hand on his arm. "As far as I can see, nobody here is against you. You just have to lighten up. V here, is probably the best friend you'll ever have. Maybe it's time you learned to appreciate that."

"Appreciate this, Bitch!" he spat out, pulling away, and extending his middle finger. And then he was gone.

Thomas and V didn't even have time to react. Suddenly Martin sprinted around the house and into the woods.

Thomas gave chase for a few paces, but quickly realized that he had no hope of catching him. "Damn!" he said as he slowed to a halt.

"Let him go," said the big man. "It's prob'ly just the booze. He must've got hold of another bottle somewhere. I've seen him like this before."

"No," said Maggie. "This time it's different. For the last few weeks he's been in another world. He hasn't slept in days. I was afraid something like this was going to happen."

"I'm so sorry Maggie," said Thomas.

"Oh, don't blame yourself, Tom. Like I said, there's something different about him lately. If it wasn't you, something else would probably have set him off."

"Do you have any idea where he might be going?"

"Ordinarily, when there's trouble, he heads for VD's house. But this time, who knows?"

V started toward the buggy. "I think maybe I'll run up and fetch Carol Ann over here, just in case," he said. "Tom, you can go or stay, but I'll feel better if she's with us."

"Maggie?"

"Oh, don't worry about me. I don't think he's crazy enough to come back and do anything."

"I don't think I'd be counting on that. Besides, there are some things I'd like to stay and talk to you about, if you don't mind."

"Okay."

"Go ahead V," he said a little louder. "But hurry back."

V slapped the reins together, said, "Gee-up" and went, rumbling down the trail.

"Maggie," said Thomas. "Did you know that Martin didn't own this place anymore?"

"Where did you hear that?"

"From Martin. I was just wondering how much you knew about it."

"He was always so secretive about anything to do with business. He always said it was one thing I shouldn't have to worry about."

"Is there some place he keeps his important papers?"

"Yes, there's a file drawer in his desk that he always keeps locked up."

"Do you think we could get into it?"

"I don't know. He wouldn't like it. I'm not even allowed to look in there."

"Desperate times call for desperate measures."

"I guess it wouldn't hurt anything." Maggie seemed almost eager.

Thomas thought he detected a hint of curiosity. It was as though she'd been looking for an excuse to see what was in that drawer.

They pried it open with a kitchen knife.

Inside, they found a stack of single-entry ledgers.

Nine of them contained entries with notes and figures. The notes were cryptic, and related mostly to business dealings; barters with neighbors, debits and credits. They served as a journal of sorts, chronicling the events of the past nine years. The previous day's entry simply said, "Fix mistake. Eliminate him."

Looking at it made the hairs at the back of Thomas' neck stand up. "May I see that for a minute?" he asked.

Maggie seemed to be in shock. She handed him the ledger and sat staring at it, as he flipped through the pages.

An April entry: "Land payment to LSIC (three to go}.....250G." In July: "Found Tommy G. in the woods. Turn him or burn him?" From August: "Big showdown. Witness problem solved. Tom wounded." And from November: "Ginny and Tom disappeared. Took money. What to do?" The narrative was salted here and there with references to Dina and Sarah. He had obviously never given up hope of enticing them to move up to his Mad River community. A few entries even contained references to his frustration, and showing that there were times when he considered Maggie as an obstacle. In one recent passage, he mused that, if the obstacle were to be removed somehow, there would be nothing to prevent Dina from coming back to him.

"I'm sorry, Maggie." Thomas was thinking how hard this must be for her.

She sighed. "More and more, especially for the past few months, I've felt like I've been living with a stranger. He's seemed so angry. Now I know why."

They heard the sound of the buggy approaching. Maggie placed the ledgers back into the desk, and closed the drawer. Thomas stood up, and they both went out to greet their friends.

When they walked out into the cold, grey day, V was in the act of helping Carol Ann down from her seat. She was dressed in her customary overalls, with a watch cap and a heavy wool jacket. "How you holdin' up honey," she said, putting an arm around Maggie's shoulder.

"Okay, I guess," said her friend. "It feels like somebody died. Right now I'm kind of numb, but later, when it really hits me, I'll probably turn into a blubbering idiot."

Thomas said, "Any sign of him?"

"Nah. Right now he's prob'ly off somewhere, plannin' his revenge." V stretched like a big cat. "I think we'll prob'ly be okay for a while. Martin is the kind who needs to have somebody on his side before he'll make a move. And right now it ain't likely that anybody's gonna join up with him."

"I hope you're right."

"Yeah, me too."

Carol Ann said, "Maggie honey, let's pack up some of your things. You'll be better off staying with me and Valentine for a little while, 'til this mess is all worked out. I've been feeling kind of lonesome up there lately, what with Christmas coming and all. I'm glad you'll be spending it with us."

Together, they packed enough of Maggie's things for an extended stay, including bedding and her favorite rocking chair. Thomas rode with them as far as the Day cabin, and struck out across country from there to the farm.

He was a bit concerned about the possibility of Martin having returned there in order to cause more trouble, but in the end, he thought that embarrassment over the outcome of his last visit would probably be enough to dissuade him from chancing an encore performance.

36 SANTA CLAUS

When he got back to the farmhouse, Virginia jumped up from her seat in the living room and ran to meet him. "Oh Tom. I was so worried…" She looked around and saw that he was alone. "What have you done with Martin?"

"He ran off into the woods before V and I could stop him. Oh, don't worry. I don't think he'll try anything until he has a chance to heal up a little. In the meantime, I thought we might take a trip down to Legget and have a little talk with Dina."

Jordan had been sitting on the couch, reading to Rebecca. He looked concerned when he heard the news of Martin's escape. Standing up he asked, "Where were you when he ran off?"

"Over at his place. Why?"

"I was just thinking, if I can get over there right away, I might be able to track him."

"That would be helpful."

"Okay then." The young man walked straight to the door, put on his heavy coat, and picked up his rifle. "Come on, Blackie old pal. Let's go see if we can find him."

The old dog, always so passive, seeming more like a rug than anything alive, jumped up and streaked to the door, his tail wagging happily. As they walked out into the cold together, Thomas yelled after them, "Good luck!" To

Virginia he said, "I should've gone with him."

"No offense, my love, but I'm afraid you might have just slowed him down," she said.

"Yeah, that's why I didn't offer. Who needs an old man tagging along."

"Oh don't be silly. It's not your age. It's him. Even when he was a little boy, Jordan was more at home in the woods than in the house. Let's get packed, so we can be ready to leave when he gets back.

What did you want to talk to Dina about? Do you think he might go down there?"

"There's something I found in his papers. It could mean there's a way out of this big mess for all of us."

It was three days later when Jordan returned. Thomas was helping Joshua replace some shingles on he roof of the barn, and suddenly Jordan was there, looking up at them from below.

Joshua grinned. "Hey Jord! You look like you've had a tough time."

"Yeah, I've been on the move ever since I left. I sure could use a meal and a nap."

"Good idea. I'm about ready to stop for lunch, myself. How about you, Tom?"

"You're the boss." Two strokes with his hammer were enough to finish nailing off the last shingle, and the job was done. "That should take care of it."

Thomas and Joshua gathered up their tools and scraps, climbed down the old wooden ladder, and then hoisted it up, onto its pegs on the wall of the barn. Josh turned to his brother and said, "So?"

"So what?"

"So did you find him?"

"Find whom?"

"Quit screwing around, Jord. Where's Martin?"

"Well, I tracked him all the way out to the Maple Creek road. There's a black pick-up parked up there, and it looks like Martin threw a big rock through the back window, and then pulled a bunch of wires out of the dash, trying to hotwire it."

"Hey!" said Thomas. "That's my truck!"

"I figured. Sorry about that. Anyhow, he didn't have any luck, and finally gave up. His tracks showed that he ended up walking down the road, toward town."

"So he's gone?"

"It looks that way, at least for now."

"Good."

Thomas was ready to leave. Virginia wanted to go with him, but Christmas was only a couple of days away, and she didn't want to miss spending it with her family. In the end, Thomas found himself swinging down the trail alone. It felt good.

Sure enough, the back window of his pick-up had been smashed out. Martin had outdone himself in pulling wires out of the dash. It took quite a while to sort them all out again, matching color-for-color, and twisting them all back together. In the end, the truck started, and he was on the road.

He drove to Eureka, and stopped at the gas station to see his friends there. Glen and his father were happy to see him. "Hey, what happened to your truck?"

"Vandals."

"Yeah, that's a problem, isn't it? Kids today don't have any respect for anything," said the father. "Let me call a guy I know."

Within a couple of hours, the window had been replaced, the broken glass had been cleaned up, the wires in the dash had been properly spliced together, and Thomas was back on the road. He figured that Martin was at least two days ahead of him, and he wondered what kind of mischief he was getting into.

He was, once again, surprised at the difference in temperature that twenty miles and a thousand foot drop in elevation could bring. Here, near the coast, it was about ten degrees warmer. The stores were all decked out in their Christmas finery, each one attempting to entice every possible shopper.

Thomas had always thought of Christmas as an excuse for people to exercise their god-given right to, temporarily at least, cross the lines of propriety and taste. It gives advertising gurus and store managers a chance to go for the jugular vein of consumerism without the impediments of subtlety and artifice. Whether they choose to display a semi-naked Jesus, bleeding on a cross, or an obese, pipe-smoking Santa Clause, holding up the latest must-have plastic collectable toy, the true religion of Christmas is essentially a writhing, naked, sacrificial orgy of desire; an homage and a tribute to the Deity of the Dollar.

It was depressing. Thomas drove away from the service station with a dark cloud hanging over his head, and another one hanging over his heart. Thinking back over his experiences of the past few months, he tried to put it all in some kind of perspective. It was impossible. He had crossed a line into a world that was alien and unfamiliar territory.

As a young man, he had made a conscious decision to give people the benefit of the doubt. He always tried to see the good in them, and to overlook their frailties and faults. Given the right circumstances and motivation, he had the feeling that he was probably capable of just as much evil and stupidity as anyone else. Everyone has regrets. We have all done things that we wish we could undo.

He really was a porcupine. Martin had actually tried to kill him, and Thomas had just continued, bumbling along as if that was okay. Even in the middle of their confrontations, Thomas had held himself back. Growing up, they had been inseparable. But a lot had happened to both of them during the intervening years.

Thomas had retreated from life. Martin had embraced it. Thomas had concerned himself with propriety, with trying to figure out what the rules are, and working within them to build an acceptable life. Martin had thrown the rules out the window. He was concerned, not with what was good for the community, but only with whatever best served the purposes of Martin Tyler. Maybe that was it. Living up there in the woods for all those years, Martin had lost sight of the fact that, in society, rules can either be self-imposed, or corporately enforced, but they are necessary.

Damn! He was doing it again. He was driving down this road, trying to make excuses for Martin's inexcusable behavior.

Thomas knew he was heading toward another confrontation, hopefully the last. He also knew that it would take all of his resolve, and all of his strength, to win, or maybe even to survive. Yet here he was, undermining that resolve, by entertaining the idea that this man, his avowed enemy, was simply the misunderstood product of ego and isolation. Why is it that some people can keep the fires of anger burning, sometimes for years, while others can't seem to keep them alive for more than a few minutes?

In spite of himself, when Thomas pulled off the freeway and into the little town of Legget, his pulse was racing. Once again, he felt like the good guy in a western movie, headed for the big showdown. He pulled up in front of the Squirrel Hole Café. The sign on the door read, "Closed."

Dina's living quarters made up the rear half of the building, so Thomas went around and knocked at the side door. No answer.

Something was definitely wrong. He walked across the street to the Flying 'A' station and bought a soda. The proprietor was a grizzled old man, with a couple of missing teeth, and a stained ball cap with the Flying 'A' logo on it. Thomas said, "It looks like rain's coming."

"Yeah, it's coolin' off... 'Might even see some snow. "That do it for ya?"

"Yeah, thanks. I was thinking about getting a bite to eat, but I see the café over there is all closed up."

"Yeah, we had a big hoo-rah over there the other day." He counted out Thomas' change. "We ain't had that much excitement around here in years."

"Oh yeah?" Thomas' pulse jumped up a notch. "What happened?"

"Well Dina… that's the owner. 'Real nice lady… Her ex came down here and made a big scene. He ain't good for much. That ain't hard to see. I guess he's some kind of big-shot though, from up north. Anyhow, I guess he was tryin' to get her to take him back, or somethin'. He went kind of nuts when she wouldn't listen, and threatened to take her little girl away with him. I could hear lots of yellin' and swearin' and then a gun went off. I called the cops, an' then grabbed my .357 an' hot-footed it over there.

When I got there Sarah… that's the girl… was lyin' on the floor with a bullet in her. Her mom was tryin' to stop the bleedin', an' they were both cryin. The ex was just standin' there lookin' at the gun like he was holdin' a rattlesnake. I asked him for it, an' he looked at me like I wasn't there, an' then handed it over. I felt like beating the hell out of him, but it looked like somebody already did, maybe a couple of days before. His eyes were all black an' blue, an' they were turnin' that sick yellow color like they do after a few days."

"Is the girl okay?"

"Yeah, I think so. She's a tough little thing. They took her to the hospital up at Scotia, an' her mom's stayin' with her 'til they let her come home."

"What about Martin?"

"I hope they fry the son-of-a-bitch."

"Do you know where they took him?"

"The cops were 'County Mounties' so they prob'ly took him up to the hoosegow up at Eureka. Why, you know him?"

"We used to be friends." Even now, Thomas was a little surprised that he'd chosen to put the friendship in the past tense.

"Well, I'd be a little more careful how I chose my friends, if I was you."

"Thanks for the pop."

"Any time."

Thomas pushed through the glass door, and out into the grey day. The wind had come up, and the temperature was dropping fast. As he put the truck into gear and drove away, it began to rain. He turned on his lights and wipers, and accelerated up the on-ramp to the northbound lanes of highway 101.

In retrospect, Martin's slide toward disaster had been inevitable. It was almost as if he had been following some kind of pre-ordained path that could only end in destruction and ruin. At any point, he could have stopped and turned it all around, but somehow he couldn't see what was obvious to everyone around him. He'd had to play it out to the end.

At the hospital, the receptionist told him that Sarah was in intensive care, and he couldn't see her unless he was a family member. He thought about trying to speak with Dina, but decided against it. She was free now, and he would just be a reminder of things she'd probably rather forget.

He drove north out of Scotia and across the bridge toward Eureka. On the freeway near the little town of Fortuna, the rain turned to snow. Virginia would be safe and snug in Joshua's farmhouse. A fire would be burning cheerily in the fireplace. He thought about just driving straight up to Mad River, but on second thought, he knew he'd have to stop at the county jail.

Martin still looked bad. The swelling had gone down, but his face still showed some rather interesting colors. Thomas pulled back an uncomfortable-looking hardwood chair, and sat down at the counter, in front of the glass.

On the other side of the long window, Martin did the same. He was wearing an orange jumpsuit that had 'Humboldt County Jail' stenciled above the breast pocket and across the back. "Hello Tom," he said. "It looks like you won."

"My god Marty. What have you done?"

"It was an accident. I just wanted my little girl. Dina had no right to keep her from me. I wasn't planning to hurt anybody. But when Sarah tried to get the gun away from me, it went off."

When Thomas came in, Martin had tried to appear disinterested, even hostile. But now his façade disappeared. "They won't tell me if she's okay or not. There was so much blood... Have you seen her? Is she alright?"

"She's in the hospital. They say she's probably going to be fine, but it'll be a long time before she's fully recovered. The bullet did some internal damage."

"But it wasn't my fault. She grabbed the gun, and it just went off."

"Marty, it was your fault. You were the one who brought the gun down there in the first place. You were living in some kind of Wild West Show fantasy world. You need to take a look around, and come back to reality here. What were you thinking?"

"It's too late for that." Martin had been leaning forward. Now he sighed and slumped against the back of his wooden chair. "They've been digging around in my past, and they came up with a big list of bullshit things to charge me with. If they can pin even a little bit of it on me, I'm screwed. I'll be here for a long time."

"Do you have a lawyer?"

"Yeah."

"Marty, I need you to tell me about LSIC."

"How the hell do you know about that?" Martin sat up again.

"I don't. I need you to tell me about it."

"Oh what the hell. I guess it can't hurt anything now. It stands for Lindel Speculation and Investments Corporation. I owe them some money."

"How much?"

"Let's see. Right now, it's about three quarters of a million dollars."

"Do they hold the title to your property?"

"Is that any of your business?"

"Maybe."

"Well, it doesn't make any difference now, anyway. With me in here, they won't get paid. And if they don't get paid, they get everything."

"Suppose I pay them off?"

"You could do that?"

"Maybe."

"Well, we'd have to get my lawyers to hash out some kind of a deal. If I ever get out of here, I'd like to have someplace to go."

"Let's do it."

"Wait a minute. Why are you even here? I've been a complete asshole to you ever since you came back up here. Hell, even when we were kids, I used to push you just to see how far you'd let me go. And up until the other day, you never fought back."

"I've been thinking about that a lot. Up until the other day, it was all just a game to you. I used to let you go on because I was fascinated, watching you work. You have a great gift. I've always been amazed at how you could talk just about anybody into giving you anything, even the shirt off his back. You could even make him feel all warm and grateful for the privilege of giving it to you. It wasn't just me. I've watched you work your magic on everyone. The problems started when you began to believe in your own bullshit. How long have you been drinking?"

"Oh, for the last year or so. I started out with a little here and a little there. I was doing okay with it up until about a month ago. I had Randy fly in a couple of cases, and you know how I can get." Martin shook his head, sadly. "If it's there, I'll drink it."

They talked for a while longer. Thomas, with his elbows on the cold, hard counter, had a feeling that the distance between them was gradually increasing. He would be on the verge of saying goodbye and Martin, sensing that, would bring up another generic topic of conversation. It was obvious that Martin was simply trying to put off the moment when he would be escorted down the long corridor and back to his cell. But sitting there, Thomas watched him grow smaller and smaller, farther and farther away.

Martin knew he was shrinking. He could feel it too. And he was afraid that, when Thomas walked away, there was a good chance that he might just disappear altogether.

When he walked through the big glass doors, and out into the street, Thomas was thinking about freedom. People are fascinated with the concept, but the reality scares the hell out of them. A life without walls requires an incredible amount of strength.

He was struck by the ironies of life. In Michigan, Thomas used to dream of freedom, while he made his living building houses. Martin, trying to break free of convention and restriction, had made a series of decisions that had led inexorably to his being locked up in a cage. Maybe Martin was right when he said that people really don't know what they want.

Right now, what Thomas wanted was to do some rapid Christmas shopping, and then get on the road. If he hurried, he figured to walk in the door of Joshua's farmhouse on Christmas morning. He found himself wondering if he should be wearing a Santa Claus hat.

ABOUT THE AUTHOR

On his fiftieth birthday, Les Dalgliesh realized that it was time to stop stalling. It came to him that there would never be a time when he could drop everything and write the novels that had been, for all of his life, meandering through his brain. The next morning, he was up at five o'clock, writing. Writing before dawn became a habit, and by the end of that year, he'd finished his first novel. By the end of the next year, he'd finished another. And for the next three years, he continued to write, every morning at five o'clock. Les grew up in the mountains of northern California where he went to a one-room school and spent the rest of his time roaming, fishing the creeks and just being. That independent spirit and longing for what lies beyond day-to-day existence comes through in his writing. He treats the natural world, his characters, and his audience with gentleness and respect. Les now lives in Northern Michigan with his wife Sarah and Emma the dog.

Made in the USA
Columbia, SC
06 January 2025